ONCE TOO OFTEN

ONCE TOO OFTEN

An Inspector Luke Thanet Novel

DOROTHY SIMPSON

SCRIBNER

SCRIBNER
1230 Avenue of the Americas
New York, NY 10020

First published in Great Britain in 1998 by Little Brown and Company
First U.S. Edition 1998
First Scribner Edition 1998

SCRIBNER and design are registered trademarks of Simon & Schuster Inc.

Manufactured in the United States of America

ISBN 978-1-5011-5375-4

To Laura,
first of the next generation

ONCE TOO OFTEN

ONE

Lamplight. Curtains drawn against the chill of an early October night. No sound but the crackle of the fire and the flutter of paper as Joan referred to one of her interminable lists. The atmosphere should have been conducive to creative thought, but Thanet was scowling as he sat gazing at his latest attempt with its numerous amendments and crossings out. He groaned, ripped the sheet off the pad, scrumpled it up and tossed it at the fire. He missed and it bounced back and lay on the hearthrug, a silent reproach – and a reminder, as if he needed one: three more days and she would be gone from them for ever.

'No good?' said Joan.

He shook his head. 'Hopeless. Absolutely hopeless. It's impossible! Keep it short, you said, that's the main thing. No more than, what? Five minutes?'

'Ten at the outside, I'd say.'

'All right. Ten. But it also has to be urbane, coherent, witty without being vulgar and contrive to sustain what we hope will be an atmosphere of conviviality and goodwill. And to be honest, the prospect of standing up and attempting to achieve all that in front of Alexander's snooty friends and relations frightens me out of my wits!'

'Don't be unfair! How can you say they're snooty if you've never even met them? Bridget says they're all very nice, the ones she's met so far, anyway.'

'Bridget sees anything to do with Alexander through rose-coloured spectacles.'

'Isn't that only natural?' said Joan gently.

9

Thanet had the grace to look shamefaced. 'Yes, of course it is. It's just that . . .'

Joan put down the sheaf of papers she was holding and took his hand. 'Look, darling, don't you think that every father agonises over his speech for his daughter's wedding exactly as you are doing now? But they all manage it, somehow.'

'That's supposed to make me feel better?'

'And to be honest, no one worries very much what the father of the bride says as long as he's brief about it.'

'You've been talking to Ben.'

Ben, their son, had just gone back to Reading for the beginning of his second year of a degree in computer studies. He was due to return on Friday, to be an usher at the wedding on Saturday.

'He said the same thing, did he? There you are, then. We can't both be wrong.'

'If you're both right and nobody cares what I say, why bother to say it at all? Why don't we scrap the speeches altogether?'

Joan ignored this as he knew she would and said, 'Speaking of Ben reminds me.' She made a note. 'He said he won't be back in time to pick up his suit on Friday. We must get it at the same time as yours. Anyway, as far as your speech is concerned, I don't know what you're worrying about. The whole atmosphere of the occasion will be working in your favour. At a wedding everyone's in a cheerful mood, predisposed to enjoy themselves and be uncritical.'

'I just don't want to let Bridget down, that's all.'

Joan grinned. 'Oh come on. Admit it. It's your pride that's at stake too, isn't it?'

She was right, of course.

'Anyway, I'm sure you're getting into a state for nothing. You'll give a brilliant speech, I know you will, and I shall be proud of you. So get it over and done with. You want to be finished with it before the invasion, don't you?'

Thanet rolled his eyes. 'How many did you say we have staying here on Friday night?'

'I think it was seven, at the last count. There's the four of

10

us, your mother, Lucy and Thomas, her fiancé. He's bringing a sleeping bag and he'll sleep on the floor in Ben's room.'

Lucy was one of the two bridesmaids, a friend who dated back to Bridget's schooldays and who now lived in York.

'I think I'll put up a camp bed at the office for the rest of the week. It'd be a lot more peaceful.'

'Coward!'

'Roll on Sunday, say I.' Thanet picked up his pen, thankful that he had only one daughter. Imagine if they'd had three or four! It didn't bear thinking about.

For over a year now, ever since Alexander had turned up on their doorstep out of the blue one Sunday morning after an absence of eighteen months, the momentum towards the wedding had been gathering pace. Thanet had found it very hard to welcome him back after the shameful way he had treated Bridget previously: a year-long relationship terminated without warning by Alexander on the grounds that he 'wasn't ready' for a long-term commitment. But Bridget had never really got over the affair and in the face of her radiant delight at Alexander's return, Thanet had been forced to capitulate; the last thing he wanted was to alienate his beloved daughter. The reservations, however, remained. If Alexander could hurt Bridget once, he could do it again.

Thanet was uneasy, too, about the fact that Alexander came from a more affluent background than their own. Although on the surface he was a good match, with a lucrative job in the City, Thanet was aware of the minefield that was the English class system and afraid that Bridget might get hurt trying to negotiate it unawares. There were undeniable advantages to the marriage, of course, not least the fact that on the strength of his mind-boggling salary Alexander had been able to take out a huge mortgage and buy a house in Richmond, apparently considered a highly desirable residential area. Bridget and Alexander had taken them to see it and Thanet had had to admit he was impressed. It was spacious, in excellent repair and even afforded a glimpse of the river from the upstairs windows. It would be a delightful area in which to live, Bridget had enthused, with both Richmond Park and the river close by.

If only, he thought now, he could somehow guarantee that she would always be as happy as this. Unrealistic, he knew, but there it was, he couldn't help feeling that way.

'What are you doing?' He peered at the paper on Joan's lap.

'Making a sort of timetable for the rest of the week.' She held it up.

So far as Thanet could see the lists of things to do grew longer and longer by the day. 'You'll wear yourself out.'

'Only a few more days and I'll be able to relax. Anyway, Bridget'll be back on Thursday to help.'

Bridget was spending a few days at the house in Richmond, hanging curtains and taking delivery of various household items.

Joan tapped the blank sheet of paper in front of him. 'Your speech, Luke! Honestly, you'll never get anywhere at this rate.'

The telephone rang.

'Saved by the bell,' said Thanet, jumping up with as much alacrity as his back would allow. About time he paid another visit to the chiropractor, he thought as he hurried into the hall.

It was Pater, the Station Officer.

'Sorry to disturb you, sir, but the report of a possible suspicious death has just come in, in Willow Way out at Charthurst. The woman fell downstairs, apparently, but our blokes are not too happy about the circumstances. I've notified Doc Mallard and the SOCOs.'

'Right. I'll get out there straight away.'

Thanet made a mental note of the directions Pater gave him, replaced the phone and poked his head into the sitting room.

Joan forestalled him. 'Don't tell me! Your speech is never going to get written!'

'Sorry, love. It'll have to wait.'

Already Thanet's pulse had quickened and as he drove out into the darkness of the countryside via the relatively deserted streets of Sturrenden, the small country town in Kent where he lived and worked, he felt a mounting sense of anticipation.

Anxiety about Bridget's forthcoming marriage forgotten, his mind was filled with the kind of pointless speculation which he was powerless to control at the beginning of a case: what would the dead woman be like? Was her family involved? Who had called the police, and why? And what were the circumstances the police officers considered suspicious?

Charthurst was about fifteen minutes' drive from Sturrenden, a large village which had, over the past twenty years, expanded considerably to accommodate a steadily growing population; possessing the dubious benefit of a main-line station to London, it was a popular choice with commuters. At this time of night there was nobody about. Only the cars parked outside the two pubs showed that there was any social life.

Thanet turned right as instructed at the second, the Green Man. The little estate where the dead woman lived was tucked in behind it, on the edge of the village. Beyond, there was a group of farm buildings and then the road narrowed to a lane bordered by high hedges. Number 2, Willow Way was obviously the house on the right-hand corner at the entrance to the estate; police vehicles and an ambulance were clustered around and the congestion was made worse by some minor roadworks at the edge of the road immediately in front of it. Figures visible at lighted windows and a small huddle of interested spectators showed that the neighbours were taking a lively interest in what was going on.

With difficulty Thanet managed to squeeze his car in behind Doc Mallard's distinctive old Rover. It was starting to rain and he turned up his collar as Sergeant Lineham came hurrying to meet him.

'What's the story, Mike?' With weary resignation Thanet recognised the onset of a familiar churning in his gut. The moment he always dreaded was at hand and there was nothing he could do to armour himself against it. Despite every possible effort and all his years of experience nothing seemed to help him bear with fortitude that first sight of a corpse. He had long ago come to accept that it was the price he had to pay for doing the work he loved.

'The dead woman is Jessica Dander, sir.'

'The *KM* reporter?'

'Yes. Apparently there was a 999 request for an ambulance. The caller just said there'd been an accident and gave the address. Didn't give his name.'

'His?'

'That's yet to be established. Anyway, when the ambulancemen arrived they found the husband crouched over the body – in a terrible state, they said.'

'By terrible state they meant . . .?'

'Distraught.'

'This was how long afterwards?'

'The call was made at 8.11. The ambulance arrived at 8.26.'

'Pretty good response time. Right. Go on.'

'Well, they thought it all looked a bit fishy. The husband swore he'd been out for a walk, had only just got in, and found his wife lying at the bottom of the staircase. But someone – either he or someone else – had made that call. So they decided to call the police and our lot weren't too happy about it either.'

While they were talking Thanet had been looking around. Housing estates varied considerably in quality and presentation, and in his opinion this one came somewhere near the bottom of the league table. Nowadays it seemed to be only the very expensive, quality-built new houses which could find buyers, but ten years or so ago, when these had been put up, mass production equalled lower prices equalled speedy sales. Here, the builder had crammed the houses together in order to fit in as many as possible and although there was a mix of detached and semi-detached, the detached ones barely merited the description: between the wall of the garage and the house next door there was room for only the narrowest of paths. The houses were depressingly uniform in style too, and the layouts inside would be virtually identical, Thanet guessed. He was surprised. He would have expected Jessica Dander to have lived in a more upmarket area than this.

'You've spoken to the husband?'

'Only briefly. Thought I'd wait until you got here. I'm not sure that was the right thing to do, though. He's in a bit of a

14

state and I've got a feeling he can't take much more tonight.'

'Right. Better see what he has to say then.' Thanet set off at a brisk pace up the short concrete path to the front door. *In a few moments now I'll see her. Don't think about it. Don't think about it.*

'Just one point, sir, before you speak to him.'

Thanet turned, only half listening, his mind on his imminent ordeal. 'What?'

'I know him, sir. The husband. I was at school with him.'

Thanet forced himself to concentrate. 'That could be useful. What's his name?'

'Manifest. Desmond Manifest.'

'She kept her maiden name for work, then.'

'Apparently.'

Inside the house the cramped hall was grossly overcrowded. Apart from the fact that there seemed to be far too much furniture for such a small space, Scenes-of-Crime Officers were already busy and Doc Mallard was kneeling beside the body, partly obscuring her from view. Hearing Thanet and Lineham come in he glanced up and nodded a greeting. Thanet swallowed, took a deep breath and moved forward to look.

She was lying on her back, one leg twisted awkwardly beneath her, arms outflung and head at an unnatural angle to her neck. Her eyes, a clear translucent green, had that fixed stillness which only death can impart. Never having met her and having seen only a black-and-white photograph of her at the head of her column in the *Kent Messenger*, Thanet was surprised for no good reason to see that her abundant curly hair was a deep, rich auburn, the colour of copper beech leaves in autumn. She was in her mid-thirties and, although her nose was a little too pointed and her lips too thin for her to be called beautiful, she was still a very attractive woman. She was small, no more than five feet three, he estimated, with a trim, compact figure, and was wearing clothes which looked expensive: a cinnamon-coloured silk blouse with loose sleeves caught in tightly at the wrist, and narrow dark brown velvet leggings. Already the cramps in his

15

stomach were subsiding, his mind becoming engaged in the how and why of her death. One of her brown suede high-heeled shoes was missing, he noticed. Involuntarily his gaze travelled up the staircase and Lineham, who had worked with him so long that words were often unnecessary, said, 'It's near the top.'

Perhaps a simple accident after all, then?

Mallard was getting to his feet. 'Yes, well, not much doubt about the cause of death, by the look of it, though I'll have to confirm that after the PM, of course.'

'Broken neck,' said Lineham.

'Precisely,' said Mallard. 'Severance of the spinal cord. But time of death, now that's a different matter. As you'll remember from that case last summer, the one where that oaf fell off a ladder – to general rejoicing, as I recall – spinal injuries can be tricky.'

'Ah yes, I remember,' said Lineham. 'You told us that unless the cord is completely severed the victim can live on indefinitely, although completely paralysed.'

'You only have to visit Stoke Mandeville to see that,' said Mallard. 'All those poor devils who've been knocked off their motorbikes or dived into shallow swimming pools.'

'You also said that even the slightest unskilled movement of the head by some well-meaning bystander could be enough to finish the person off,' said Thanet.

'Which is why paramedics take such extreme care in dealing with such cases,' finished Lineham.

'Bravo! Total recall!' said Mallard. 'Well, you see what I'm getting at here, then. Did anyone move her head?'

Thanet and Lineham exchanged glances.

'Her husband was kneeling beside the body when the ambulancemen arrived,' said Lineham.

'Well, you'd better check with him, then.'

'We shall, of course,' said Thanet. 'But even though you can't be precise, could you just give us some idea as to time of death?'

Mallard looked at Thanet over the top of his gold-rimmed half-moons and raised his eyebrows. 'You know I always hate committing myself at this stage, Luke.'

Thanet persisted. 'Just a rough estimate?'

Mallard shrugged. 'Oh well, if I must. Some time within the last two and a half hours, I'd say.'

Thanet glanced at his watch. Nine-twenty p.m. Between 7 and 8.26, when the ambulance arrived, then. 'Thanks, Doc, that narrows it down a bit.' Though it didn't help with the question of whether she died immediately, or later because her head had been moved. 'Where's her husband?' he asked Lineham.

The sergeant nodded at a closed door to the right of the hall. 'In there.'

'You said he's in a bad way. Has his doctor been sent for?'

'Yes. I rang straight away when I saw the way things were going. But he was out on a call. His wife said she'd give him the message as soon as he got in.'

Thanet glanced at Mallard. 'Would you mind hanging on while we interview him? In case you're needed?'

'Not at all.'

'Good. I'll just have a word with the SOCOs and then we'll go in. I assume they got all the pictures they wanted before you examined her?'

Mallard nodded.

'In that case, the ambulance can take her away. We don't want her husband to have to see her again like this, if we can help it.'

It was a sad fact, Thanet knew, that in cases of domestic murder the person most likely to have committed the crime was the spouse. He also knew, from long experience, that preconceived ideas could get in the way. He had no intention of condemning Manifest before he even set eyes on him.

But he was still eager to meet him.

TWO

The sitting/dining room stretched from the front of the house to the back but even so was not very large – some ten feet wide by eighteen feet long, Thanet guessed. He noticed that like the hall it was crammed full of furniture – good-quality stuff, too, though the scale was all wrong for a house like this. At the far end a long oval mahogany dining table with eight matching chairs looked ridiculously pretentious in this setting and most of the space in the rest of the room was taken up by two vast sofas and a couple of equally plump armchairs, all of them upholstered in expensive-looking fabrics. There was a lavish display of entertainment equipment: a huge television set and video housed in an antique-style cabinet, and a CD player with enormous loudspeakers and hundreds of CDs stored in shoulder-high vertical racks nearby. All around the walls, tables, chairs and even two size-able desks stood cheek by jowl, with books, lamps and ornaments covering every available surface. Thanet was beginning to get the picture. Either the Manifests had come down in the world, or they were living in temporary accommodation between moves.

Desmond Manifest was sitting in one of the big armchairs, leaning forward with elbows on knees and head in hands. He was still wearing outdoor clothes, a Barbour and a green-and-cream-checked woollen scarf. He raised a dazed face as they came in, his eyes moving slowly from one to another, coming to rest on Lineham. But he didn't speak.

Thanet dismissed the uniformed constable who had been waiting with Manifest until they arrived and then nodded at

Lineham. At this stage it made sense for the sergeant to interview the man, as he knew him.

Lineham introduced Thanet and Doc Mallard and they all sat down. Manifest acknowledged them with no more than the merest flicker of an eyelid and remained in the same position as if incapable of further movement. He was a little older than his wife, a big man with heavy jowls and an unhealthy pallor which could have been due to shock. He looked as though he hadn't shaved that day and his hair straggled untidily over his collar. Definitely a man who had seen better days, Thanet thought. The interesting question was whether it was professional or domestic problems which had brought about this deterioration.

'You'll appreciate we have to ask you a few questions, Des?' Lineham glanced at Thanet to check that the informality was acceptable.

Thanet blinked approval.

Manifest took a while to respond but eventually he nodded slowly, sliding back in his chair and stretching his arms along the armrests. His fists, however, remained clenched.

'Would you tell us what happened this evening?' said Lineham.

Manifest opened his mouth as if to speak, but no sound emerged. He closed it again.

'Des?' said Lineham.

Manifest tried again. 'I . . . I went for a walk.' His voice was hoarse, as if rusty with disuse.

'How long were you out?'

No response, just a blank stare.

Lineham tried again. 'What time did you leave?'

The man's forehead creased as if the question were some immensely complicated and difficult inquiry. 'After supper.'

'Could you be a little more precise?'

Manifest compressed his lips and the frown deepened. 'I . . . I . . . Is she really dead?'

Lineham glanced at Thanet. 'I'm afraid so, Des. I'm so sorry. And I'm sorry too to have to bother you with questions at a time like this. But we really do need to know, you see.'

'She was just lying there,' whispered Manifest. 'All . . . all crumpled up. I saw her as soon as I pushed the door open. But why?' His gaze suddenly became fierce. 'I don't understand. I mean, why was he *there?* He should have been here.'

'Who? Who should have been here?'

Suddenly Manifest folded his arms across his chest and began to rock to and fro. 'Oh God, Jess, I can't bear it. Oh God, what shall I do?' He clutched at his head, then, still holding it as if to cling on to his sanity, leaned forward and continued rocking and moaning, 'Oh God oh God oh God oh God oh God oh God!.'

Lineham glanced at Thanet and raised his eyebrows. Thanet looked at Mallard, who frowned, pursed his lips and shook his head. 'Sorry,' he said. 'I think you ought to stop. He needs to take a sedative and rest.'

'But he can't stay here by himself in that state,' said Thanet. 'We'll have to find someone to sit with him. See if you can get him to suggest someone, Mike.'

But Manifest was beyond reason, it seemed. Lineham could get no sense out of him.

'Any bright ideas then, Mike? You seem to know the family.'

'Only slightly. But he has got a younger brother who lives locally, I believe. His number should be in the phone book.'

'See if you can get hold of him.'

'Right.' The phone was in the hall and Lineham went off to make the call, returning a few minutes later. 'He'll be over as soon as he can.' He crossed to Manifest, who was still sitting hunched forward, face hidden. 'Des, Graham will be here soon to keep you company. But we think you ought to rest now. Dr Mallard here will give you something to help you sleep, then we'll take you upstairs.'

At the top of the stairs the door to what was obviously the main bedroom stood open but Manifest directed them with a nod towards a room at the back of the house. At first Thanet attributed this choice to a natural delicacy: Manifest did not want to sleep in a room which perhaps more than any other in the house would remind him of his wife. But Thanet changed his mind when he saw that the back bedroom, which was just as cluttered with furniture as the sitting room, bore signs of permanent occupation: one of the two single beds was already made up and there was a pair of pyjamas on the pillow. Manifest collapsed on to it and rolled over on to his side, turning his face to the wall. They covered him with the duvet from the other bed and left him.

'Separate rooms,' murmured Thanet, outside on the landing.

Lineham nodded. 'I noticed.'

'Let's take a look at the main bedroom.'

This was so crowded with furniture that there was barely room to move around the king-sized bed. Thanet counted two dressing tables as well as two double wardrobes. 'Why all the clutter?' he asked Lineham. 'Do you know?'

The sergeant pulled a face. 'Their last house was much bigger, a lovely converted oast out at Marden and I suppose they couldn't bear to get rid of it all when they had to move.'

'What happened?'

'Des was made redundant about five years ago and so far as I know he's never managed to find another job. The trouble is, he has no qualifications other than experience in the work he was doing. It's a sad story. He went straight into the City after A levels and during the Thatcher years he was really raking it in. We all thought he had it made. Then when the recession came, suddenly he was out on his ear, just like that. Turned up for work one day to find his desk had been cleared. No warning, nothing.'

As Lineham was speaking an icy chill had crept through Thanet's veins. Could the same thing happen to Alexander?

'It must be awful when you're used to earning huge sums like that, suddenly to find yourself on the dole,' said Lineham, innocent of the discomfort he was causing.

'That's terrible,' said Thanet. 'Can they do that? Kick you out without warning?'

'They can and they do, apparently. Imagine what it must be like, living on that sort of knife edge, never knowing each morning whether you're going to discover that you're suddenly a mere unemployment statistic!' Lineham was moving about the room, looking into drawers, picking up and putting down bottles and jars on one of the dressing tables. He peered at a label. 'Mmm. Chanel. She obviously had expensive tastes. It must have been a terrible shock for her, thinking she'd married a wealthy man only to find she'd suddenly become the breadwinner. I wonder how it affected their relationship. It obviously wasn't very good.' He nodded at the single set of pillows in the bed and twitched back the sheets to reveal Jessica's solitary silk nightgown, neatly folded.

'Quite. But he could have found some sort of job, surely.'

'The trouble with people in his position is that they're afraid to take low-paid work in case it doesn't look good on their CV when they're trying to find something more lucrative. So they end up doing nothing.'

'I don't think I could bear that. It must be so demoralising. Though I can understand the dilemma.' How would Alexander react, if his high-powered job were snatched away from him? And how would Bridget? With an effort Thanet forced himself to concentrate on what he was supposed to be doing. He opened a wardrobe door. The array of expensive clothes inside was now explained, all purchased no doubt in better days.

'They hadn't been married that long when it happened, either,' said Lineham.

'Oh?'

'I've been trying to remember exactly when the wedding was. I think it was the year Mandy was born, so it must have been nine years ago.'

'Did you know his wife personally, then?'

'No. Oh, I met her briefly, once or twice, but that's all. Des and I were never close friends. It's just that he was in my form at school and from time to time I'd hear about him from one of the others on the grapevine. You know how it is.'

Thanet nodded. He knew. He too had been brought up and educated in Sturrenden and although he had done his stint away, had been glad to return and settle here. He loved the town, liked the area, and over the years had built up a network of acquaintances in all walks of life. News of former classmates invariably filtered back to him too, sooner or later, especially if they lived locally. 'What's his background?'

'Pretty ordinary. Working class. His father was a bus driver and they lived in a council house. Still do, I believe. He's retired now. They were both so proud of Des. It must have been a terrible blow for them when he ended up on the dole.'

'What about the brother?'

'Graham? He's a carpet-fitter. Self-employed. Very efficient. Fitted all our carpets, as a matter of fact, and I can thoroughly recommend him. Ironic, really. It was Desmond who was supposed to be the shining success but it's Graham who's managed to weather the recession relatively unscathed. Come to think of it, it was probably when Graham was laying our bedroom carpet that I heard about Des.'

While they talked they had drifted out on to the landing and now they paused at the top of the stairs to see if there was any indication of how the accident had happened. At Lineham's request Jessica's shoe had been left where it was until Thanet had seen its position. It still lay against the staircase wall, three steps down from the top.

'Doesn't seem to be any obvious reason why she should have fallen,' said Lineham. 'No frayed carpet or uneven floorboards.'

'Quite. The heel of the shoe is pretty high, though. If she turned over on it, lost her balance . . .'

'The only explanation, if it was a simple accident,' agreed Lineham. 'Of course, if she was pushed . . .'

Thanet sighed. They'd been here before, in at least two previous cases. And, he reminded himself, in both of them they'd managed to get at the truth in the end.

Downstairs Lineham picked up the telephone. 'It might be worth dialling 1471.' He listened, raising his eyebrows at Thanet and nodding as he jotted the number down. 'It's a local one,' he said. 'Do you want me to try it?'

'Might as well.'

Lineham dialled again and a moment later said, 'Ah, I believe you rang this number earlier, sir. I'm speaking from the Manifests' house. This is the police. I'm afraid there's been an accident. Would you mind confirming what time you rang? And your name and address please? Thank you. And what is your connection with this household?' He listened for a moment, then covered the receiver and said to Thanet, 'He's her brother-in-law. Rang at 7.31 according to the recorded message. Do you want me to give him the bad news?'

Thanet considered. 'Let me have a word with him. What's his name?'

'Covin. Bernard.'

Thanet took the receiver. Covin must be married to Jessica's sister, who would no doubt be able to fill them in on the dead woman. It would be useful to talk to her as soon as possible. He broke the news of Jessica's death as sympathetically as he could and arranged to see him later. He lived in Nettleton, about ten minutes' drive away.

He had just put down the receiver when the door opened and the uniformed constable looked in. 'Mr Manifest's brother is here, sir.'

'Send him in.'

The first thing you noticed about Graham Manifest was his ferocious squint. Apart from that he was a younger, fitter version of his brother. He had the same stocky build, square face and dark curly hair, but he moved lightly on his feet and it was obvious there wasn't a spare ounce of fat on him. He was wearing jeans, trainers and a dark blue anorak streaked with rain. 'This is terrible!' he said, one eye looking at Lineham and the other, apparently, at Thanet. 'Where's Des, Mike?'

Lineham introduced Thanet, then said, 'Upstairs. Asleep, we hope. He's been given a sedative.'

'How's he taking it?' As he spoke Graham slipped off the anorak and shook it. Droplets of water spattered everywhere.

'Let's go into the lounge, shall we?' Lineham waited until they were all seated before saying, 'Badly, I'm afraid. Not surprising, of course. But people react differently, you can never tell.'

Graham was nodding. 'He always was potty about that woman.'

'You didn't like her?' said Thanet. He knew he shouldn't find the squint disconcerting, but he did. He tried to focus on Graham's good eye.

'Couldn't stand her. Oh, I know you shouldn't speak ill of

24

the dead – though frankly I don't see why not, if they deserve it – but she was a real cow.'

'In what way?' said Lineham.

'Well, look at this place!' Graham's eyes swivelled alarmingly as he waved at the superfluous oversized furniture stacked around the walls. 'Why couldn't she have just accepted that Des had lost his cushy job and wasn't going to get another one, and made the best of it? A lot of people would be bloody grateful to have a roof over their heads, let alone a nice place like this. But no, they had to live all the time with the reminder that she was expecting him to hit the jackpot again one day soon, that this was only a temporary arrangement. I mean, look at this stuff! Poor old Des! It must be like camping out in a posh department store!'

'Are you saying she married him for his money?'

'You bet I am. She was all sweetness and light for the first few years, wasn't she?'

'And she changed, when he lost his job?'

'Well, not to begin with.' Graham was grudging. 'Not while she was still expecting him to pick up something equally well paid any minute. But as soon as she began to realise that wasn't going to happen, it was a different story. You ask Sarah – my wife. She'll tell you I'm not making all this up. No, there's no doubt about it, she was bad news for Des, was our Jess.'

'Though he didn't think so, apparently,' said Thanet.

'He was always making excuses for her. She could walk all over him and he wouldn't lift a finger to help himself, and that's the truth.'

'And did she?' said Thanet. 'Walk all over him?'

Graham's good eye glared fiercely at Thanet. 'It used to make me mad, the way she treated him. "Do this, do that. Fetch this, fetch that." As if he was a pet poodle or something. I don't know how he stood it.'

And maybe, in the end, he couldn't, thought Thanet. Maybe one day, this evening in fact, Desmond Manifest had reached the point where he had had enough. He had seen his chance and the temptation had proved too much for him: one little push and he would be a free man again.

Lineham was thinking the same thing, Thanet could tell.

'We stopped coming over in the end,' said Graham. 'Unless we could be sure she wouldn't be here.'

'But it sounds as though your wife was quite friendly with her at one time,' said Thanet.

Graham pulled a face and shrugged. 'Sarah was never that keen, but she made an effort, for Des's sake. Jessica was all right on the surface, nice as pie when she wanted something or things were going her way, but you only had to cross her to see the claws underneath. She was never afraid of speaking her mind, whether it would hurt or not. I could never decide if she genuinely didn't know how the things she said affected people or if she just didn't care. Des always said it was because she'd had to learn to stick up for herself. She'd had a rotten time when she was young, he said.'

'Do you know anything about that?' said Lineham.

Graham shook his head. 'Couldn't have cared less, to tell you the truth. Just kept out of her way as much as possible.'

'Your brother said something odd when we were talking to him earlier,' said Thanet. 'He said, "I don't understand. Why was he there? He should have been here." Have you any idea what he meant or who he was referring to?'

Graham thought for a moment or two before saying, 'Haven't a clue.'

They decided to go to Covin's house in separate cars, as it was now 10.30 and Thanet couldn't see much point in returning to the Manifests' house tonight. He was pleased to find that the rain had eased off to a light drizzle. It wouldn't have been much fun floundering about unfamiliar terrain in the dark in heavy rain. Lineham said he knew the way and Thanet followed the sergeant's tail-lights through the empty lanes. In Nettleton there was no street lighting and many of the houses were already in darkness. The black-and-white timbered façade of the combined shop and post office was illuminated, however, presumably to deter prospective burglars. They passed the church at the far end of the village street, with the row of cottages opposite where Thanet had once solved one of the most fascinating cases of his career, and half a mile further on turned left at a sign saying 'HUNTER'S GREEN FARM'.

Here the road surface was covered with lumps and clods of mud from the passage of farm vehicles and there was a constant stuttering sound as Thanet's tyres picked them up and hurled them against the wheel arches. Thanet could imagine Lineham, who was very car-proud, muttering about the mess they would be making. On either side were tall hedges, concealing what lay beyond.

They passed the looming bulk of the farmhouse with lights in its upstairs windows and as directed continued up the track for several hundred yards further to a smaller house next to a number of large outbuildings. A light had been left on over the front door, presumably for their benefit. They parked in front of one of the barns and got out. Looking around Thanet could now see that they were surrounded by orchards. A fruit farm, then.

'Honestly!' said Lineham, bending down to peer at the splatters of mud on his car. 'Look at that! What a mess!'

Thanet was grinning. 'Don't be such an old woman, Mike. No harm done. You should expect to find mud in the country.'

'Preferably not on my car!' said Lineham.

'Anyway, you can't possibly see properly in this light. Do stop fussing! At least it's stopped raining.'

They started to walk towards the house but Thanet paused. 'What do you think he meant, Mike?'

Lineham understood at once. He and Thanet had worked together for so many years that they were rather like an old married couple in this respect: frequently picking up long afterwards a train of thought left unpursued earlier.

'Sounded to me as though he had expected someone, a man, to be at the house and he wasn't. Des had seen him somewhere else, somewhere he hadn't expected to see him.'

'Looks that way, doesn't it? What do you think of Manifest as a suspect, Mike? You know the man. Do you think he was capable of pushing her? The worm turning and all that?'

'I really couldn't say. People change. I knew him as a schoolboy. I haven't a clue what he's like now.'

There was an uncharacteristic acerbity in Lineham's tone and Thanet glanced at him uneasily. Lineham had become increasingly short-tempered of late. He was having problems with his mother again. She was tired of living alone and had been dropping stronger and stronger hints that she would like to move in with Lineham and Louise. The trouble was that neither of them could face the prospect, Louise because she was just as strong-minded as her mother-in-law and Lineham because he knew that with both women under the same roof he would constantly be the rope in a tug-of-war between them. Meanwhile the situation was deteriorating rapidly. Both women were becoming increasingly impatient with Lineham, his mother because she wasn't getting the invitation for which she was angling, Louise because Lineham was procrastinating. Thanet sympathised with his sergeant's predicament but felt that the matter would have to be resolved shortly. The strain on Lineham was beginning to tell and, sooner or later, if he didn't act, Thanet would have to sit down with him and try and get him to make a decision.

But now was not the moment. Covin must have heard their cars draw up, and had come to the door.

THREE

'Evening. Come in.' Covin stood back to let them in, then
ushered them through to a sitting room which stank of cigarette smoke. It was conventionally furnished with fitted
carpet, three-piece suite and the ubiquitous television set,
which was tuned in to a late-night current affairs programme.
A dying fire flickered in the hearth and Covin crossed to
poke it and put another log on before switching the television
off and inviting them to sit down. He chose what was obviously his favourite armchair – on a small table nearby stood
an empty mug, a packet of cigarettes, a disposable lighter
and an overflowing ashtray. He tapped out a cigarette and lit
up. 'Hope you don't mind.' He flapped his hand in a futile
attempt to disperse the clouds of smoke.

Thanet elected to sit on the sofa. 'It's your house,' he said,
knowing that Lineham would mind, very much, but that
there was nothing they could do about it.

Lineham retreated to an upright chair against the wall, as
far away from Covin as he could get. He took out his notebook.

Covin gave the notebook a nervous glance. 'I'm not quite
sure why you wanted to see me.' He took a deep drag at his
cigarette. His fingers, Thanet noticed, were stained a deep
yellow but outwardly at least his addiction didn't seem to have
affected his health: his colour was good, his eyes bright and
his dark hair a luxuriant curly thatch which many men of his
age would envy. Thanet put him in his early fifties.

'We're just trying to fill in some background,' Thanet said
reassuringly. 'Mr Manifest is naturally very distressed and has

had to be sedated, and as you are married to Mrs Manifest's sister, we thought you might both be able to help us.' He laid slight emphasis on 'both' and glanced hopefully towards the door. 'I hope your wife hasn't gone to bed yet.'

'I'm afraid my wife died two years ago, Inspector.'

'I'm sorry.'

'No need to apologise. How could you be expected to know?'

'So you live here alone?' Thanet's eyes flickered towards the mantelpiece where there were a number of photographs, mostly, so far as he could make out, either of a woman and a girl or of a young girl alone, at various stages of her childhood. In the largest and most colourful picture she was posing on skis against a background of snowy mountain peaks.

'Yes.' Covin followed Thanet's glance. 'Well, most of the time, anyway.' He lit another cigarette from the stub of the old one.

'That's your daughter?'

'Yes. But she's away at university.'

'Oh, which one? My son's at university too. Reading.'

'So is Karen.'

'So she's just gone back.'

'Yes. This evening, as a matter of fact.'

Ben had gone yesterday. 'You must miss her.'

Covin shrugged. 'You have to put up with it, don't you?'

Thanet was trying to get the feel of the man but so far he wasn't succeeding. He certainly hadn't warmed to him and for some reason felt as though he were having to drag information out of him despite the fact that Covin had answered his questions readily enough. Thanet was sufficiently experienced to know that every good interviewer uses his own reactions to the interviewee as a tool, so he now tried to work out why Covin should be having this effect on him. Was it because the man was naturally morose or because he was used to leading a solitary life? Or was he holding back for some other reason? If so, of course, it might have absolutely no connection with their investigation.

On the other hand it might.

'This phone call you made to your sister-in-law earlier this evening, what was it about?'

'It wasn't actually about anything. I didn't get through.'

'Why didn't you leave a message on the answerphone?'

'Can't stand the things. As soon as the recorded message began, I rang off.'

'What time was this, exactly?' Though Thanet knew of course.

'I'm not sure. Is it important?'

'It could be.'

Covin stubbed out his cigarette, but it was only a few moments before he was shaking another out of the packet. 'I think it must have been about half seven. I know it was just after Karen left, and I remember looking at the clock when we finished supper. It was just gone twenty past then, and she went soon afterwards.'

'Rather late for her to be leaving, wasn't it?'

'She was driving down. She borrowed my car.'

'So, what was your reason for ringing your sister-in-law?'

'Karen asked me to. She'd intended to go round to see her aunt before she went back to Reading but she just hadn't managed to, and she wanted me to ring and say sorry, give her her love.'

'How well did you know your sister-in-law, Mr Covin?'

Covin shrugged, his mouth tugged down at the corners. 'Pretty well, I suppose. We more or less brought her up.'

'You and your wife, you mean? How was that?'

'Jess's father died when she was six, in an accident at work. Eileen – my mother-in-law – got decent compensation so she didn't have to go out to work and everything was fine for a couple of years, until she got breast cancer, same as Madge, my wife. They say it's often hereditary, don't they? Anyway, Eileen struggled on for another couple of years and then she died, so Jess came to live with us. We'd been married about five years by then.'

'Your wife must have been considerably older than her sister.'

'Yes, she was. Sixteen years. She was twenty-six when her mother died.'

'So your sister-in-law had a pretty rough time, really, losing both her father and her mother within – what? – four years of each other.'

Covin shrugged. 'I suppose so. Though you could say she was lucky she had someone to take her in. Otherwise she'd have had to go into care.'

'I have the feeling you didn't like her much, Mr Covin.'

'She wasn't the most appealing child in the world. She was always whining, clingy, wanting her own way and making a fuss if she didn't get it. And my wife was inclined to spoil her, which only made things worse.'

It didn't sound as though Covin had been the most sympathetic of father substitutes, thought Thanet. And Jessica had obviously been a source of conflict between him and his wife.

'She took advantage of my wife's good nature,' Covin went on. This obviously still rankled, even after all these years. 'She was always asking for things we couldn't afford. Had expensive tastes, even then. But when she was earning, later on, and it came to spending her own money, it was a very different story. Madge used to make excuses for her, call her thrifty, but I say she was just downright mean.'

'I understand she was quite well off for a few years at least, after she got married.'

Covin gave a bark of cynical laughter. 'Yes, and that was a laugh, when he lost his job and she found she was having to support two people on her salary instead of one.'

'You think she married him for his money?'

'Perhaps not entirely,' Covin said grudgingly. 'But I'd say it was a major factor, yes.'

'But she did stay with him.' Lineham intervened for the first time.

Covin looked surprised, as if he'd forgotten the sergeant was present. 'Yes. I was never quite sure why. I think to begin with she thought he'd just walk into another job pretty quickly.'

'But he didn't,' said Thanet.

'No.'

'So why do you think she did stick with him?' persisted Lineham.

'How should I know? Just waiting until a bigger fish came along, I should think.'

'You mean she was actively looking?' said Thanet.

'No idea. I told you, I didn't see enough of them to know much about their private life.'

'So you don't know if she had any boyfriends? Her husband hasn't dropped any hints?'

'No. You'd have to ask him.' Another cynical laugh. 'Though they do say the husband's often the last to know, don't they? Look, I don't want to speak out of turn, but why all the questions?'

'We always have to be careful, in cases of sudden death, Mr Covin.'

'What do you mean, careful?' Covin glanced from Thanet to Lineham and back again. 'I thought you said it was an accident?'

'I said that she had fallen down the stairs,' said Thanet.

Covin stared at him for a moment. Then in went another cigarette and this time his hand was shaking as he lit it. He inhaled deeply, then said, 'Are you implying what I think you're implying?'

'I'm not implying anything. At this stage we have no idea what happened and we shall have to wait for the post-mortem results before we are even certain of the cause of death. But meanwhile we can't afford to sit around twiddling our thumbs, just in case the matter is not as straightforward as it seems.'

Covin was puffing furiously and even though Thanet was a pipe smoker himself and used to a certain amount of tobacco smoke his eyes were beginning to sting and water. He spared a sympathetic thought for the way Lineham must be suffering.

'You're saying someone might have pushed her, aren't you?'

'I'm saying that at this point we have to keep an open mind.'

'Which is why you're asking all this stuff about Des and whether or not Jess was running around with someone else.'

'Please, Mr Covin, there's no point in jumping to conclusions, I assure you. All we're trying to do is find out as much

33

as possible about your sister-in-law. So, if you wouldn't mind answering just a few more questions, fill in a little more background for us . . .'

'Go on, then. I've got nothing to hide.'

'I wasn't suggesting that you have.' No point in becoming exasperated. It was always a shock for witnesses to realise that they might, however marginally, be involved in a potential murder investigation and their reactions varied widely, from complete withdrawal to belligerence. 'So, if we could very briefly go back to what you were telling us. Mrs Manifest came to live with you when she was ten and stayed until . . .?'

'She started work.'

'How old would she have been then?'

'Sixteen.'

'She left school after she took her O levels, then?'

'Yes.'

'Where did she go to school?'

'Sturrenden Grammar.'

'And where did she work, when she left?'

'The *Kent Messenger*. She'd done a week's work experience there the summer before, and enjoyed it.'

Thanet was surprised that Jessica had been taken on straight from school like that. Nowadays there was such competition for reporters' jobs that he understood it was virtually impossible to get one without a degree. But it was – what? – twenty years or so since Jessica Manifest started work. Perhaps things had been different then. In any case, she probably hadn't started reporting straight away. No doubt there'd have been some kind of apprenticeship. All the same, if she had been reasonably bright, as she must have been . . . 'As a matter of interest, why didn't she stay on at school, to take her A levels?'

Covin leaned across to stub out his cigarette in the ashtray which was now so full that he had difficulty in doing so. He got up and emptied it into the fire. 'Oh, you know what kids are like at that age. She was fed up with school, wanted to start work, earn some money of her own. And, like I said, she was pretty good at getting her own way, if she really wanted something.' He didn't sit down again but stood with his back to the fire, hands clasped behind his back.

A hint that the interview had gone on long enough? Thanet had no intention of ending it until he was ready. 'Just one or two more points, then. Would you mind telling me what you did, after you finished supper this evening? That was just after twenty past seven, I believe you said?'

Covin was lighting another cigarette, but he didn't sit down. 'That's right.'

'Presumably your daughter then had to load her things into the car?'

'No, she did that earlier, before supper, so she was all ready to go.'

'So it must have been about 7.30 when she left?'

'About then, yes.'

'Then you tried to get through to your sister-in-law . . .'

'I thought I might as well do it right away, while I was thinking of it.'

'Quite. And then?'

Covin shrugged. 'Nothing much. I sat around, watched the telly.'

And that was as much as they could get out of him. There was, he assured them, nothing more to tell.

'What do you think, Mike?' said Thanet, when they were outside.

Lineham was standing with his head thrown back, taking in great gulps of fresh air. 'Honestly, I thought I was going to suffocate in there! It was the worst atmosphere I have ever been in my entire life! And I bet our clothes absolutely reek of cigarette smoke.' He sniffed experimentally at his sleeve. 'Faugh! Disgusting. I'm certainly not leaving these indoors all night, they'll stink the house out.'

'What will you do, Mike?' said Thanet, grinning. 'Undress in the garden? That'll intrigue the neighbours. I can just see the headline . . .'

'Give over, sir.' Lineham was not amused. He stalked across to his car then turned to say, 'I bet my hair stinks, too. I'm going to have a shower before I go to bed.'

Privately, Thanet resolved to do the same. But all he said was, 'Mike! I've got the message. And believe me, I sympathise.'

'It's a wonder he's still walking around, if you ask me! He ought to be six feet under, by rights.'

'There is no justice,' agreed Thanet. 'And now, if you wouldn't mind turning your attention to the matter in hand for a few minutes . . .'

'Sorry, sir. OK. What were you saying?'

'Look, it's getting a bit chilly. Let's sit in your car for a few minutes, shall we?' He waited until they were settled before picking up on the conversation. 'I was just wondering what you thought of Covin – apart from disapproving of his smoking habits.'

'They may not be entirely irrelevant though, sir, may they?'

'What do you mean?'

'Well, you could tell he always smokes a lot, from the way the room stank, but he surely couldn't chainsmoke like that all day? Apart from anything else, it would cost an absolute fortune.'

'He did seem very tense, I agree. And Jessica obviously wasn't exactly his favourite person.'

'A bit far-fetched, though, surely, sir? I mean, what would he be doing there in the first place? And why suddenly shove her down the stairs after all these years?'

'It does seem unlikely. But we only know what he has actually told us. He may have a very powerful motive about which we know nothing at the moment. I certainly had the feeling he was holding back on something.'

'So did I.'

'What, I wonder?'

Both men were silent, thinking.

'Of course, it might have nothing to do with Jessica's death,' said Thanet. 'I suppose it could be connected with his daughter. What was her name? Karen.'

'In what way?'

'Well, it does seem odd that she's driven herself back to Reading. It isn't as though she has a car of her own. Most students I know are either driven back by their parents along with all the gear they seem to need to take with them, or they travel by public transport, looking like pack mules. But say that was what they originally intended, that her father should drive her. And then say they had a row and she walked out and drove off in a temper . . . He could be on tenterhooks in case she had an accident on the way. That could account for his being tense, and for the fact that we both felt he was holding back. He wouldn't have wanted to tell us he'd had a row with Karen, would he? He'd regard it as none of our business.'

'But she'd have arrived by now, surely.'

'Maybe. But if she hasn't rung to let him know and there's no phone in her digs so he can't ring her to find out . . .'

'Mmm. You could be right.'

'Or, let's face it, there could be half a dozen other reasons why he happens to be uptight tonight. Maybe he had a nasty letter from his bank manager this morning. Maybe he's just been sacked. Maybe he's just learned he's got some fatal disease . . .'

'Like lung cancer, for example.'

'Quite. But in any case, I think we ought to check the times he gave us with Karen. It won't do any harm. Jerry Long's stationed in Reading now. Give him a ring in the morning.'

'With respect, is there any point, sir? Even if she does confirm that she left about 7.30, Covin would still have had plenty of time to get over to the Manifests' house, if he was involved. That anonymous 999 call didn't come in until 8.11, as I recall.'

'I know. Still, it's worth a phone call, I think.'

'OK. I'll ring him first thing. Mind, it's in Covin's favour that he made no attempt to hide the fact that he didn't like Jessica, isn't it? If he'd had anything to do with her death he'd surely have kept quiet on that score.'

Thanet pursed his lips. 'Unless he hoped that's what we'd think.'

'Bit subtle, for him, don't you think?'

'Perhaps. You know, if it weren't for that call to the emergency services we might well have accepted without question that this death was a straightforward accident. But someone made that call and according to the ambulance crew it wasn't Manifest. When they arrived at 8.26 he told them he'd only just got in.'

'If he's telling the truth.'

Never overlook the obvious, thought Thanet. Here was a marriage long gone sour, a husband sorely provoked by his wife. Perhaps they needn't have bothered to interview Covin at all. Still . . . 'First thing in the morning check the number that call was made from.'

'I can do it tonight, if you like.'

'No. It'll keep.' Thanet had had enough for one day.

At home, Joan had gone to bed, leaving the light on in the hall. Beside the telephone were two more gaily wrapped parcels which must have been dropped in during the evening. So many had arrived over the last couple of days that Bridget was going to have a positive orgy of present-opening when she got back.

These reminders of the wedding resurrected Thanet's worries about his speech and he fell asleep once again rehearsing his proposed opening. His dreams were anxiety-ridden: he was at the reception and first he found that he had mislaid his notes and then, when he finally stood up to address the blurred sea of faces which seemed to stretch away to infinity, he discovered that he had forgotten to put on his trousers.

Next morning, when he went downstairs to make their tea, he found a Post-it note stuck on the handle of the kettle saying, *Check bows on bridesmaids' dresses* and there was another on the mirror in the bathroom saying, *Ring printer.* Over the last week these little self-reminders had been appearing everywhere. The truth was that with a house to run and her full-time job as a probation officer Joan simply didn't have time to deal with all these last-minute details and the fact that she was writing them down whenever and wherever they occurred to her was a measure of the strain she was under. Bridget really should have stayed at home this week to give her a hand.

'Is there anything I can do to help?' he asked at breakfast and felt a guilty relief as she shook her head. 'Well, do try not to overdo it, darling.'

If only, Thanet thought as he started the car, Alexander's parents were less upper middle class. It was natural that he and Joan didn't want to let Bridget down in front of her new in-laws, and equally natural that this anxiety should be an extra pressure upon them both. He wasn't looking forward to meeting them for the first time at the family dinner which had been arranged for Friday evening at the Black Swan, where the Highmans would be staying and where the reception was to be held next day.

With a determined effort he put thoughts of the wedding out of his mind and tried to concentrate on the day ahead. At least it looked as though it might be fine. Overnight the clouds which had brought yesterday's rain had begun to break up and there was a promising brightness to the east.

Lineham invariably arrived at work before him and today was no exception.

'So,' said Thanet, taking off his coat. 'What's the story? Anything interesting come in from the house-to-house inquiries?' He sat down at his desk.

'A couple of things. The next-door neighbours are away for a few days, unfortunately, but another neighbour saw a red Volkswagen Polo parked just up the lane around half past seven last night. He passed it when he was coming home.'

'Any details?'

'I'm afraid not, except that it was newish. He said the back was that rounded shape which came in in '95. Apparently it was only there for a very short while – ten or fifteen minutes, he thinks. He got to thinking it was rather odd, that it should be parked there like that, and looked out again about a quarter of an hour later to check if it was still there. But it was gone.'

'Was there anyone in it?'

'First he said yes, then he said no, then he said he couldn't be sure because it was dark by then, and he was concentrating on turning into the estate.'

'Pity.'

'However,' said Lineham, and Thanet could tell that the sergeant was looking forward to imparting the next piece of information. 'Inquiries at the Green Man turned up some potentially useful stuff. Apparently, because the lane is so narrow, people often use the pub car park even if they're not paying customers, and, as you can imagine, the publican isn't too pleased about this. In fact, it makes him hopping mad, and he's taken to trying to catch them out – not always easy, partly because he's often busy behind the bar and partly because although he recognises most of the cars belonging to regular customers, when there are strangers in the pub it's hard to tell whether the cars are legitimately parked or not.

'Anyway, though none of them was there for long, last night there were three cars which didn't belong to customers – well, one was a pick-up. A white Ford. But there was also a Mercedes which he thinks he's seen around but which hasn't actually parked at the pub before, and a Nissan which is apparently a persistent offender. He'd taken the number of that one and I've checked it on the computer. Belongs to an Alistair Barcombe who lives in Sturrenden.'

'Excellent. That's a bit of luck.'

'There's more. Another neighbour says that she's seen a young man hanging around lately. She's been dithering about reporting him to the Neighbourhood Watch but she hasn't because she thinks he looks familiar and she wondered if in fact he lives somewhere on the estate and she'd be making a fool of herself. Anyway, she's sure she's seen him before somewhere, but she can't think where. Says if she does remember, she'll let us know.'

'Good. That the lot?' Thanet glanced at his watch. Time for the morning meeting. 'It'll have to wait.'

The morning meeting was Superintendent Draco's way of keeping his finger on the pulse of his domain. A fiery little Welshman, he had initially made himself unpopular by the demands he made upon his staff but gradually they had come to regard him with affectionate respect. They had supported him wholeheartedly throughout his wife's long struggle with leukaemia and had rejoiced with him when against all the odds she had made a good recovery. Draco adored her and now that she was restored to health he was back on the top of his form, crackling with energy and 'sticking his nose into everything' as Lineham frequently complained.

Today, however, the meeting was soon over. Immediately afterwards Draco was leaving for Heathrow. Since 1989, the Foreign Office had been helping Eastern European countries to establish new systems of law and order by examining existing ones and today a group of delegates from Poland was arriving on a two-day visit to study different aspects of the British criminal justice system. Extraordinarily enough, for some reason Thanet could not remember (a Polish grandmother?) Draco spoke Polish and had been asked to accompany the group as an interpreter. Within ten minutes Thanet was back in his office. He plumped down in his chair and said, 'Where were we, Mike?'

Lineham put down his pen. 'Just two more points, sir. One, Doc M. says today's impossible for the PM. Promises he'll fit it in first thing tomorrow.'

Thanet shrugged. 'Ah well, can't be helped.'

'And the other thing is, I thought you might be interested to know that Louise was at school with Jessica Manifest – Jessica Dander, as she was then.'

Thanet sat up. Now that *was* interesting. 'Was she indeed? What does she have to say about her?'

'That Jessica didn't mix very well and had the reputation for being unsociable. There were a couple of girls she was friendly with, one in particular, a Juliet Barnes – Juliet Parker then – but on the whole she tended to keep herself to herself.'

The phone rang and Lineham picked it up. 'Jerry Long,' he mouthed at Thanet. 'Rang him earlier.'

You couldn't hope for a much swifter response than that, thought Thanet. Long must have sent someone out to see Karen Covin right away.

In fact he had gone himself, but Karen was out. He had spoken to her roommate, however, and she had said that Karen had arrived about 10.15 last night, that she had been rather subdued and her roommate suspected an argument with her father.

'Just as we thought,' said Thanet. 'Anyway, her arrival time is about right.'

'The roommate was a real chatterbox, apparently,' said Lineham. 'Jerry found it hard to get away. She says she and Karen are good friends, go on holiday together and so on. He heard all about their summer holiday hiking in Scotland, their plans to Interrail around Europe next year and go to India the year after. He asked if we'd like him to go back later and speak to Karen herself, but I said no. Was that right?'

'I think so. There doesn't seem much point at the moment. We can always get back to him if necessary. Did Louise tell you anything else of interest?'

'Well, she did say that Jessica was very bright, and that everyone expected her to go on into the sixth form and probably to university. They were all surprised when she left after her O levels.'

'Does this Juliet Barnes lives locally?'

'I'm not sure. I think so, from the way Louise spoke about her. I could find out.'

'Right.'

'Do you want me to ring her now?'

'Oh no, tonight will do. We've enough on our plates for today.'

'So,' said Lineham. 'What first?'

'I think Desmond Manifest comes top of the list, don't you?'

FOUR

There was a Council transit van parked just beyond the sectioned-off area in front of the Manifests' house and two workmen were sitting inside drinking from the tops of Thermos flasks and reading tabloid newspapers. A spade and a pickaxe lay near the hole in the road as evidence of good intentions though so far as Thanet could see nothing had yet been done this morning. Beyond was parked a bright red Datsun. Had the next-door neighbours returned? Thanet wondered.

'Hard at it, as usual,' murmured Lineham as they walked past the van. 'It makes me mad,' he went on as they waited on the doorstep for a response to their ring. 'It's taxpayers' money they're wasting!'

The door was opened not by either Desmond Manifest or his brother, as Thanet had expected, but by a burly man in his sixties, with greying hair and a square face with an aggressive thrust to the jaw. Desmond's father, perhaps?

It was, and he was none too pleased to see them. 'My son isn't well enough to talk to you.' And he started to close the door on them.

Lineham acted swiftly, stepping forward to hold it open.

'Mr Manifest,' said Thanet. 'I don't think you understand. We really have to speak to your son. If he's not prepared to talk to us here, I'm afraid he'll have to accompany us back to Headquarters.'

Manifest hesitated and then grudgingly stood back to allow them in.

In the hall stood a diminutive woman with arms folded

43

across her chest and one hand pressed to her mouth. Frightened eyes peered out at them from a shapeless nest of badly permed hair. 'It's the police,' said Manifest. 'They want to talk to Des. Is he up?'

The woman shook her head.

'Go and tell him, then.'

Without a word she turned and scuttled up the stairs.

'You'd better wait in here.'

By daylight the overcrowded sitting room looked subtly different – shabbier. Now Thanet could detect signs of wear in the upholstery, and the surfaces of the wooden pieces were slightly clouded, as if they hadn't been polished for a very long time. Strange, he thought, how possessions can say so much about their owners. These spoke of aspirations abandoned, of dreams destroyed, above all of a mistress who didn't care about them any more. And her husband? Had she cared about him? Or he about her?

Manifest senior was determined not to be hospitable. He did not invite them to sit down and stood on the threshold, arms folded, watching them intently as if he expected them to pocket the non-existent silver. His attitude was understandable, Thanet told himself, trying not to be irritated by such unwarranted hostility. The man was simply being protective. After all, how would he, Thanet, feel if Ben had suffered a mortal blow? Remember how furious he had been with Alexander when Bridget had been so hurt by his rejection?

'Mr Manifest,' he said, 'I can understand your wanting to ensure that your son is not upset any further, but we really do have to speak to him. You must see that.'

'I don't see nothing of the sort! She fell downstairs, didn't she? Simple accident. So why all the fuss? Why can't you leave well alone?'

'Look, sit down for a moment, will you? Please?' he persisted, as Manifest remained obdurate. 'Perhaps we ought to explain just why it is so important.'

Manifest moved at last, reluctantly going to perch on the edge of an upright chair against the wall near the half-open door.

Thanet glanced at Lineham and they both sat down.

'I don't suppose you're aware of the circumstances of your daughter-in-law's death,' said Thanet.

His wife entered the room. She moved so quietly Thanet hadn't heard her come downstairs. 'He's getting dressed,' she said to her husband.

He acknowledged what she had said with a nod. 'Go on,' he said to Thanet.

'Just after ten past eight last night someone phoned the emergency services.' Blast. He had forgotten to ask Lineham if he had checked the number that call was made from. And Lineham had forgotten to tell him. He glanced at the sergeant and raised his eyebrows, hoping Lineham would understand.

'That call was made from this number,' said Lineham. 'By a man.' *Sorry*, he signalled to Thanet.

Was it indeed? thought Thanet.

'And when the ambulance arrived at 8.26, fifteen minutes later,' Lineham went on, 'they found your son kneeling over the body. He told them he had just come in.'

'So who made that phone call?' said Manifest.

'Precisely,' said Thanet. 'So you see, the matter is not quite as straightforward as it might appear.'

'I still don't see why you have to bother Des.' Manifest glanced up at his wife, who was standing beside him, one hand on his shoulder. They looked, Thanet thought, rather as though they were posing for a Victorian photographer. 'I can't see how he can help you, if he wasn't here when it happened. I don't want him upset any more than he already is. He's in a right old state, isn't he, Iris?'

She nodded, her thin face a troubled mask.

'Though I can't say we feel the same. Do we, Mother?'

A shake of the head this time.

'You weren't fond of your daughter-in-law?' said Thanet.

'Good riddance, I say. We both do, don't we?' Manifest did not wait for a response this time before saying, 'Nothing but trouble, she brought him.'

'Trouble?'

'With her airs and her graces, wanting this, wanting that. All over him, she was, when he was doing well, but the minute

45

he lost his job . . . He was made redundant, you see. Disgusting, the way it was done, wasn't it, Iris? Anyway, it was a different story then. Treated him like dirt, she did. You'd think she'd never heard of the marriage vows. For better or for worse, my foot! No, once he's got over the shock it'll all be for the best, you'll see.'

'Dad? What are you saying?' Desmond Manifest came in. His hair was wet from a shower but he hadn't bothered to shave and he still looked slightly dazed. He was wearing jeans and a sweatshirt.

Manifest looked discomforted. 'Nothing much, son. Just chatting to the Inspector here.'

'Yes, well, thank you, Mr Manifest. We'd like to talk to your son now.'

Manifest didn't take the hint. He remained seated, as if he were welded to the chair. His wife glanced uneasily at him and then at Thanet. She took her hand from his shoulder and started to move away but he snatched at her skirt to restrain her and gave Thanet a defiant glare.

'Alone,' said Thanet.

'We have every right to stay.'

'Dad! I'm not a child, you know.'

Ah, thought Thanet, you may not know it, but you are. To them, anyway, and always will be. 'If you'd like your parents to stay . . .?'

'No, thank you.'

'Mr Manifest?' said Thanet.

The old man rose reluctantly. 'If you want us,' he said to Desmond, 'we'll be in the kitchen.'

Desmond touched him on the shoulder. 'I know. Thanks.'

When they had gone he said, 'He means well.'

'I realise that. Please, sit down, sir.'

Desmond chose the same chair as the previous evening and glanced uneasily at Lineham, who was opening his notebook.

'There are a few points we'd like to clear up,' said Thanet. They had decided that he should conduct this interview. Last night, when Manifest had been so vulnerable, it had helped that Lineham was a familiar face. This morning it could be a

46

disadvantage. 'First of all, someone rang for an ambulance last night, from this number. Was it you?'

'No. I was wondering about that. I told you – told someone, anyway, I'm afraid it's all a bit of a blur – I'd only just got in when they arrived. Who did ring?'

'That's what we're wondering.'

'What did they say?'

Thanet glanced at Lineham.

'Just that there'd been an accident, and the address,' said the sergeant.

'I wonder who on earth it could have been. And why didn't they wait for the ambulance to arrive? And how did they . . .?' Desmond's eyes narrowed. 'Hang about . . .'

'What?'

'I was going to say, how did they get in? But I've just remembered . . . When I got home the door was open. My God, how could I have forgotten that?'

Because, thought Thanet, assuming that you're innocent, every time you've had a flashback to last night you'll have seen nothing but that image of your wife lying crumpled at the foot of the stairs. 'Because you were in a state of shock,' he said. 'But it does explain something that was puzzling me.'

'What was that?'

'Last night, you didn't say, "I saw her as soon as I opened the door." You said, "I saw her as soon as I pushed the door open." The implication is that it already was.'

'There you are, then.'

'How wide open was it?'

Manifest frowned. 'Just a few inches, I think.'

'You'd been for a walk, you said.'

'That's right.'

'How long a walk? What time did you leave?'

Manifest pressed his thumb and forefinger into his eye-sockets, then looked up, blinking as if the light were too bright for him. 'About twenty past seven.'

'And you didn't get back until twenty-five past eight?'

'So?' The first hint of aggression there.

'You were walking for over an hour.'

47

'I like walking.'

'Where did you go, exactly?'

'The way I usually go.'

Lineham scribbled as Manifest outlined the route. It might be necessary for someone to walk it later.

'Did you stop at all on the way?'

Something flickered behind the man's eyes and there was the merest hesitation. But it was enough to alert Thanet. 'No.' He crossed his legs and his foot twitched.

Thanet was well aware that people are more practised at controlling their facial muscles than their extremities. 'You didn't call in at a pub for a drink, for example?'

Again that hesitation. 'I was going to, but I changed my mind.'

'Oh? Why was that?'

A shrug. 'Just didn't feel like it, I suppose.'

He was lying, definitely. But why? It was worth probing a little further, irrelevant as it might seem. 'Was it the pub you usually go to?'

'Sometimes. Sometimes I go to the Green Man, down the road.'

'It depends on whether you're going for your usual walk, I suppose.'

'Yes. Look, what the devil has this got to do with . . . with . . .'

'I'm just trying to get a clearer picture of last night,' said Thanet soothingly. 'And I'm afraid that might mean asking questions about all sorts of things which appear irrelevant. Just bear with me, will you?'

Manifest didn't argue, so Thanet went on, 'So, you'd been for your usual walk. For some reason you decided not to call in at the pub as you often do – what time would that have been, by the way?'

'I'm not sure, exactly. I've never timed it.'

'Approximately, then?'

'Ten or a quarter past eight?'

'The pub is well over half way, then? You said you left here at 7.20 and if you reached the pub at 8.15 and got home again at 8.25, just before the ambulance arrived, it must be only about ten minutes' walk away from here by the shortest route.'

'Oh, I see what you mean. Yes. I never do the circuit that way around.'

'Which pub did you say it was?'

'The Harrow.'

And Manifest hadn't wanted to tell him that, either, but hadn't known how to refuse. What was going on here? 'So you got home about ten minutes later. Would you tell me what happened then? I'm sorry. I know this is going to be painful for you.'

Manifest compressed his lips, narrowed his eyes and frowned, remembering. 'So far as I can recall,' he said slowly, 'there was nothing out of the ordinary until I got close to the front door. Then I saw it was ajar and that did alarm me. Jess would never have left it open when she was alone in the house at night. I called out to her as I pushed it open and then I . . . There she . . .' Manifest swallowed hard, over and over, as if to suppress incipient nausea.

Thanet waited for a few moments while Manifest got himself under control again, then said, 'Now, I want you to think carefully. Did you touch your wife at all? Move her in any way, to even the slightest degree?'

This was very important. If he had, it was possible that Jessica might have been alive until that moment, that an understandable but fatal effort to check whether or not she really was dead, or a spontaneous gesture of despairing love, such as gathering her up in his arms, might have finally severed a badly damaged spinal cord. In which case, Manifest might in all innocence have caused her death.

But he was shaking his head emphatically. 'I saw a St John's Ambulance film once and it said if it looks as though someone's neck is broken the last thing you should do is touch them. And it was obvious right away . . . I mean, the angle of her head . . .'

'Good,' said Thanet. 'You did exactly the right thing. Now, I have to ask you this. Do you know of anyone who might want to harm your wife?'

Manifest pushed a hand wearily through his hair. 'The

49

obvious explanation, so far as I can see, is that it was a burglary which went wrong. And even so, of course, it might have been a pure accident.'

'Quite. Well, we shall see. It's early days yet.'

Manifest hesitated, then said slowly, 'But there is one other possibility.'

'Oh? What?'

'My wife was convinced that someone had been following her lately. I'm afraid I didn't believe her – thought she was imagining things. I never saw any sign of anything like that. But perhaps I should have listened, paid more attention. If I had . . . Oh God, if I had, perhaps she'd still be alive.' And he buried his face in his hands.

Thanet and Lineham exchanged glances.

'Des,' said Lineham. 'Could you tell us a bit more about this?'

Manifest shook his head but he did straighten up again and take several deep breaths in an effort to calm down.

'Try, will you?' Lineham urged. 'It could be important.'

'There's nothing more to tell, really. She did make a complaint to the police, but nothing came of it.'

'Did she ever describe the man to you – I assume it was a man?' said Thanet

'We both assumed it was a man. But no, that was half the trouble. It was just an impression, really. A feeling she had. And twice at night she was convinced she'd seen a prowler outside, watching.'

'In the garden, you mean? Looking through the windows?'

'Once she thought she'd seen a movement in the back garden. I went outside to look, but there was no one there. And another time she thought she saw someone behind the hedge across the road. But that time I was out.'

'I see. Well, we'll look into it. There's only one other point to clear up at the moment, I think, then we'll leave you in peace. When we were talking to you last night, you said – let me see if I can remember the words exactly: "I don't understand. I mean, why was he *there*? He should have been here." What did you mean?' Thanet could tell immediately by the guarded look which had appeared in Manifest's eyes as he was speaking that another lie was coming.

'I can't imagine. I was very confused. I didn't really know what I was saying.'

'Well,' said Lineham as they walked down the path to the gate. 'I don't know what you think, but if he had anything to do with her death he's missed his vocation. He should be on the stage.'

One workman was now pecking away half-heartedly at the hole with his pickaxe while the other stood by, leaning on his spade.

'Don't overdo it, will you?' murmured Lineham after they were past them. 'On the other hand,' he went on, returning to what he was saying, 'it's obvious he was lying in his teeth when you asked him about the pub.'

'Yes. I wonder why?'

'I was thinking about that. What if he wasn't as fond of his wife as people are making out? After all, she didn't treat him too well by all accounts, did she? And what if he'd found himself another girlfriend, was in the habit of meeting her in the pub, and didn't want to mention the pub because he thought if he did we might check up and find out about her?'

'Possible. But it also occurred to me . . . You know what we were saying, about him having seen someone somewhere he hadn't expected to see him, someone he had in fact expected to be with Jessica . . . What if he'd intended calling in at the pub, but had seen – either through a window or after he'd gone in – the person he had thought would be here, and that was why he changed his mind about having a drink and came home instead?'

'Yes. That would make sense. In which case . . .'

'Quite,' said Thanet. 'We need to find out who that someone was.'

'But if that's so, why didn't he tell us about this person? What possible reason could he have for not mentioning him?'

'If we find out who, we might find out why.'

'Shall we go to the pub, ask some questions?'

'No. We'll get someone else to do that. We've got too much

51

to do today. But first, I want to nose around here a bit. Let's take a look behind that hedge, shall we? See if there are any signs of this prowler.'

'If he exists,' said Lineham.

'Quite. If Manifest had nothing to do with his wife's death he's certainly feeding us plenty of red herrings – open front doors, watchers in the dark . . . Over that five-barred gate, I think?'

'I suppose the prowler could be the young man that neighbour mentioned.'

'That's certainly a possibility.'

'But what I don't understand,' said Lineham as they climbed the gate and worked their way along behind the hedge, 'is why Des goes out walking in the evenings, when he's got all day to do it in. It does sound as though he made a habit of it.'

'Unless he has a girlfriend, as you suggested.'

'Oh, I don't know. On second thoughts I admit the girl-friend idea is unlikely. He does seem genuinely cut up about his wife's death.'

'Perhaps it was simply that she'd got fed up with him,' said Thanet, 'and wanted the place to herself in the evenings. Remember the separate rooms? Or that he regularly went out when she had a visitor he wanted to avoid.'

'The mysterious someone!' Lineham had been poking around in the hedge with a stick and now he straightened up with a jerk. 'Yes! That makes more sense. What if it was a lover, sir?'

'And Manifest went out on the evenings he was expected, leaving him a clear field? Sounds a bit far-fetched to me.'

Over the hedge Thanet saw Desmond Manifest's father leave the house and fetch something from the Datsun. The car didn't belong to the neighbours then.

'Just say I'm right, though,' Lineham persisted. 'Say she and her lover quarrelled and he pushed her down the stairs. He panics, rings for an ambulance, then scarpers . . .'

'And Manifest gets back a quarter of an hour later, realises what has happened and decides to cover up for him? I really think we're moving into the realms of fantasy here.

Anyway, it doesn't add up, Mike. If you're right about all this, the lover was sitting in the Harrow and Manifest saw him there.'

'But it all depends on the timing, sir! You said yourself that the Harrow was only ten minutes' walk away. That's only a couple of minutes by car. This chap could have arrived at the house after Des left at 7.20 and while Des was walking for the next fifty-five minutes there'd have been plenty of time for him and Jessica to have quarrelled and for him to have driven to the pub afterwards so that he was sitting there calm as you please for Des to see when he got there at 8.15!'

'True. Well, we'll see. It shouldn't be too difficult to unearth him if he exists. All this, of course, assumes that Manifest didn't do it himself.'

'I still think that unlikely. Though I agree, we shouldn't rule it out. It all depends, really, on whether he was telling the truth about the front door being open. Otherwise he might well have rung for the ambulance himself and simply have been pretending that he'd just arrived before they did. What do you think, sir?'

'At the moment I'm inclined to give him the benefit of the doubt. Doc Mallard didn't seem in any doubt that he was genuinely in a state of shock last night, and if the business about the door was a ploy to divert suspicion from himself, it was a pretty subtle one. Just to slip in that he pushed it open and leave it to us to pick up –'

'But he didn't, sir. He was the one who brought it up this morning. He wouldn't have known that you were going to mention it anyway.'

'I still think there would have been a temptation for him to make more of it last night. Anyway, it's pointless to speculate any further at this stage. Let's get a few more facts under our belt first.'

'Look at this, sir!'

Their little foray had been rewarded. At a point directly opposite the Manifests' house the ground was trampled, the grass flattened, and there were a number of cigarette butts.

'Roll your own,' said Lineham, taking a polythene bag from his pocket and slipping it over his hand so as to pick them up without touching them. 'Not many people smoke those these days.'

'We'll check to see if she did file a complaint.'

'I was wondering, sir . . . That unauthorised parking at the pub . . . You don't think the owner of that Nissan –'

'The same thought had occurred to me. What was his name?'

'Barcombe. Alastair Barcombe.'

FIVE

The owner of the Nissan lived in one of the little Victorian terraced houses on the Maidstone Road in Sturrenden. These had been built in the days when their peace would have been disturbed by nothing more intrusive than the gentle clopping of horses' hoofs and the rumble of carts, but now, in addition to local traffic, a never-ending line of lorries, cars, vans and buses streamed past on their way to the Channel ports, to the huge passenger station for the Channel Tunnel trains at Ashford, to the new industrial estates which had sprung up to the south of that town and to the Tunnel car terminus on the M20. That the beautiful county of Kent, the so-called garden of England, had become little more than a through-route to Europe, never failed to anger Thanet and all those who, like him, loved the county and had known it before so much of it had been sacrificed to the god of transport. It still boasted some of the most beautiful gardens, the most historic castles, the loveliest landscapes in England, but its long-suffering inhabitants couldn't help wondering where it was all going to end.

Double yellow lines and the narrowness of the road meant that it was impossible to park in front of the house and they had to drive some way past and turn off the main road to find somewhere to leave the car before walking back. The sun had broken through at last but Thanet scarcely noticed, he was too preoccupied with trying to take shallow breaths in order to avoid filling his lungs with the exhaust fumes with which the air seemed saturated. The houses were small, with only the narrowest of pavements to protect them from passing vehicles. Here and there an optimistic gardener had managed to gouge out a hole in which to plant a climber, but coated with the dust constantly thrown up by passing traffic the shrubs had failed to thrive.

'Don't know how people ever manage to sleep at night living on a road like this,' said Lineham as they waited for an answer to their knock, raising his voice to make himself heard over the roar of a passing lorry. 'It must be impossible to have the bedroom windows open. If you weren't deafened you'd be suffocated.'

'I suppose you get used to it,' said Thanet. 'But I agree, I'd hate it.' So often, when interviewing people in their homes, he gave heartfelt thanks for his own comfortable if modest home. Though this one, he had noted, was much cherished: the windows sparkled, the paintwork was in pristine condition, and the brass knocker, the letterbox and even the keyhole cover shone with much polishing.

'House-proud,' said Lineham, reading his mind.

Thanet nodded as the door opened.

'Mrs Barcombe?'

'Yes?' She was tall, thin and bony, clutching a duster and a spraycan of polish to her chest and was dressed like a char-woman from a forties comedy, with a turban over her hair and a floral crossover apron of the type Thanet would have expected to be virtually unobtainable nowadays. Perhaps she made them herself, he thought irrelevantly as he introduced himself.

She immediately looked alarmed. 'Police?' Her eyes darted from one to the other. 'What's happened? Is it Kevin?'

'No. Please don't worry. These are merely routine inquiries. Er . . . May we come in for a moment?'

She looked down at their feet and Thanet saw that not only was she herself wearing carpet slippers but that two more pairs, men's, were lined up to the right of the door. A thick sheet of plastic carpet protector ran down the centre of the narrow hallway. Mrs Barcombe evidently carried her war against dirt to the kind of extremes he would find impossible to live with. On the whole Thanet tried to accommodate him-self to the lifestyles of those he had to interview on the principle that there was no point in arousing unnecessary antagonism, but he drew the line at taking off his shoes. He watched her struggle to overcome her desire to request just that, and waited with what he hoped was an expression of polite expectation.

Eventually she capitulated. 'I suppose so,' she said grudgingly.

They followed her through a door on the right into a sitting room where there were antimacassars and arm-protectors on the three-piece suite and every surface shone, sparkled or twinkled. There was a strong smell of Brasso and furniture polish overlaid with air freshener but no evidence of any occupation – no books, newspapers, magazines, no knitting or needlework, not even a television set. Thanet guessed that the room was rarely used. Pride of place was taken by a photograph of a young man, no more than a boy really, set precisely in the centre of the mantelpiece. It was obviously a holiday snap – he was leaning against some railings with a background of beach, sea and sky. If the owner of the Nissan was Alistair Barcombe, this, presumably, was Kevin.

'Is Mr Barcombe in?'

She shook her head. 'He's at work.'

'Where is that, Mrs Barcombe?'

'Bentall's, in the High Street.'

A men's outfitters, in the town.

'May we sit down?'

She nodded and sank into a chair herself, still clutching the duster and spraycan. Comfort objects perhaps, thought Thanet. 'He drives to work?'

'No, he walks.'

Thanet waited.

She fidgeted with the duster, then said, 'It's not far into the town from here, it's not worth getting the car out. Then there's the parking. If you can find a space you have to pay through the nose for it.'

'Where do you keep your car? Some distance away, I imagine?'

'We rent a garage, round the back.'

'Does your husband take it out much in the evenings?'

'Has it been stolen or something, and smashed up? Is that what all this is about?'

'No, not at all. Does he? Take it out in the evenings?'

'Well, sometimes, yes.'

'And last night? Did he take it out last night?'

'No, he stayed in at home with me. We watched the telly.'

Thanet believed her. Which left Kevin – who, he guessed, was the apple of her eye. He would have to be careful. He stood up. Lineham, taken by surprise, was a little slow to follow and gave Thanet a questioning glance. 'Well, thank you, Mrs Barcombe,' said Thanet, smiling. 'I don't think we need to trouble you any further at the moment.' He turned away and in so doing pretended to notice the photograph for the first time. 'Is this your son? Kevin, did you say his name was?'

She was already on her feet, relief making her almost garrulous. 'Yes. Well, adopted son, as a matter of fact. We've always made a point of making no secret about that. I always think it's a mistake not to be open about it, don't you? You hear of such terrible stories when the children learn about it late in life. We told our Kevin very early on, and whatever people say to you about adoption, don't you believe it. No son of our own could have been more to us than he is, nor treated us better. He's never given us a moment's worry.'

But the shadow behind her eyes denied what she was saying.

Thanet smiled. 'I'm delighted to hear that. It's rare enough, with young people carrying on the way they do these days.' He began to move towards the door. 'Does he work locally?' His tone was casual, as if he were merely expressing a polite interest.

'At Snippers, in the High Street.'

'Oh. That's where my wife has her hair done. She started going there last year and says she's never had it cut so well in her life before.'

Mrs Barcombe looked gratified. 'That's why Kevin was so pleased to get in there. They do a really good training, he says.'

'He's apprenticed, I suppose.'

'Halfway through.'

They were on the doorstep by now, about to leave, when Thanet turned as if an afterthought had just struck him – a technique which always amused him when he watched the Columbo films but which could occasionally, as now, prove useful. 'He drives, I suppose? Kevin? And borrows your husband's car sometimes?'

But he saw at once that his tactic had failed. A tiny frown appeared on her forehead and her eyes grew wary. 'Yes. Why?'

'Did he borrow it last night, by any chance?'

She hesitated, clearly torn between a reluctance to lie and anxiety that she might incriminate her son. 'I'm not sure.' She was still holding the spraycan and now, with a sudden movement, she tucked it under her arm and began to twist the duster into a tight spiral with hands reddened and coarsened by too much unnecessary housework.

'He doesn't always ask your husband's permission, if he wants to borrow it?'

'I don't always hear. If I'm in another room or something.'

'Of course. But he did go out last night?'

'Yes.' The answer was grudging.

'And what time did he leave?'

'I'm not sure.'

'A rough estimate?'

She sucked in her breath in exasperation. 'About a quarter to eight, I suppose.'

'I see. Well, thank you again, Mrs Barcombe.' And they left her staring after them.

As soon as they were out of earshot Lineham said, 'He obviously did borrow it last night, don't you think?'

'Looks like it.' Thanet glanced at his watch. Twelve-twenty. 'We'll have a bite to eat, then go and see what he has to say.'

Over a beef-and-pickle sandwich and a pint at a nearby pub Lineham said, 'And what was all that stuff about adoption?'

'Yes, I wondered that.'

'Something gone wrong there, you think?'

'It did sound rather as though she was trying to convince herself as well as us.'

'I was surprised she mentioned it at all.'

'I don't know. It sounded to me as if she was genuine in saying they'd never made a secret of it. It all came out as though it was something she told people automatically. But as for Kevin "never giving a moment's trouble", well, I'm not so sure.'

They drove into the town centre and, leaving the car at Headquarters, walked along to Snippers. It was a unisex salon but Thanet had never set foot inside before, preferring to have his hair cut the old-fashioned way in a barber's shop with a striped pole outside. Such places were becoming harder and harder to find but Sturrenden still boasted two and Thanet had been going along month after month to the same one for longer than he cared to remember; despite Joan's occasional proddings he had no intention of abandoning a practice of such long standing. He made a mental note, *Must fit in a haircut before Saturday.*

Inside he was surprised to see that the one feature he invariably associated with salons where women had their hair done was absent. There was not a single dome-shaped hair-drier in sight. The place was open plan and several stylists were at work, cutting, wielding combs, hand driers and styling wands. All but one, an older man, were young. Pop music blared out and the air was full of the mingled scents of shampoo, hair-spray and another more acrid ammoniac smell. Thanet found it very difficult to envisage Joan fitting in to this environment. On the other hand the place obviously had a wide appeal – the clients seemed to range from teenage to elderly.

'Can I help you?' The receptionist was in her teens with tousled hair streaked with green and red. She was wearing a black top with irregularly shaped holes cut out of it, revealing unappetising glimpses of pallid skin beneath.

'We'd like a word with Kevin Barcombe, please.' Briefly, Thanet flashed his warrant card. 'Police,' he murmured. He saw no point in causing unnecessary embarrassment.

She frowned. 'I'll get him.'

After a quick word with the older man, who gave them a

sharp look, she went to the back of the shop where the boy in the photograph was working not on a customer but on a model head. He was putting its hair up into an elaborate plait which began high on the back of the head and his absorption was total. He started when the girl approached him and left his work with reluctance.

'Is there anywhere private we can talk?' said Lineham, when they had introduced themselves.

'There's an exercise room upstairs. I'll have to ask Dennis.'

This was the older man, the owner presumably. He nodded and Kevin led them to an upper room equipped as a gym. Various exercise machines stood about and Lineham glanced at them with interest. 'I didn't know you had these here.'

'They're chiefly used in the evenings and at weekends. People come to work out. Look, what's all this about, then? I ain't done nothing – so far as I know, anyway.'

'We're just making some routine inquiries,' said Lineham. 'This shouldn't take long.'

'Good. It don't do my image much good, do it, to have you coming here like this?'

Thanet wondered what 'image' Kevin had of himself. Neither of his most memorable features was attractive – carrot-coloured hair and the dense crop of freckles which so often accompanies it.

'We understand you borrowed your father's car last night.'

'So? No crime in that, is there?'

But Thanet was sensing that beneath the bravado the boy was nervous. Was it possible that he really had been involved in Jessica Dander's death? Or was it simply that he had never been questioned by the police before and found the process alarming? Even innocent people often did, as Thanet was well aware.

'Of course not. Where did you go?'

'Sally's.'

A nightclub which had recently opened in a disused ware-house on the edge of town. According to Kevin he had left home at 8.15 and gone straight there. He had stayed until just after midnight, then returned home. A number of friends, he said, would confirm his story.

On the way out Thanet paused at the desk and inquired if Jessica Dander – or Jessica Manifest as she might have called herself – had been a client at Snippers. Apparently she had.

'So,' said Lineham as soon as they were outside, 'he knew her, by sight, anyway. He could be the prowler, don't you think? And if he's the prowler . . .'

'Let's not jump to conclusions, Mike. I agree, he could be. But let's get a little more evidence before making up our minds.'

'But he's involved somehow, isn't he? Otherwise, why lie about the time? There's a discrepancy of half an hour between the time he says he left home and the time his mother gave us. What's more, it covers part of the period we're looking at. Doc Mallard put the time of death between 7 and 8.26, and if Kevin left home at around 7.45 he could have been in Charthurst by eight.'

'Motive?'

Lineham grinned. 'Give me time and I'll come up with one.'

'Meanwhile we'll check the time of his arrival at Sally's, though I don't know if we'll get much joy. It's pretty popular, I believe, and usually heaving with people.'

'I'm not so sure. There might not have been many there so early in the evening. Things don't usually hot up until much later, I believe.'

'Well, we'll see.'

'So, what's next on the agenda, sir?'

'A visit to the *KM*, I think, in Maidstone.'

'Great.' Lineham loved driving, the further the better.

Thanet was relieved to have a brief respite too, to sit back and enjoy the mellowness of the early autumn landscape. This was the moment when the land was poised between one annual cycle and the next. The harvest was long since over and the year was winding down, but already some of the fields had been ploughed and sown with winter wheat, their chocolate-brown furrows etching graceful curves across the contours of the earth. Soon the tender green shoots would appear but meanwhile nature was preparing itself for its most spectacular display, the blaze of autumn colour which was already beginning to tint the patches of woodland which flanked their route.

At this time of day the roads were relatively clear and by just after 1.30 they were pulling into the car park at Maidstone Police Station in Palace Avenue. A few minutes' walk took them to the *Kent Messenger* offices which were in Middle Row, a narrow block of buildings between Maidstone High Street and Bank Street, one of the oldest streets in the town.

The reception area was light and airy with access from both streets. Behind a large square inquiry counter were two receptionists, one of them working the switchboard. The other looked up and smiled at their approach, but her expression quickly changed when she heard why they were there.

'We still can't believe it. You never think it'll happen to somebody you know.'

'You knew her well?'

Like Jessica the woman was in her thirties, with a broad, flat-featured face and short, straight blonde hair.

'Not really well. She wasn't a friend, if that's what you mean, but she had worked here for ages.' She turned to the other woman. 'Someone was saying this morning that they thought Jessica had worked at the *KM* longer than anyone else here, weren't they?'

Her colleague nodded.

'So you're bound to feel it, even if you didn't particularly . . . even if you weren't particularly close.'

So the receptionist hadn't liked her. It might be worth talking to her later. Meanwhile it was time for the appointment they had made with the news editor.

'I believe Mr Anderson is expecting us.'

The receptionist rang through and within minutes Colin Anderson had arrived and was whisking them upstairs. The narrow staircase led into the main editorial office. This too was light and airy and stretched the whole width of the block, with high windows overlooking both streets. Reporters were busily tapping away at their computers or answering telephones surrounded by a sea of paper piled up on desks and overflowing from bins, cardboard boxes and wire baskets. A large map of Kent hung on the wall. Anderson nodded at an empty desk. 'That was Jessica's.'

'Perhaps we could take a look at it later.'

'Of course.'

He led them through a door at the far end of the room and up a further flight of stairs into an interview room. When they were all seated he said, 'Now, how can I help you? I'm not sure what you want of me but I gather from your visit that you are not satisfied Jessica's death was an accident. Are you treating this as a murder investigation?'

Thanet and Lineham had already agreed that as the senior officer Thanet should conduct this interview. They felt that in view of his position Anderson would expect it. So Thanet began by saying, 'First of all I would like your assurance that anything said in this interview will remain confidential. As you know, we always try to cooperate with the press and we shall continue to do so in this instance, especially as we do appreciate that you must have a particular interest in the case, since Mrs Manifest – or Miss Dander, as I suppose I should call her here – was a colleague of yours. We'll do our best to keep you up to date with developments, but I'm sure you understand that we can't release information which might prejudice the investigation.'

Anderson nodded. He was in his forties, with horn-rimmed glasses which gave him an earnest, studious air, and hair which was already receding at the temples. Like the other reporters downstairs he was in shirtsleeves. 'Understood.'

'So, yes, we have to say that we are not satisfied as yet that her death was an accident. There are one or two circum-stances, which I can't reveal to you at the moment, that are giving us reason to doubt that it was.'

'So. Fire away. Jessica might not have been very popular but no one would have wished that on her.'

'She wasn't? Popular?'

'Not particularly.'

'Why was that?'

'She was a bit impatient. Offhand.'

'So she didn't have any close friends at work?'

'Not really, no. Oh, she rubbed along well enough with people but she was a bit of a loner, that's all.'

'How important are personal relationships in a place like this?'

'Well, there's a certain amount of teamwork, obviously, there has to be. But at the same time there's always rivalry, even between friends. Everyone has the same aim, to get their story and their name on the front page.'

'Was Jessica ambitious?'

'To a degree, yes, you have to be in a job like this. In many ways she was a model employee. She was a good writer and she was hardworking, punctual, efficient, reliable. You always knew that if you asked her to do something it would be done thoroughly and well. Not brilliantly, perhaps, but there are plenty of times when it isn't brilliance that's needed.'

'Is that why she stayed with the same paper for so long – since she was sixteen, in fact? Because she didn't have that little extra edge of talent? It's pretty unusual to stay as long as that, isn't it?'

'Yes, it is. And yes, perhaps that was why. Maybe she didn't want to risk trying for one of the nationals.'

'Risk?'

'Perhaps she was afraid of failure. Maybe she felt secure here.'

'You think she was an insecure sort of person?'

Anderson shrugged. 'Underneath, I'd say she probably was.' He leaned back in his chair, considering, then shook his head. 'She wasn't easy to understand. She was dedicated to her work, as I say, very intense about it. But she found it difficult to ease up, she was prickly, didn't have much sense of humour, and hated being teased. On the other hand, I know she had a softer side, and this certainly came over in some of the features she wrote. They were what she was best at. Her news sense wasn't so good.'

'What do you mean by that, exactly?'

Anderson laughed, revealing two crooked front teeth. 'The classic way to explain that is to tell the story of the editor and the new reporter. He sends her out to cover a wedding and when she comes back she tells him there wasn't a story. "What do you mean?" he says. "There wasn't a story because there wasn't a wedding," she says. "The bride didn't turn up."'

Thanet and Lineham laughed.

'So,' said Thanet. 'This softer side –'

The telephone rang. 'For you, Inspector,' said Anderson, handing it over.

The Manifests' next-door neighbours had returned and were at Headquarters, asking to speak to Thanet. He glanced at his watch. He was almost finished here. 'Tell them I can be back by around 2.45. Apologise for keeping them waiting and suggest they go and do a bit of shopping or something.' He handed the receiver back. What had he been saying? 'This softer side. It came over in what she wrote?'

'Yes. Especially when she was working with disabled people, or those who had suffered a tragedy or were in some terrible predicament. Nowadays our reporters do a tremendous amount of their work by phone, but sometimes we want pictures and personal interviews, and photographers who've worked on those sort of stories with Jessica tell me she was a different person when she was talking to people like that. And I suspect that was because she found it easy to relate to them, because underneath she may have felt just as vulnerable as they are. Perhaps she had a tough time as a kid, I don't know.'

'She came to the *KM* straight after her O levels. I imagine that's pretty unusual nowadays.'

'Oh yes! Very rarely happens any more. There's tremendous competition for jobs in journalism, even among graduates; a prospective employer can usually pick and choose. But – what? – twenty years ago it was a different matter. The office was based at Larkfield in those days and she'd have been taken on as an editorial assistant – that's a grandiose title for someone who runs errands and makes the tea, draws up the chemists' rotas and so on. Then I imagine she'd have graduated to junior reporter, perhaps in another paper within the group, and probably have moved around a bit before ending up here.'

'How did she get on with the opposite sex?'

Anderson smiled. 'That's an interesting question.' He took off his spectacles and rubbed his eyes before putting them back on. 'She wasn't above turning on the charm when she wanted something, but she definitely didn't put out signals that she was available, so to speak.'

'Some men regard that as a challenge.'

'True.'

'But to your knowledge none of them got anywhere?'

An emphatic shake of the head. 'No. And when she married Desmond, of course, the comment was that she had obviously been saving herself for someone rather better off than a mere reporter. Not that we didn't feel sorry for her when it all fell apart.'

'Did her husband's unemployment make any difference to her work?'

'I'd say she was a little more . . . driven, I suppose is the word. I imagine she felt it was especially important that she keep her job, as she was now the breadwinner.'

'Did she ever talk about it?'

'No. If she'd wanted to, there were a number of sympathetic ears around. But we didn't feel it was up to us to broach the subject. It's a pretty sensitive issue, after all.'

Thanet thought of the made-up single bed in the Manifests' back bedroom, of the solitary pillow in the marital bed. 'We understand the situation was a considerable strain on her marriage. Do you happen to know if she looked for consolation elsewhere?'

For the first time Anderson hesitated.

'What?' said Thanet.

He chewed the inside of his lip. 'I don't want to drop anyone in it unnecessarily.'

Thanet sighed. 'There's not much point in holding anything back. We'll find out in the end anyway. It'll just take longer, that's all.'

He shrugged. 'I suppose that's true. Well, the rumour was she was having an affair with Adam Ogilvy, the estate agent.'

Thanet knew at once who he meant. Ogilvy was a well-known figure in the area. 'He drives a silver Mercedes, doesn't he?' The charge of adrenaline made it difficult for Thanet to keep his tone casual and refrain from exchanging glances with Lineham.

But Anderson was no fool. 'Yes. Why?'

'I'm sorry, I can't say at the moment.'

They learnt nothing more of interest, either from going through Jessica's desk or from talking to the receptionist, who merely confirmed what Anderson had told them about the former reporter's relationships with her work mates.

'So,' said Lineham, the minute they were out in the street. 'Adam Ogilvy, eh? Car owner number two by the look of it.'

'Yes. Looks as though you were right about the lover after all. No need to say, "I told you so"!'

Lineham grinned. 'Wouldn't dream of it, sir.'

'Though it's beyond belief that Manifest went out in the evenings so as to leave his wife's lover a clear field!'

'Sounds like it, though, from all that "Why was he there when he should have been here" stuff.'

'Well, we'll find out sooner or later, no doubt.'

'I assume we'll go and see him now? Ogilvy?'

'We have to go back to the office first.' Thanet told Lineham about the appointment with Manifest's neighbours.

'I wonder what's made them come rushing into town to see us the minute they got back,' said Lineham.

'Well, we'll soon find out.'

SIX

Back at Headquarters a uniformed constable on his way out gave them a wide grin and there was more than a hint of amusement in Pater's greeting when they inquired about Manifest's neighbours.

'The Bartons? They're in interview room four. They didn't go into the town, said they were quite happy to wait.' Pater exchanged a conspiratorial look with a colleague.

'What's going on?' said Thanet.

Pater's smile broadened. 'You can see for yourself, sir. They're . . . er . . . meditating.'

Thoroughly intrigued by now Thanet and Lineham went straight to interview room four and opened the door. The Bartons were both standing on their heads, side by side against the far wall. Their eyes were closed and they gave no sign that they had heard anyone come in. Thanet cleared his throat and when that had no effect said, 'Mr and Mrs Barton?'

Their eyes opened in unison and they righted themselves with an ease he guessed was born of long practice, landing up side by side as if awaiting further instruction. They were in their sixties and quite remarkably alike – could certainly have been taken for brother and sister. They both had slightly hooked noses, deep-set eyes and sported identical hairstyles. They were dressed alike, too, in maroon tracksuits with navy trim, and if it hadn't been for the fact that one of them was slightly smaller than the other and had two unmistakable bulges in her upper torso, Thanet might well have thought them both male. 'I believe you wanted to see me.' He introduced himself and Lineham. 'Sit down, won't you? I'm sorry to have kept you waiting.'

'Oh, not at all, Inspector. We really didn't mind. We have many ways of improving the shining hour, haven't we, Ellie?'

His wife nodded vigorously. 'It really didn't matter at all.'

Thanet waited until everyone was settled, then said, 'So, how can I help you?'

They exchanged glances and then Barton said, 'We thought we ought to come and see you –'

'About Jessica, being as we're next-door neighbours –'

'And hearing the police were involved –'

'And that it might not have been an accident.' Mrs Barton finished what turned out to be the first joint sentence of many and they looked at Thanet expectantly.

'Quite,' he said, wondering if this double act was the norm.

Barton leaned forward confidentially. 'Only being so close you can't help hearing –'

'And seeing –'

'What's going on,' finished Barton.

'Of course,' said Lineham.

Mrs Barton screwed up her face anxiously. 'We mean, we wouldn't want you to think we're the type who spend all their time –'

'Looking over the neighbours' wall.'

They gazed at Thanet earnestly.

'We quite understand,' said Thanet. 'The houses are very close together.'

'And the gardens!' said Mrs Barton. 'They're very close too. In the summer –'

'You just can't avoid overhearing.'

'And we like Desmond,' said his wife. 'He's there much more than she is – was –'

'So naturally, we see much more of him.'

'Both of us being retired.'

'Naturally,' Thanet agreed.

'And we felt sorry for him,' said Mr Barton.

Thanet felt the first quickening of his pulse. 'Oh? Why was that?'

'We're not gossips, you know,' said Mrs Barton. 'I mean, we've never breathed a word of this –'

'Not to anyone. But we think we were probably the only ones to know. And we wanted you to understand –'

'What she was really like.'

'They say the police always suspect the husband first, don't they?' Mrs Barton gave hers a fond glance. 'Though why that should be I can't imagine.'

Barton reached across to squeeze her hand. 'Not everyone is as lucky as us, my dear. And in any case, we know Desmond is in the clear.'

'He was out for a walk, he told us.'

'Lucky for him, wasn't it?'

'Awful for him to come back and find . . . find . . .' Mrs Barton shuddered. 'It doesn't bear thinking about.'

Patience, Thanet told himself. We'll get there in the end. Let them tell it their own way. They obviously had scruples to overcome and this was never easy.

'Still,' said her husband, 'I suppose it's not surprising, in the circumstances.'

They needed a little prod. 'What circumstances?'

There was a brief silence and then Mrs Barton leaned forward and said in a hushed tone, 'She was carrying on, you see.'

'And not behind his back, either.'

Their indignation was gathering pace.

'Openly!'

'Disgraceful, it was. The fellow would come to the house –'

'When Desmond was there –'

'When we *knew* he was there.'

'And once or twice –'

'If we were just coming back from a walk –'

'We'd see the bedroom light go on –'

'Just after he arrived –'

'And we'd see them both –'

'This man and her –'

'Both up there –'

'Bold as brass.'

'It was awful,' said Mr Barton.

71

'So humiliating.'

'In the end Desmond took to going out just before he arrived. We didn't blame him, did we, Ellie?'

She shook her head. 'Poor man.'

'Do you know who this man was?' said Thanet.

'Drives a great big silver car,' said Mrs Barton.

'A Mercedes.'

Ogilvy. Further confirmation that the rumour Anderson had heard was correct.

'I wonder why none of the other neighbours have mentioned him,' said Lineham.

'Television!' Mr Barton almost spat the word out. 'We won't have one in the house.'

His wife was nodding. 'Got better things to do with our time, haven't we, love.'

'And he always came in the evenings when they'd be glued to *Coronation Street* or some other such rubbish.'

'That's why we said we thought we were probably the only ones to know. We've never heard a word about it from anyone else.'

'How long had this been going on?' said Thanet.

They consulted each other with a glance.

'Four months?' said Barton.

'Four or five,' said his wife.

'Well,' said Thanet, starting to get up, 'thank you very much. We appreciate your taking the time and trouble to come in. You've been most helpful.'

They didn't move.

He sat down again. 'There's something else you wanted to tell us?'

Another wordless consultation.

Shall we?

We did agree.

'Well,' said Barton hesitantly, 'as a matter of fact there was.'

'And we're absolutely certain no one else knew about this, either.'

'We never realised such things went on.'

'Shocked, we were, that first time we found out about it.'

They stopped.

'About what?' said Thanet gently. This was hard for them, he could see that. They certainly weren't aiming for dramatic effect and there was no pleasure for them in the telling either.

But they had to make an oblique approach.

'We were in the garden, weren't we, Ellie? A lovely day it was, so peaceful.'

'We'd been working hard all afternoon –'

'And we sat down for a cup of tea.'

'And then she started,' whispered Mrs Barton. 'Shouting –'

'Screaming –'

'Terrible things.'

'Horrible.'

'They were inside at first –'

'In the kitchen –'

'But then they came out –'

'Into the garden –'

'And we heard this noise, didn't we, Bill. A sort of –'

'A thwacking sound. That's what it was.'

'At first we thought one of them was beating a carpet –'

'With one of those old-fashioned carpet beaters, you know?'

'But then we began to wonder –'

'Because it wasn't a dry thud, it was a wet thud –'

'If you see what we mean.'

'And all the while she was calling him names –'

'Saying how useless he was –'

'And the thuds were coming in between every word.'

'So naturally we couldn't help wondering what on earth was going on.'

'Desmond wasn't making a sound.'

'And there's a gap in the fence.'

'A sort of broken bit.'

'So we went and looked through.'

They paused – not, Thanet thought again, for effect. They were genuinely reluctant to say what they had seen. By now, of course, he had guessed what it was and so, he suspected, had Lineham. He gave an encouraging nod.

Mr Barton leaned forward and lowered his voice, as if by doing so he could diminish the shocking nature of what he was about to reveal. 'She was hitting him,' he said. 'With a rolled-up towel. We think it was wet.'

'It made this horrible squelchy noise every time it hit him.'

'And he was just standing there –'

'With his shoulders hunched –'

'And his hands over his head –'

'To protect it.'

'If I hadn't seen it,' said Barton, 'I wouldn't have believed it. A grown man, just standing there and taking it, like that!'

'In the end she just flung the towel on the ground and stalked back into the house. I could never feel the same about her after that.'

'When was this?' said Lineham.

'Not long after they moved in,' said Barton. 'Three years ago?'

'And this wasn't the only incident of this kind you noticed, I gather?' said Thanet.

'No. The only reason we're telling you is because we wanted you to know –'

'What she was like when she lost her temper.'

'Someone else might not have been so ready to put up with it –'

'Being treated like that.'

'Someone like her fancy man, for instance.'

'And if they had an argument –'

'At the top of the stairs –'

'It would only need a little push –'

'If you caught her off balance.'

'Quite,' said Thanet.

'Well,' said Lineham when they had gone. 'So Desmond was a battered husband. That's a turn-up for the book, isn't it? And what a pair! I've never seen anything like it.'

'I suppose it's called being of one mind,' said Thanet with a grin.

'You can say that again. They obviously carry on like that all the time. And I really don't think it even entered their heads that they were making things look black for Desmond!'

'I know. It certainly gives him an even stronger motive. In

fact he seems to have had plenty of provocation, one way and the other.'

'She sounds a nasty bit of work to me. Flaunting her lover like that.'

Thanet grinned. 'Flaunting. That's a good old-fashioned word, Mike. But I agree. Not very nice.'

'What gets me is that he put up with it! The beatings, too! It just shows how little you know about other people. I'd never have put him down for such a wimp!'

'Anyway, I think we can take it now that a lot of what we guessed was correct. She did have a lover and Manifest did go out for walks in the evening because he wanted to avoid him. So let's say, for the sake of argument, that that's what happened last night, that he had nothing to do with her death and he's telling the truth when he says he went out around 7.20 and didn't get back until just before the ambulance –'

'Meanwhile lover-boy turns up on his white horse, so to speak. But he can't park in front of the house because of the hole in the road, so he parks at the pub instead, where his car is noticed by the owner.'

'Why didn't he simply park further up the road?'

Lineham's mouth turned down at the corners and he raised his shoulders. 'Because he didn't want to draw attention to himself and people in a street like that always tend to notice cars that are parked directly in front of their houses?'

'Possibly,' Thanet conceded.

'Anyway, when he gets to Jessica's house Desmond has already left. They go up to the bedroom as usual, but they have a row. They argue, she falls, he's horrified and dials 999 for an ambulance. Then he scarpers to the pub, to give himself an alibi –'

'Where he's seen by Desmond –'

'Who can't understand why he was there instead of with Jessica.'

Thanet laughed. 'Do you realise we're doing a Barton?'

'A what?'

'Finishing each other's sentences.'

Lineham grinned. 'So we are. We'll have to watch it or we'll be standing on our heads next.'

SEVEN

The distinctive purple and green 'For Sale' boards of Ogilvy and Tate were a familiar sight in the area. It was an old-established family firm with many branch offices in the larger villages around. Its main premises, in Sturrenden, occupied a prime site in the High Street, not far from Snippers. Thanet glanced into the hairdressing salon as they passed by but without actually stopping and peering in he couldn't make out if Kevin was inside or not.

The estate agent's double shop front was crammed with photographs of houses for sale. The property market had had a rough ride since the heady, hectic days of the eighties, when houses sold like hot cakes and the scramble to buy pushed prices higher and ever higher. The subsequent collapse, in 1988, had resulted in hundreds of thousands of people being left to suffer the trauma of 'negative equity', a bland-sounding term for the harrowing situation of having bought a property which was worth far less than the mortgage taken out to purchase it. During the long stagnant period which followed estate agents were forced to tighten their belts. Branch offices closed, staff were made redundant and even the giant Prudential Insurance Company decided to pull out of the property market. Things had picked up over the last year or two, especially in London and the South East, but many firms were still licking their wounds.

'I wonder how badly affected he was by the recession,' said Thanet as they paused to look in the window.

'Look at that one!' Lineham was admiring an imposing modern house 'newly completed and in a select, tranquil environment'.

'Bit out of your price range, isn't it, Mike?' Thanet peered more closely. 'I don't know, though. It has got a granny flat.'

Lineham hastily moved away and pushed open the door.

Inside there were fitted carpets and four little islands of desks where negotiators sat talking into telephones or busying themselves with paperwork. One of them slipped on his jacket and rose to greet them. He was in his late twenties, neatly dressed in pinstriped suit, white shirt and discreet tie. His look of eager welcome faded at the sight of Thanet's warrant card. 'Mr Ogilvy is out, I'm afraid.'

'When will he be back?' said Lineham.

'I don't think he'll be coming back into the office this afternoon.'

'Where is he, exactly?'

'Visiting a prospective client, near Ashford.'

Must be an important client, thought Thanet, for the boss himself to visit him.

'Will he be going straight home afterwards?'

'I imagine so, yes. I'm not sure.'

Reluctantly he handed over Ogilvy's home address.

At the door Thanet glanced back. The young man was already dialling. Ogilvy's mobile, perhaps?

'So, what now?' said Lineham.

'We'll wait. Go and see him at home. Meanwhile we might as well catch up on some paperwork and save time later.'

Thanet took advantage of the open air to light up. Apart from a few puffs in the car on the way to work this morning he hadn't had a pipe all day. To his disgust Sturrenden Police Headquarters had recently become a smoke-free zone. Smokers had first been relegated to a designated smoking area (i.e. the bar) and then, when the bar closed, found themselves ousted altogether. In the face of gentle nagging from Joan and Lineham's aversion to tobacco smoke in any shape or form he had in any case cut down substantially on his smoking but he resolutely refused to give up altogether, partly because he enjoyed it so much, but also because a core of stubbornness in him refused to be emotionally black-mailed into doing so.

Back at the office there was a message to say that the

landlord of the Harrow had been out when the officer called and another attempt to interview him would be made later.

'Better get him to check if Ogilvy was there last night too.' Thanet lowered himself carefully into his chair. Over the last hour he had become increasingly conscious of the dull ache in the small of his back and now he again thought that he must try to fit in a visit to the chiropractor. Like millions of other people Thanet had suffered from back trouble for years. None of the treatments he had undergone had had any lasting beneficial effect until a year or two ago, when he had given in to Joan's urging and, without any expectation of relief, had gone to a chiropractor. To his amazement she had worked wonders for him and treatments were now very rarely necessary. This, however, he decided, especially with the wedding coming up, was one of those occasions. He glanced at his watch. Three-forty-five. Perhaps he ought to take advantage of this brief lull and give her a ring now, just in case she might be able to fit him in. He reached for the phone. He was in luck. She had just had a cancellation for four o'clock. If Inspector Thanet could come along straight away . . . 'I'll be there,' he said. A quarter of an hour later he was submitting himself to Janet Carmel's expert ministrations. She was in her thirties, tall and slim with very direct blue eyes and long fair hair braided into a thick plait. As usual she was wearing a tracksuit and training shoes.

'You've been doing very well,' she said, as she followed her usual routine of testing for the vulnerable area. 'It's five months since your last visit.'

'Amazing!' said Thanet. 'I never thought I'd go that long without needing to see you.'

'Ah,' she said. 'Yes. That's it. Turn on to your right side, please.'

Fifteen minutes later Thanet emerged, feeling as if he were walking on air.

'That woman is an absolute miracle,' he said to Lineham. 'She is just incredible.'

Lineham, who had worked with Thanet in the days when he had been severely incapacitated, grinned. 'She certainly does wonders for your temper.'

'Temper? Me? Nonsense!'

'While you were out I checked on that prowler business. Jessica did file two complaints, one on September 28th, one on October 4th. Uniformed branch investigated but with no results.'

'I wonder if it was Kevin,' said Thanet. 'Say he'd developed a thing about her, from seeing her at the salon. She was a very attractive woman.'

'Bit long in the tooth for him, though, wasn't she? He's only, what, twenty, twenty-one?'

'Oh come on, Mike, don't be naïve. Older women and younger men are all the fashion these days. And in Victorian times it was considered quite the thing, I believe, to be initiated into the mysteries of sex by a woman with a bit of experience.'

'Are you suggesting that's what happened here?'

'No, not necessarily, especially if she was already having an affair with Ogilvy. Let's face it, there's no doubt he would have been a much more attractive prospect. It does sound as though wealth was something of a magnet for her and a hairdresser's apprentice doesn't exactly fall into the right category. On the other hand, open admiration is always flattering. She might quite innocently have smiled on him a little too warmly, fed his fantasies with false hopes.'

'But surely, if it was Kevin who was following her she would have recognised him?' Lineham shrugged, answered his own question. 'Not necessarily, I suppose, if he was careful not to get too close. Well, if you're right, and he was there last night . . .'

'Who knows what he might have seen? Exactly. Which is why I want to go gently on him at the moment, until we have a clearer picture. Now, if there's nothing else, I must try and get some of these reports done before we go.'

It was a quarter to six when they turned in between the stone pillars at the entrance to the drive of Ogilvy's house.

'Wow!' said Lineham.

'Stop drooling, Mike!'

But Thanet had to admit, it really was a lovely house. As Goldilocks would have said, it was neither too big nor too small, but just right, a Georgian gem of perfect proportions, with two tall sash windows on either side of the porticoed front door and five above. Its elegance was enhanced by the simplicity of its setting, a wide straight gravelled driveway flanked by young copper beeches and terminating in a perfect turning circle in front of the house.

'I suppose in his position he had the pick of the market,' said Lineham.

'I imagine so.'

'Doesn't exactly look as though he had to tighten his belt too much over the last few years, anyway.'

'Quite.'

As they reached the circle Thanet saw that the drive branched off it, left and right, maintaining the symmetry imposed by the house, and he glimpsed outbuildings behind and a car parked in front of them beside a horse box hitched to a Land-Rover. Lineham pulled up near the front door and they got out.

'Just a moment, Mike,' said Thanet with a jerk of the head, and they walked back to the corner of the house. 'I thought so,' he said. 'It's a red Polo.'

They looked at each other, remembering the red Polo a neighbour claimed to have seen parked near Jessica's house the night she died. 'Mrs Ogilvy's?' said Lineham. 'I wonder if it's the same one.'

'Bit too much of a coincidence, if it's not.'

'That's what I was thinking.'

The door was opened by a girl in her late teens. The perfect oval of her face was emphasised by the way she wore her dark hair, sleeked back into a pony-tail. She was casually dressed in jeans and sweatshirt and was carrying a little dark-haired girl of about two who stuck her thumb in her mouth when she saw the two strangers. Had Ogilvy taken a child bride?

'Mrs Ogilvy?' he said.

The girl laughed, showing teeth of the degree of perfection normally seen only in toothpaste advertisements. She shook her head. 'I am Chantal.'

Even in those few syllables her nationality was obvious.

'And this is Daisy,' she added, giving the baby a little bounce and planting a kiss on the top of her head.

'Hullo, Daisy,' said Thanet, smiling. The child was enchanting, with huge brown eyes and a tumble of curls tied up in a bright red ribbon.

She turned her head away and buried her face in the girl's shoulder.

'Is Mr Ogilvy at home?' Thanet thought he might not be. There was no sign of the silver Mercedes. If not, he was prepared to wait.

But Ogilvy must have put his car away because Chantal stood back and invited them in. 'I will fetch him. Wait here a moment, please.'

They were in a wide hallway with a generously proportioned staircase running up the right-hand wall. Oriental rugs glowed on polished floorboards and framed prints hung on the walls above the dado rail.

Chantal disappeared through a door on the left and they heard a murmur of voices. A few moments later she emerged with two boys of about eight and five beside her, closely followed by a man. She went off up the stairs with the three children and Ogilvy came forward to greet the two policemen. He was in his early forties, with brown hair that was over-long at the back and already thinning at the temples. He had discarded his suit jacket and his trousers were held up by braces decorated with Rupert Bears, a fun present from his wife or daughter, Thanet guessed. Despite the *déshabille* he still contrived to look well groomed: shoes highly polished, blue-and-white-striped shirt still crisp, discreetly patterned tie firmly knotted. Introductions over he led them back into the drawing room which was as beautifully proportioned as the house and elegantly furnished with a large Persian carpet, swagged and tailed curtains at the tall windows, and comfortable sofas and chairs complemented by carefully chosen pieces of antique furniture.

A woman rose and switched off the early evening news as they came in.

'My wife, Inspector. Penny, this is Inspector Thanet and Sergeant . . .?'

'Lineham.'

Mrs Ogilvy acknowledged them with a nervous nod and an attempt at a smile before returning to her seat on the sofa. She was a good ten years younger than her husband, with long straight blonde hair and speedwell-blue eyes. Thanet liked her at once. Despite her obvious anxiety there was a candour about her, an openness of expression which appealed to him. She was dressed for riding in well-cut breeches and Puffa waistcoat.

'Sit down, Inspector, please,' said her husband.

'May we have a word in private, sir?'

'That won't be necessary. My wife and I have no secrets from each other.'

Thanet glanced at Mrs Ogilvy but she wouldn't meet his eyes. She was hating this, he could tell. 'It's up to you, of course.' He and Lineham sat down.

Ogilvy stood looking at Thanet, waiting for him to speak.

Deliberately, Thanet allowed the silence to prolong itself.

Ogilvy shifted from one foot to the other, then cleared his throat. He had a high colour which Thanet thought looked distinctly unhealthy and was slightly overweight too, not drastically so but enough for his belly to bulge over the waistband of his trousers.

'How can I help you, Inspector?'

'I expect you realise why we've come.'

Ogilvy glanced uneasily at his wife who refused to look at him. She was plucking nervously at a loose thread on the arm of the sofa on which she was sitting. 'It's Jessica, I suppose,' he said. 'We heard about it on the news this morning. Though I don't quite understand why the police are involved. The report said she had fallen down the stairs.'

'That's right. But there are one or two circumstances which make us question whether it was an accident.'

Mrs Ogilvy made an inarticulate little sound and pressed her hand against her mouth.

'Such as?' said her husband.

'I'm not at liberty to say.'

Mrs Ogilvy spoke for the first time. 'Inspector . . . are you saying someone might deliberately have pushed her?'

'Let's just say we're keeping an open mind at the moment.'

Her eyes flickered to Ogilvy and back to Thanet. 'But . . . but that would mean . . .'

Thanet and Lineham exchanged the briefest of glances. *She's wondering if her husband did it.*

As if she had tuned in to their thoughts she said, with more spirit than she had shown before, 'You're surely not suggesting my husband had anything to do with it?'

'Mr Ogilvy's car was seen in the vicinity of Mrs Manifest's house around the time she died,' said Lineham.

'And so,' said Thanet softly, 'was yours, Mrs Ogilvy.' Not strictly accurate, but worth a try.

They stared at him but did not deny it.

'All right,' said Ogilvy, 'I was there. I admit it. But I only stayed ten minutes, then I left. And I assure you that she was certainly alive and kicking then.'

'What time did you arrive?'

'Seven-thirty.'

And Manifest had left at 7.20. That made sense, if he had wanted to avoid Ogilvy. 'And you left ten minutes later, you say. At 7.40, then.'

'Approximately, yes.'

'Why did you stay such a short time?'

Ogilvy shifted uncomfortably. 'I had come to a decision.' He stopped.

Thanet waited.

Ogilvy glanced at his wife. 'We . . . my wife and I . . . we'd discussed the matter and I had decided to end my – er – relationship with Mrs Manifest.'

Translation: his wife had found out what was going on and given him an ultimatum.

'You verify this, do you, Mrs Manifest?'

'Of course.' She compressed her lips and folded her arms across her chest as if to contain the distress which this conversation was clearly causing her.

'Could we go back a little then, sir. Would you tell me exactly what happened, from the moment you arrived at the house.'

Ogilvy shrugged. 'I got there about half seven, as I said. There was a bloody great hole in the road so I couldn't park outside. I parked at the pub instead and walked back.'

'Why not park a little further up the road into the estate?' said Lineham.

'I didn't want to attract too much attention. People always notice if you park in front of their houses. They seem to think the road belongs to them. And my car isn't exactly unobtrusive.'

'Go on.'

'There really isn't much to tell.'

'Presumably you didn't walk straight in, tell Mrs Manifest you wouldn't be seeing her again and walk straight out again?'

'No, of course not.'

'Well then. In detail, please.'

'I knocked at the door,' said Ogilvy. 'She opened it. I went in. Is this enough detail for you?'

Thanet ignored the sarcasm. 'That's fine. Do go on.'

Reading between the lines of Ogilvy's no doubt heavily edited account Thanet imagined the conversation must have gone something like this:

> '*Adam! It's lovely to see you.*'
> '*No, not upstairs, Jess. Let's go in here.*'
> '*Why?*'
> '*I can't stay tonight.*'
> '*Why not?*'
> '*I . . . Look, let's sit down for a minute, shall we?*'
> '*What's up, Adam? There's something wrong, isn't there?*'
> '*No. Yes. Yes, there is. Penny's found out about us.*'
> '*So? That's wonderful! Terrific! I've hated all this hole-and-corner stuff. Now we can be together at last.*'
> '*Hang on, Jess. I never said anything about splitting up with Penny.*'
> '*But that was what you intended, wasn't it? Eventually?*'
> '*You don't understand. I simply can't afford to run two households. The last few years have been hell in my business. But we've managed to survive and now, at last,*

84

we're starting to pull out of it —'

'Well, that's fine, then, isn't it? I can wait a bit longer.'

'But it'll be ages before we're properly on our feet again. Years, maybe. I have to put the business first. It's what we all depend on.'

'I haven't exactly noticed you going short. You still have your house, your cars, your horses, private schools for James and Henry and no doubt Daisy in due course.'

'It's essential to keep up appearances in order to maintain confidence in the business. If people saw me selling my house, sending my kids to state schools and driving a Ford instead of a Mercedes the word would go round in no time that I was on the ropes.'

'I see. So what, exactly, are you trying to tell me? That we're finished, is that it?'

'Yes. I'm afraid so. I'm sorry, Jess.'

'Sorry! I thought we had something special, but no, it sounds as though as far as you're concerned all it comes down to in the end is money, money, money.'

'That's not true. Of course it was special!'

'But not special enough. What a fool I've been! I was just a nice little bit on the side, wasn't I? You never had any intention of giving up your wife, your children, your home and life-style for me, did you? Get out. Go on, get out.'

'Jess, don't be like this. I hoped we could still be friends.'

'Just go, Adam, will you. Now.'

'And I can assure you that, as I said before, she was absolutely fine when I left,' Ogilvy concluded.

But if Jessica had gone straight upstairs after opening the door and Ogilvy had followed her and a similar conversation had taken place at the top of the stairs instead of in the sitting room as Ogilvy claimed, it would be only too easy to imagine it ending in disaster.

'Did the telephone ring while you were there?' said Lineham.

Ogilvy stared at him. 'Yes, now you come to mention it, it did. Soon after I got there. But she didn't answer it, said the answerphone was on.'

Not surprising that Jessica had considered her conversation with Ogilvy of more importance, thought Thanet.

'Did Mrs Manifest come to the front door with you?' said Lineham.

'No, she didn't. Why?'

'Did you shut it behind you?'

'Yes, I think so. I must have. Yes, I'm sure I did. Why?' Ogilvy asked again.

'So,' said Thanet to Mrs Ogilvy. 'Where were you while all this was going on?'

She flinched at becoming the focus of attention. 'In my car,' she said with a lift of the chin.

'Waiting for your husband, presumably.'

'Of course.'

'Why?'

'I don't understand what you mean.'

'Why were you waiting for him?'

'Well, obviously because I wanted to hear how he'd got on.'

'Why didn't you accompany him in his car, then?'

She bit her lip and glanced at her husband. It was obvious what had happened. Ogilvy had promised her that the meeting with Jessica would be brief and she had followed him to see if he had kept his word.

'I . . . I didn't make up my mind until after he had left.'

Her husband came to her rescue. 'You thought it would be nice for us to go out for a drink together afterwards, didn't you, darling? Which is what we did,' he added, turning to Thanet. 'When I came out I saw my wife's car and realised she was waiting for me.'

'Where did you go for this drink?' said Lineham, though they were already pretty certain of the answer.

'To the Harrow. You can check if you like. There weren't many customers, they'll probably remember us.'

'Why not the Green Man? Your car was already parked there.'

'We wanted to go a bit further away.'

In case Jessica or her husband came in, thought Thanet. Ogilvy wasn't to know that it was to the Harrow that Manifest usually went.

They had, he said, arrived about 7.45 and stayed until around 8.30. Manifest claimed to have passed the Harrow about 8.15, so it was just as they had thought: he had probably intended to go in but had changed his mind when he spotted Ogilvy and his wife there.

Ogilvy claimed that they had arrived home at about 8.45.

'Is there anyone who can confirm these times?' This wasn't really necessary at this stage but Thanet wanted an excuse for a word with Chantal. Nannies have a pretty good idea of what goes on in a household.

'Chantal?' said Mrs Ogilvy to her husband.

'I'll fetch her,' he said.

'I'd better come with you, to look after the children.'

'Just one more point, Mrs Ogilvy,' said Thanet quickly as she started to move towards the door. 'Could you see Mrs Manifest's front door from where you were parked?'

'No, I couldn't.'

'And after your husband came out? Did you get out of the car?'

'No. He came across to speak to me.'

'Which way was your car facing?'

'Towards the village.'

'So you had to turn around, to drive to the Harrow?'

'Yes.'

'Where did you turn?'

'I backed into the road leading into the estate.'

'Did you happen to notice then if the door of Mrs Manifest's house was open?'

'No. I was watching that I didn't back into some traffic cones that were in front of her house.'

'I see. Thank you.'

Lineham waited until they had gone, then said, 'He must have been crazy, to run the risk of losing all this, those lovely children and that nice wife of his.'

'Yes, I liked her too. She doesn't trust him, though, does she? Following him like that to Jessica's house. And I'd say she wouldn't put it past him to have shoved Jessica down the stairs.'

'I agree.' Footsteps could be heard on the staircase and

Lineham lowered his voice. 'I wonder when she found out about them.'

Ogilvy came back in with Chantal. 'There's no need to be nervous,' he said to her. 'Just answer whatever questions the Inspector asks.' He sat down on the sofa as if to underline the fact that he had no intention of leaving.

Thanet could have insisted, but decided not to make an issue of it at the moment. He could always come back later if necessary. He suspected Chantal wasn't too keen on her employer, which could prove useful. She quickly confirmed the times of departure and arrival Ogilvy had given them and they left it at that.

'All very well,' said Lineham when they were back in the car, 'but I'd say he definitely goes on our list. We've only his word that Jessica was alive when he left.'

'Quite. Put Bentley on to investigating his background. Mrs Ogilvy's, too.'

'You don't suspect her, surely?'

Thanet shrugged. 'Just being thorough. They could be covering up for each other.'

'So, where now, sir?'

'I think it's time we had another go at Desmond, don't you? He's got rather a lot of explaining to do.'

EIGHT

They consulted the map to work out the most likely route for Ogilvy to have taken to get to the Manifests' house in Charthurst and discovered that it went past the Harrow.

'Explains why they chose that particular pub,' said Lineham. 'It was the first one they came to on the way home. And he must have passed it many times.'

Thanet agreed. 'Might as well call in, as we're going by. It's past opening time, the landlord should be there now.'

'Though I still don't get it,' said Lineham as he started the engine. 'Just think about it. You know your wife is expecting her lover so you obligingly go out. When you get home the front door is open and you find her dead at the bottom of the stairs. Then you learn someone rang for an ambulance from your own number. I mean to say, what would you think?'

'You forget, he was confused. He'd seen Ogilvy in the Harrow with his own wife only ten minutes before.'

'It doesn't take much intelligence to work out that Ogilvy'd have had plenty of time to visit Jessica first, though, does it? I really can't see why he didn't put us on to him straight away. Especially as it would have let him off the hook himself!' Lineham shook his head. 'I just don't understand him.'

'I've a feeling there's a lot we don't yet understand about him – or about Jessica either, for that matter.'

At the Harrow the landlord confirmed that Manifest was a regular customer, calling in two or three evenings a week. 'Though Des isn't exactly what you'd call a big spender. Only ever has one drink and makes it last more than an hour, usually. Not surprising, really, being as he's on the dole. I don't mind, he's a good bloke.'

'What about last night?' said Lineham.

'Ah, now that was very peculiar. He started to come in through the door then turned around and went straight out again!'

'What did you think?'

A shrug. 'That he'd seen someone he didn't want to meet, probably. It happens.'

'Any idea who?'

'No.'

'What time was this?'

'About a quarter past eight? Something like that.'

'And were you busy at the time?'

'Not particularly.'

'So do you remember if there was anyone in at the time who wasn't a regular customer?'

'A few, yes.'

'Who, for instance?'

The man frowned. He was big and beefy and didn't look as though he'd have much trouble controlling difficult clients. 'Couple of American tourists, a businessman on his way home, a commercial traveller asking if we had a room for the night . . .'

'No one else?'

'Well, there was Mr Ogilvy, the estate agent. He's not exactly a regular, I suppose, but he's not a stranger either.'

'Was he alone?'

'With his wife. At least, I assume it was his wife, hadn't seen her before, he's usually by himself. A real looker, blonde hair, blue eyes.'

'Did Mr Ogilvy see Mr Manifest?'

'Don't think so. He was sitting sideways on to the door.'

'What time did Mr Ogilvy and his wife arrive?'

Another shrug. 'I don't time people's arrivals and departures, you know!'

'Approximately, then.'

'Oh, I don't know. They'd been here a little while before Des looked in, anyway.'

'What d'you mean by "a little while"? Five minutes? Ten?'

'No. Half an hour, more like.'

This fitted what they had been told.

'You didn't happen to notice if he came by foot or by car, did you?' It had occurred to them that if Desmond had borrowed Jessica's car this would have altered the time scenario considerably.

'On foot, as usual.'

'You're sure?'

'Positive. Like I said, things were quiet and I thought it was so peculiar he hadn't come in I went across to the window to see what he was doing. The car park's around the back, as you know, but he was walking off in the direction of Charthurst.'

'You could see him clearly? It was pitch dark.'

'We're well lit up, at the front. And he always wears one of those fluorescent safety straps. It was him all right.'

Lineham left it there.

'So,' said Thanet when they were back in the car, 'neither Manifest nor Ogilvy made that phone call.'

'There are only three possibilities,' said Lineham. 'Either someone else had a key and let himself in . . .'

'Unlikely, don't you agree?'

'Yes, I do. Or, Jessica was alive when Ogilvy left, as he claims, and she later opened the door to someone else.'

'Possible.'

'Or Ogilvy did in fact kill her but didn't shut the door properly and someone else got in, found the body and made the phone call.'

Thanet sighed. 'I think you'd better stop, Mike. It seems to me there are an infinite number of possibilities and at the moment we haven't a hope in hell of proving any of them.'

In any case, they had arrived. Allowing for the stop at the pub the drive to Willow Way had taken thirteen minutes.

'Looks as though the parents have gone,' said Thanet. The red Datsun was no longer there.

'Mmm.' The hole in the road in front of the Manifests' house was still roped off and Lineham was peering into it. 'A day's work for two men and it still looks exactly the same! How do they get away with it?'

'If it annoys you so much why don't you complain to the Council? Come on, Mike,' said Thanet as he approached the front door. 'We haven't got all day. I really have to finish my speech for Saturday tonight.' He rang the bell.

Lineham was grinning as he hurried up the path. 'I'm looking forward to hearing it.'

'I'll remind you you said that, when Mandy gets married!'

Amanda, the younger of Lineham's two children, was nine.

'I'm not going to start worrying about that yet!'

'I shouldn't be too sure of that. The expense is unbelievable!'

'I took out an insurance when she was born,' said Lineham smugly.

'Mike, has anyone ever told you that sometimes you are completely and utterly insufferable?'

'You have, sir.'

Grins gave way to solemnity as the door opened.

'Oh, it's you,' said Manifest with weary resignation, standing back to let them in. He was wearing the same clothes as this morning and still hadn't bothered to shave. Thanet wondered what he had been doing all day. It was always difficult in a case like this to tread the tightrope between suspicion and sympathy. If Manifest had had nothing to do with his wife's death and was genuinely in mourning for her, he deserved every consideration, but they couldn't afford to allow compassion to cloud their judgement and let a possible murderer off the hook.

There was an appetising smell in the hall and Manifest walked ahead of them into a cramped kitchen which was furnished with a cheap range of units, a huge refrigerator and a flap table neatly laid for one against the wall. With three men in the room there would have been no room to move and Lineham hovered in the doorway.

'I'm sorry if we're interrupting your supper,' said Thanet.

Manifest stooped to turn off the oven on the electric cooker. 'It's all right. I'm not hungry anyway. My mother insisted on preparing it, but . . . Let's go back in the other room, shall we?'

In the sitting room Thanet came straight to the point. 'Why didn't you tell us about Mr Ogilvy?'

Manifest blinked, then sighed. 'Didn't take you long to find out, did it?'

'That's beside the point! Witholding information in a possible murder investigation is a serious matter! If someone did push your wife down those stairs, don't you want to find out who it was?'

Manifest said nothing, merely hung his head like a schoolboy being reprimanded by the headmaster and stared glumly down at his clasped hands.

'You knew he was expected last night, didn't you, Des?' said Lineham. 'And you didn't go into the Harrow for a drink because when you arrived you found he was already there. And you couldn't understand it. That was why you said, "Why was he there? He should have been here", wasn't it? We actually asked you about that this morning. So why didn't you tell us?'

There was a long pause and then Manifest raised his head and held the gaze of first one then the other. 'If your wife had been having an affair,' he said, 'would you have found it easy to say so to a bunch of policemen?'

So, it was partly loyalty to Jessica which had held him back, thought Thanet, and partly a desire to hold on to the last vestiges of his privacy. If you have just received a mortal blow the last thing you want to do is expose yourself to further humiliation. 'You're right, of course,' he said. 'I'd have hated it. On the other hand, you must see that if we are to make any progress we have to be in full possession of the facts. And we've wasted a great deal of time finding out what you could have told us in the first place.'

'I suppose I should have realised it would only be a matter of time before you did find out. Jessica wasn't exactly . . . discreet. I just wanted to give myself a bit longer to think things over.'

'What things?'

'To try to understand it all.'

'What happened last night, you mean?' said Lineham.

Manifest shook his head and sat back in his chair. 'Oddly enough, not that so much, no. More what went wrong between us.'

Thanet wasn't surprised. He had seen this before – how someone who had suffered a catastrophic blow sometimes tried to avoid thinking about it by obsessively raking over the past. The psychiatrists probably had some jargon to describe the process – displacement activity, perhaps? Nor did it surprise him that Manifest apparently wanted to talk. If what the Bartons had said was true – and Thanet could see no reason for them to lie – Manifest must have been humiliated beyond measure by her openly taking her lover to bed while he himself was in the house. Thanet didn't think Manifest would have confided this to anyone and doubted that he would do so now, but in the long, dragging days of unemployment he must have spent many an hour brooding on the situation. Now that Thanet and Lineham knew about his wife's infidelity maybe the urge to talk about it at last was irresistible. 'And did you come to any conclusions?' he said.

Manifest rose, walked across to the window and stood gazing out as if to get a clearer view of the past. 'Only that it was mostly my fault,' he said.

'Oh come on, Des,' said Lineham. 'It's never just one person's fault.'

'Mostly, I said.' He turned around to face them, and leaned back against the windowsill. 'I mean, look at this.' His gesture took in the cluttered room, the cramped little house, the neighbourhood. 'She didn't expect this when she married me, did she?'

'But she did promise for better or for worse,' said Lineham.

'And she stuck to me when it all fell apart! She never gave up hope, you know, that it would all come right again.'

Thanet wondered whom he was trying to convince. Himself, probably. Thanet's own guess was that Jessica had been preparing to abandon ship with Ogilvy, an altogether better prospect. He thought that in Jessica's eyes her husband had probably become irrevocably a loser. He wondered if Desmond really had been a battered husband (but again, why should the Bartons lie?) and if so, whether the abuse had begun early in the marriage when Manifest was still a success or whether it had been born of Jessica's anger and frustration at the disastrous turn of events.

'The trouble was,' said Manifest, 'that Jessica needed security. And I really do mean needed it, like most people need food and drink. And unfortunately I couldn't give it to her any longer. That was why I appreciated so much the fact that she stood by me.'

To the extent that he was prepared to put up with whatever treatment she felt like dishing out? thought Thanet. 'Why was that, do you suppose? Why did she need security so much?'

Manifest lifted his shoulders. 'I imagine it was to do with the fact that she lost both her parents when she was quite young. Her father died when she was six and her mother four years later. She went to live with her sister, who was much older than she was and married by then.'

'Yes. We've talked to her brother-in-law.'

Manifest pulled a face. 'Bernard.'

'You don't like him?'

'He's all right, I suppose. I just can't stand the way he smokes like a chimney and stinks like an ashtray.'

Lineham shifted in his chair, obviously longing to voice his agreement.

'Strange that it should have affected her so profoundly,' said Thanet. 'Obviously it's pretty traumatic for a child to lose both parents one after the other but at least she did have close family to take her in. If she'd gone into a children's home and been shifted from pillar to post it would have been a different matter.'

'I know.' Manifest had relaxed considerably by now. He returned to his chair and sat down, stretching out his legs and clasping his hands loosely in his lap. 'But there it was. It took me a long time to realise that the Jessica we saw on the surface – so self-assured and confident – was quite different from the person underneath.'

'What was she like underneath, then?'

'Insecure, as I've said. Pessimistic. Gloomy. Often depressed. And angry. For a long time I couldn't understand why she would blow up about quite trivial matters and then, eventually, it dawned on me. There was this constant anger always simmering away beneath the surface, just waiting to erupt the moment something triggered it off.'

Thanet thought of the scene in the garden which the Bartons had described. An anger, then, which occasionally erupted into violence. An anger which might last night have erupted at the wrong moment, against the wrong person?

'Anger about what?'

Manifest shrugged again. 'Life in general, I suppose. I've had a lot of time to think about things over the last few years but I've never reached any cut and dried conclusions. I don't suppose you ever can, as far as people are concerned. They change all the time, according to circumstances and how life treats them. Look at me, now! You'd hardly recognise me as the man I was five years ago.'

Thanet hesitated. There was something he badly wanted to ask and he didn't know if Manifest would ever again be in the mood to talk so frankly about his wife. In Thanet's experience people often regretted such confidences later and tended to withdraw. He decided to risk it. 'Look, sir, there's a question I'd like to put to you. But it could be painful.'

'Go ahead. I don't suppose it'll affect me too much. I'm still pretty numb at the moment.'

'How do you think your wife would have reacted if Ogilvy had told her that he was breaking off the affair.'

Manifest tensed. 'Did he?'

'He says he did.'

'Last night?'

'Yes.'

'So that was why he didn't stay long. Poor Jessica! I suppose he'd found himself someone new. He was in the Harrow with a woman.'

'That was his wife.'

'Oh. What was she doing there?'

Thanet shook his head. 'I'm sorry, I can't go into all the

96

ins and outs of the situation now. You haven't answered my question. How do you think Mrs Manifest would have reacted?'

Manifest stared at him. 'I don't know.'

'Would she have been crushed? Or angry? Pleaded with him?'

'No! She wouldn't have pleaded! She had too much pride. And she wouldn't have wanted him to know if she was really upset. She'd have kept that till later, when she was alone. But yes, she would have been angry. Furious, in fact.' He sat up with a jerk. 'My God, is that what happened? They had a row because he was leaving her, and he shoved her down the stairs? It all makes sense now.'

'It's much too early in the investigation to jump to conclusions, sir. That's the danger of being in possession of only half the facts.' Thanet hoped he hadn't been imprudent. He didn't want Manifest to do anything rash like rushing off to accuse Ogilvy.

'But don't you see?' Manifest jumped up out of his chair and began to pace about, swerving to avoid those pieces of furniture which projected into the limited free space. 'It must have been him! He's the one who made the phone call! Then he scarpered, before the ambulance got here, so he wouldn't be involved, the bastard!'

'He assures us that your wife was alive and well when he left.'

'Well he would, wouldn't he!'

'And,' said Lineham, 'the phone call was made at 8.11, only a few minutes before you yourself saw him in the pub with his wife. What is more, the landlord confirms that they arrived at around the time Mr Ogilvy claims, a quarter to eight.'

But Manifest was not deterred. 'OK, so he didn't make the phone call. But he still could have been involved in her death, before he left for the pub. Someone else must have found her and rung for the ambulance.'

'Who?' said Thanet, thinking *the prowler?* 'And how would he have got in? Mr Ogilvy swears he shut the front door behind him.'

'You've only got his word for that. Maybe he didn't. Or maybe he thought he had and the latch hadn't caught. It doesn't always.'

'The point is,' said Thanet, 'that all this is speculation. We have to wait and see what the scientific evidence tells us. Then we might have a clearer picture.'

Lineham waited until the front door had shut behind them and then said, '"Poor Jessica" indeed! Imagine being sorry for your wife because her lover had given her the push! Talk about weird!'

'I think he really cared about her, in spite of everything,' said Thanet as they got into the car. 'In fact, I think he's still in love with her.'

Lineham buckled his seat-belt, started the engine and switched the lights on. Dusk was now beginning to fall. 'I don't know about that, but I do think we're beginning to get a clearer picture of what went on last night, don't you?'

'Yes. Though there are still too many gaps for my liking.'

'Of course, the fact remains that he's right about Ogilvy. He could have done it before he left for the pub.'

'Has it occurred to you the same could be said about him?' said Thanet. 'All right, we know he couldn't have made the phone call, but we've only got his word for it that he was striding about the countryside in the dark between 7.20 and 8.15. What if he set out on his walk as usual, then thought, what the hell, I've had enough of this, I'm going back to have it out with them?' Thanet could tell by the expression on Lineham's face that he didn't like this idea.

'What would be the point, sir? If they were . . . brazen enough to go to bed together with him still in the house, they're not going to listen to him if he finally loses his temper with them.'

'To relieve his feelings, get it off his chest?'

'Possible, I suppose.' But Lineham still sounded unconvinced.

'But then, when he got there, Ogilvy had already left and Jessica was by herself. But Manifest had worked himself up to the point of having it out with her and that was what he did.

With tragic results.' Having put the theory into words it seemed to Thanet that it was all too likely a scenario.

But Lineham was still reluctant to accept it. 'I think I agree with what you said earlier, sir,' he said, turning the tables. 'It's too early to jump to conclusions.'

Thanet grinned inwardly. *Very neat, Mike.* Then he yawned. 'I'm sure you're right. Anyway, I don't know about you, but I think we've had enough for today.'

'Can't wait to tackle that speech, eh, sir?'

Thanet grinned. It was a pleasure to see Lineham in a good mood, engrossed in the case. The sergeant had always loved his work. Maybe this was just what he needed to give him a sufficient boost in morale to lift him out of his impasse and help him to resolve his problems at home. With any luck Thanet wouldn't have to intervene after all.

It was a cheering thought and his spirits lifted further at the thought of an evening – what was left of it – at home alone with Joan. He was therefore not very pleased to find a strange car in the drive. 'Who on earth . . .?' he muttered, as he parked in the road.

Joan must have heard his key in the lock and came out into the hall to meet him. A savoury smell made Thanet's mouth water and his stomach give a protesting rumble at the thought of nourishment being further withheld. In response to his raised eyebrows and expression of dismay as he gestured towards the sound of voices in the sitting room, Joan whispered, 'James and Marjorie. Called in with a present for Bridget.'

Thanet scowled. 'Better say hullo, I suppose.' He was fond of James and Marjorie and was normally pleased to see them, but not now, at the end of a long day, when he was tired and hungry. He put his head around the door and greeted them with a smile.

Despite their declared intention of leaving at once it was another three-quarters of an hour before they did so.

'Poor you. You must be starving.' Joan went straight into the kitchen and took his supper out of the oven. She took the cover off the plate and a delicious aroma of lamb casserole with herb dumplings filled the air.

He sat down. 'That smells good.'

Half an hour later, with a cup of coffee beside him and his pipe drawing well he was a different man.

'How's the case going?' said Joan companionably. She was stretched out full length on the sofa with her shoes off. Tonight, she had announced, she was not going to do one single chore connected with the wedding.

Thanet had always discussed his work with her. Some policemen, he knew, shut the door on their working life the minute they got home, but he had never found it possible to do that. Joan was completely trustworthy and she had often helped him to see his way through a difficult case. He knew too that it helped her to cope with the often unreasonable demands his job made upon her if she felt, in however limited a way, a part of it.

'You have your hair cut at Snippers, don't you?'

'Yes. Why?'

'I was surprised, when we went there today. I wouldn't have thought it was your kind of place.'

She laughed. 'What is my kind of place, exactly?'

'Something a bit more, well . . .'

'Conventional?'

'Perhaps, yes. All that pop music –'

'Dull?' Joan persisted.

'Of course not!'

'Fuddy-duddy, in fact?'

'Perish the thought! You know I love the way they do your hair. It suits you perfectly. It's just that the atmosphere was a bit, well, brash, I suppose.'

'I agree,' said Joan.

'You do?'

'Unreservedly. But as far as I'm concerned, I'd be prepared to put up with anything so long as they cut my hair as well as they do.' Joan ran her fingers through her mass of curls. 'They're the first place I've been to that could tame this lot. Dennis is a brilliant cutter.'

'Ah so, you have Dennis, do you?'

'Yes. Why all the interest, anyway? What were you doing there?'

'One of the apprentices is hovering on the fringe of this case. Kevin Barcombe.'

'Oh yes. He's washed my hair occasionally.'

'What do you think of him?'

The silence lasted a little longer than Thanet would have expected.

'Joan?' he said.

'I'm thinking. As a matter of fact, though I haven't consciously admitted it to myself before, I don't particularly like him.'

Thanet's brain clicked into a higher gear. 'Why not?'

'That's what I was trying to work out a moment ago. And the truth is, I don't know. He just makes me feel uneasy, that's all.'

'But why? This could be important, darling. Please try to think.'

She hesitated a moment longer, then said, 'It's his eyes, I suppose.'

'Ah! "The windows of the soul", as the saying goes. What you mean is, you find him creepy.'

'Yes.'

'Because you have a nasty feeling that something rather unpleasant is going on in his mind.'

'Yes.'

'Because of the way he looks at you?' Thanet found his hackles rising.

'No, that's the puzzling thing, that's not it. It's nothing to do with me, specifically, which is why I haven't given it much thought. And it's not the way he looks at other women, either. No, sorry, I'm not sure what it is exactly. Just an uneasy feeling, as I said. Why the interest, anyway?'

Thanet explained and Joan said, 'So, a prowler. Now yes, that would just about fit the bill, I think.'

They talked for a while longer about the case and then Thanet said, 'The frightening thing is that for the Manifests the whole thing fell apart because of something completely outside their control.'

'Him losing his job, you mean? Why frightening?'

'You do realise that he was in the same line as Alexander, don't you?'

101

'Oh. I see.' Joan swung her feet on to the ground and sat up. 'So of course you're wondering, what if the same thing happened to Bridget and Alexander?'

'I can't help asking myself that. I mean, that huge mortgage they've got . . . What on earth would they do if Alexander were to turn up for work one day and, like Desmond Manifest, find his desk had been cleared – which is, I understand, how it's often done?'

'So I've heard. It must be shattering. And I've no idea what they'd do. But look, Luke, you're just going to have to accept that if it came to the worst and that did happen, they'd simply have to cope with it in their own way. If we thought of every possible thing that could go wrong for them before they've even started, we'd go mad.'

'I suppose so.'

She left the sofa and came to kneel on the floor in front of him. She took his hand. 'You're finding this very hard, aren't you? To let her go.'

It was difficult to admit it, even to himself. He sighed. 'You're right, of course.'

'It's nothing to be ashamed of! She's always been your little girl and, let's face it, she always will be, in a way. But at the same time she's a woman now, and you have to allow her to be one.'

'I know, I know, I know! I'll manage it in the end, I'm sure. If only I were happier about Alexander.'

'Alexander is all right. He's kind –'

'Kind, after the way he ditched her!'

'He was younger then. Commitment is a frightening thing. Young people these days seem to find it very difficult. If he wasn't ready for it, it was only right for him to say so. I know Bridget was hurt but far better that he should go into marriage sure in his own mind that he's doing the right thing, than rush into it too soon and always wonder if he had. But now . . . No, I think they'll be fine. He's loyal, patient, hardworking . . .' She smiled up at Thanet. 'Just like you, in fact.'

'Like me!' Thanet was astounded. The successful, glamorous Alexander, just like him! 'Rubbish!' he said.

'I mean it. Come to think of it, that's probably why Bridget chose him.'

'For a sensible woman you do talk a lot of nonsense sometimes!' But secretly, the thought pleased him and he tucked it away for future examination.

NINE

'I remember Bridget once saying to me that she had decided she wasn't going to get married at all, she was going to be a career woman,' said Thanet to his reflection. 'It goes without saying that that was before she met Alexander.' He adjusted his tie. 'In fact, she was only six years old at the time.' He paused, then consulted himself. 'Too feeble? No, I don't think so. But I must get the timing right. A pause before "In fact".'

He had stayed up late last night putting the final touches to his speech and was now running through it for the second time this morning.

'Luke? You're getting behind.' Joan was calling up the stairs.

He checked the time. So he was. He slipped his jacket on, stuffed wallet, keys, loose change, pipe and tobacco pouch into his pockets and hurried downstairs.

Joan was in the hall, putting her coat on. 'I've got to get in early,' she said. 'One of my clients is starting a new job this morning and I want to see him before he goes to work.'

'Have you had any breakfast?'

She nodded. 'A piece of toast and a cup of tea.'

'Are you all right?' Despite her evening off she was still looking tired, he thought.

'Fine. How's your back this morning?

Thanet moved experimentally. 'Much better, thanks, after that session yesterday. When is Bridget arriving?'

'I'm not sure. Some time this afternoon, I think.'

'Good.' He kissed her. 'See you this evening, then.'

In the kitchen he made himself a cup of coffee to accompany what Joan called his breakfast cocktail, an approved (by her) mixture of various cereals, fruit and yoghurt. Except on high days and holidays bacon and eggs were a thing of the past. At first Thanet had protested about the healthy regime she had instituted but by now he had got used to it – enjoyed it, even, though he had no intention of admitting it. By twenty past eight he was in the car on his way to work enjoying a few puffs of his pipe, speech forgotten, focusing on the day ahead. It was a crisp autumn morning with clear skies, bright sunshine and a touch of frost in the air. His spirits rose. While he deplored the senseless waste of human life, the challenge of a new case always excited him. He enjoyed the way it stretched him, forced him to exercise all his skills, all his ingenuity, all his patience. He liked meeting new witnesses, working out fresh lines of inquiry and following them through to their logical conclusion. Above all he enjoyed that incomparable feeling of elation when the days of striving finally bore fruit and he knew the mystery was solved. And this time, of course, there was the added bonus that with Draco away he wouldn't have the Superintendent breathing down his neck. He wondered what new information was awaiting him on his desk. By the time he got to work Lineham would no doubt have sifted through the reports as usual.

But surprisingly, Lineham wasn't there.

Thanet checked what had come in. A neighbour who regularly walked his dog at that time had been returning home at about twenty past seven on Tuesday evening and had seen Desmond Manifest set out on his walk 'as usual'. This backed up what the landlord of the Harrow had told them.

Much more interesting was the fact that Kevin Barcombe apparently hadn't arrived at Sally's, the nightclub, until around 8.30. The doorman was a client at Snippers and knew him by sight. He remembered the time because he was keeping a close eye on it; his mother had been rushed into hospital that afternoon and he had been told he could ring and inquire how she was any time after 8.30 p.m. Kevin had been the last person to come in before he made the phone call.

Thanet sat back and thought. Kevin claimed not to have left home until 8.15, but Thanet was much more inclined to believe his mother, who said he had left at 7.45. Thanet worked out a possible scenario: Kevin drives to Charthurst, arriving at about eight. By this time Ogilvy would be cosily ensconced in the Harrow with his wife. Kevin parks at the pub and takes up his post behind the hedge opposite the Manifests' house.

Then what?

Say Jessica had fallen or been pushed down the stairs during a quarrel with Ogilvy and say Ogilvy had not shut the front door properly behind him as he claimed. Manifest had said that the catch was faulty. After a few minutes Kevin realises that the door is ajar. He goes to investigate, discovers the body, phones for an ambulance and leaves. Yes, the timing of the phone call would be right, and if he left immediately Kevin would have been back in Sturrenden in time to have arrived at the nightclub at around 8.30.

Alternatively –

'Sorry I'm late, sir.' Lineham arrived, out of breath.

'Nice lie-in, Mike?'

'Very funny. It's my mother. She rang before breakfast, said she'd had one of her "turns". I had to go and check.'

'Of course. Was she all right?' Mrs Lineham's 'turns' had haunted Lineham throughout his working life, had almost prevented him getting married at all. It was tempting to believe that she was invariably crying wolf but she was getting old and one of these days no doubt it would be serious, even fatal. In the very nature of things it would be the one occasion when Lineham decided to ignore her cry for help. He simply couldn't risk it and Thanet sympathised.

'Yes. It was just a dizzy spell. It had more or less passed off by the time I got there.'

'Good. Listen, Mike.' Thanet related the scenario he had just visualised, studying Lineham as he did so. The sergeant looked tired, exhausted, even, with deep pouches beneath his eyes and a grey tinge to his skin. Perhaps he should speak to him about his dilemma after all. He didn't want to interfere in what was, after all, a private matter, but things couldn't go on like this. On the other hand, Lineham was still functioning efficiently. Thanet could hardly take one late arrival as an excuse to broach the subject in view of the fact that Lineham was almost invariably at his desk before anyone else and never complained about late hours or extra duty. No, he would have to wait. If Lineham started slipping up, then that would be a different matter.

The sergeant was nodding. 'Yes. It could have happened like that. But if Kevin was there, there's no reason to think he didn't do it himself. Say Ogilvy left the door open, Jessica didn't realise, Kevin saw his opportunity to get in, and took it. Jessica is in her bedroom, hears footsteps on the stairs, comes out, sees Kevin, gets frightened –'

'Et cetera et cetera. Quite. Yes, it's possible, I grant you.'

'Anything else come in, sir?'

'The PM's been confirmed for this morning, that's all.'

'So, what next?'

'I was thinking . . . I'd like to get a bit more background material. Did you get the address of that schoolfriend of Jessica's – what was her name? – from Louise?'

'Barnes, sir. Juliet Barnes. Yes, I did.' Lineham fished out his wallet and extracted a slip of paper. 'She lives at Ribbleden. But if you want to see her this morning, she works as a chiropodist in the town.'

'How convenient!'

The morning meetings conducted by Draco's deputy were always brief and before long Thanet and Lineham were stepping out into the sunshine. Another bonus of this case so far, Thanet thought, was that a number of the witnesses worked in the town. He sometimes felt he spent half his working life driving around and it was pleasant to walk along Sturrenden's picturesque High Street occasionally acknowledging a smile or a hand raised in greeting. By now it was virtually impossible for him to take even the shortest stroll through the town without seeing someone he knew.

The chiropodist's practice was based in a terraced house just off the High Street. The receptionist, a prim starchy woman in her mid-fifties, was not amused at the prospect of having Mrs Barnes's list of appointments disrupted and it took patience, persistence and diplomacy to convince her that they really did need to see her employer as soon as she had finished with her current client.

Juliet Barnes herself was a different matter and without hesitation ushered them through into her surgery. 'Aren't you married to Louise Stark?' she said to Lineham as they went.

'Yes. You were at school together, I believe.'

'That's right. I see her around occasionally.'

'So she said.'

'It's about Jessica Manifest of course, Mrs Barnes – Jessica Dander, as you knew her,' Thanet said, as soon as the door was shut behind them.

'Yes, I heard what had happened. It's dreadful, really dreadful.' She was tall and well built, statuesque almost, with broad high cheekbones, shining blonde hair cropped short and earnest hazel eyes. She was wearing a white medical coat and exuded an air of professional efficiency. 'Do sit down.' She waved a hand at the only two chairs in the room and propped herself against the windowsill.

She waited until they were seated, then said, 'But why on earth have you come to see me? I haven't seen Jess in years. Well, I've seen her, of course, round and about, but we never used to meet on purpose or spend time together.'

'We're trying to fill in on Mrs Manifest's background, actually,' said Thanet. 'And we understand that you and she were close friends, when you were at school.'

'Yes, we were, at one time. But you know what it's like when you're young. You drift in and out of friendships; some last and some don't. Ours didn't, I'm afraid.'

'We're thinking particularly of the year you took your O levels,' said Lineham.

'My goodness! That's – what? Twenty years ago now! It hardly bears thinking about!'

'I know,' said Thanet, smiling. 'But if you could cast your mind back . . .'

'I'll try. What do you want to know?' She shifted uncomfortably against the window-ledge and Lineham stood up. 'Wouldn't you prefer to sit down?'

She smiled at him. 'Very well. Thank you. Though without wishing to be unhelpful I do hope this won't take too long. I have a full list of appointments this morning and if I fall too far behind I won't get a lunch break.'

'We'll be as brief as possible,' said Thanet. 'If you would cast your mind back, then, to that summer, the summer when you were sixteen. You and Jessica were friends at that time, I believe?'

She nodded.

'Now, we understand from Sergeant Lineham's wife that Mrs Manifest – we'll call her Jessica for convenience – was very bright, and you all expected her to stay on at school to take her A levels and go on to university, that in fact everyone was surprised when she left school that summer.'

'Yes, that's true. I was as surprised as anyone. I mean, she'd made her A-level choices and everything.'

'So what happened, do you think? What made her change her mind?'

'I really don't know.' Juliet's forehead creased as she frowned, remembering, and her eyes narrowed as if she were peering into the past. 'All I can recall is that when school broke up at the end of that summer term I was looking forward to doing all the usual things with her – playing tennis, swimming, going for bike rides and so on. Jess was especially keen on swimming and during the previous Easter holidays we'd gone every day. But for some reason she went cold on me and whenever I rang up to suggest we go out she had some excuse ready. I was really upset about it at the time and I'd just decided I wouldn't bother about her any more when she rang to say she was going to stay with an aunt in Bristol for the rest of the holidays. Then she wrote to say she loved Bristol, it was a great city, and she much preferred living with her aunt than with her sister and brother-in-law – and who could blame her? – and she'd decided to stay on there.'

'Why do you say, "who could blame her?"'

'She couldn't stand him. Her brother-in-law. What was his name? Bernard.'

'Why not? Any particular reason?'

'Have you met him?'

'Yes.'

'Well, there you are then. He's a creep, isn't he? And that stink, those perpetual cigarettes . . .'

'Was she going to continue her studies in Bristol?'

'I don't know. But I do know that things went wrong. The aunt fell ill, so much so that Jess couldn't cope alone and Madge – that's Jess's sister – had to go and help look after her, even had to stay over Christmas. Bernard went to join them over the holiday, I believe. Anyway, when the aunt got better Madge came back but Jess stayed on. And then, a month or two later, the aunt had a relapse and died unexpectedly so Jess came back to Sturrenden.'

'To live with her sister again, I presume.'

'At first, yes. But Madge's baby had arrived by then and I think Jess felt a bit *de trop*. She landed herself a dogsbody job on the *KM* and as soon as she was earning she moved out into a bedsit in Maidstone. You had to hand it to her. She really worked her socks off – went to journalism classes at nightschool and slowly climbed the ladder until she was a fully fledged reporter. You had to admire her for that.'

An inflection in that last sentence made Thanet say, 'I sense a reservation there.'

She grimaced. 'Yes, I suppose so. To tell you the truth; one of the reasons why we lost touch is that I decided I didn't particularly like her. She was very ambitious, of course, nothing wrong in that, but she became much too materialistic for my taste.'

There was no point in asking her to elaborate. Thanet didn't want to waste her time and he felt that she had told them as much as she knew. They thanked her and left.

'Interesting,' said Thanet as they emerged on to the street.

'Yes. I wonder –' Lineham dodged to avoid a young woman with a pushchair and Thanet saw that it was the Ogilvy's nanny, Chantal, with Daisy bundled up against the autumnal chill in bright red bobble hat and miniature ski-suit.

He seized his chance and minutes later they were seated in one of Sturrenden's many teashops, ordering coffee. 'I hope we're not holding you up too much, Mademoiselle . . .?'

'Chantal, please.' The perfect teeth flashed at him again as she took a box of breadsticks from her shopping bag and presented one to Daisy, safely ensconsed in a high chair. Daisy took it and holding it like a sword swiped the air with it once or twice before taking her first bite. 'No, not at all. So long as I perform my duties I am free to do how I wish.'

'Have you been with the Ogilvys long?'

'I come when Daisy is born.' She reached out to remove Daisy's hat, smiling at her. She was obviously fond of her charge.

The coffee arrived and there was a pause while it was served.

'Au pairs don't usually stay as long as that,' said Lineham.

Chantal took a sip of her coffee and grimaced slightly. 'I did not intend to. But Penny – Mrs Ogilvy – is very kind and she offer me more money to stay. And I think, well, why not? But I must move on soon.'

'Why is that?' said Thanet. 'This coffee's not very good, is it?'

'I understand that the coffee in England is much better than it used to be. But sadly, not everywhere. You must not stay with a family more than two years,' she went on, answering his question. 'It becomes too hard to leave the children. I know I will miss Daisy so much already. I keep on putting it off.'

'Your English is excellent,' said Lineham.

Another dazzling smile. 'Thank you. I try, and Penny help me. I ask her to correct me and she does. That way, I learn.'

'You're obviously fond of her, too,' said Thanet. It was a pity, for his own purpose. The girl might be too loyal to talk.

'Yes. I am.'

'But you're not so keen on her husband.'

Chantal gave him a startled look then a rueful smile. 'Oh dear. It is so obvious, then?'

'Not at all. We are trained to notice these things. You do understand why we're interested in him, don't you?'

She frowned. 'Yes. Don't do that, *chérie*.' Daisy had started sucking the breadstick and was now wiping the chewed end up and down the front of her ski-suit, leaving brown trails. 'If you don't want any more, give it to Chantal.'

Daisy handed it over with an angelic smile and said, 'Want my book.'

Chantal wiped the little girl's hands with a damp flannel which she produced from her bag then rummaged in it again. 'Say please.'

'Please.'

Chantal's hand emerged holding a book which she duly presented to Daisy. '*The Very Hungry Caterpillar*,' she said. 'It's her favourite.'

Lineham shifted impatiently, but Thanet was happy to let Chantal set the pace. He judged, however, that she was now ready for him to be frank with her. 'You know that Mr Ogilvy was involved with the journalist who died? That he admits to visiting her that evening? And that there is a question mark over her death?'

'She fell down the stairs, didn't she? You are suggesting he might have pushed her?' Chantal's eyes opened so wide that the whites showed all around the irises.

Thanet felt he had to reassure her. 'We really don't know at present and even if he did, we don't believe for a moment that he is a danger to anyone else. In fact, there are several possible suspects. But we do need to find out as much as we can about all of them. So if there is anything you can tell us, to help us . . .?'

She shrugged. 'In France everything is so different. A mistress, *pouf*, it is no big deal, as you say. But here . . . Penny was very upset, when she find out.'

'When was that?'

'On Tuesday.'

Thanet's pulse quickened. The day of the murder.

'She go to a coffee morning and when she come home she go straight up to her bedroom and shut the door. She does not come down for lunch and when I see her later her eyes, they are red from weeping. Then, when Mr Ogilvy come home, there is a quarrel.' She paused to extricate Daisy's finger from one of the holes in her book.

Don't stop now, begged Thanet silently. 'You heard what was said?'

Chantal lifted her slim shoulders. 'I was curious,' she

admitted. 'I do not like to see Penny unhappy. I wondered what had upset her. So when I hear them start to argue, yes, I listen. It is my affair, after all. If there is something wrong between the parents, it will affect the children.'

'Quite. So what did you hear?'

'I couldn't hear every word, you understand, but Penny, she was accusing him of being unfaithful and he was not denying it. She was very upset, she was crying and shouting. She is not usually like that. Usually she is calm and patient.'

Thanet waited. Across the table he could see Lineham silently urging her on. Daisy was mercifully quiet at the moment but the attention span of a two-year-old is brief, as they were both aware, and the next interruption might be the signal for Chantal to decide that it was time she gave her charge her full attention again.

'She tell him he must choose between this woman and her. She say that if he choose the woman she will fight for her home and her children and he would soon find he wouldn't be able to live – how do you say? – in the style to which he was accustomed. The business, you see, has not been good during the recession. Mr Ogilvy has been very worried at times. Just after I come, two years ago, things were so bad they were talking about selling their house.'

'I see,' said Thanet. And he did.

So did Lineham. 'So,' said the sergeant, outside, after they had waved Daisy on her way, 'someone spilled the beans at that coffee morning. Mrs O. presented him with an ultimatum and he knew which side his bread was buttered. No matter what Jessica said he wouldn't have given in.'

'Let's go and have another word with him, while we're in the town,' said Thanet. 'And we mustn't forget that we have only their word for it that his wife didn't get out of her car that evening.'

'You're still wondering if she was involved?'

'It's difficult to see how she could have done it by herself,' said Thanet. 'They must have gone off together afterwards, as they claim, or how could she have known he was at the Harrow?'

113

'She could have spotted his car there, as she went by. It is on their way home.'

'True. But I don't see how he could have missed seeing her car when he left Jessica's house. I shouldn't think people normally park there, the lane's too narrow, I think she deliberately parked where she did so that he would see her.'

'So what are you suggesting, sir?'

'Well, say she was too on edge to bear just sitting still in the car, waiting for him to come out –'

'Yes!' said Lineham eagerly. 'And say Jessica had gone straight upstairs and Ogilvy had followed and his wife saw them in the bedroom – the Bartons said Jessica often didn't bother to draw the curtains, if you remember –'

'Quite. She might not have been able to resist the temptation to go and try to break up the tête-à-tête by knocking on the door.'

'No, she wouldn't have done that, surely?'

'Who knows? She was obviously in a state about the whole business. People often act out of character when they're deeply upset, do things they would never dream of doing under normal circumstances. And if Jessica opened the door . . . No, I don't think I can believe in this scenario.' They had come to a halt outside the premises of Ogilvy and Tate. 'Anyway, let's see what Ogilvy has to say for himself, if he's in.' Thanet was studying the advertisements. 'Look, your house hasn't been sold yet.'

'My house! At that price? Ha ha.' But Lineham paused to take another look at the photograph before following Thanet inside.

This time Ogilvy was in and they were ushered straight into his office. It was furnished with high-quality office reproduction furniture, a black leather executive swivel chair behind the desk and photographs of his wife and children in silver frames. He rose with a smile as they came in. 'Inspector. How can I help you?'

His bonhomie disappeared in a flash, however, when Thanet said, 'We find you've been less than frank with us, Mr Ogilvy.'

TEN

Ogilvy's eyes darted from one to the other. 'What are you talking about?' He sat down behind his desk again as if to establish who was in charge here and flicked his fingers at a couple of chairs nearby.

Thanet and Lineham moved them so that they were facing him squarely and sat down. The battle lines were drawn. Thanet could almost hear Ogilvy thinking: *What have they found out?* 'I'm talking about your account of what happened on Tuesday evening.'

Ogilvy's eyes narrowed.

'And specifically about the conversation with your wife, before you left to visit Mrs Manifest,' said Thanet. Was that a flash of relief he saw before Ogilvy's expression hardened?

'Conversations with my wife are a private matter,' snapped the estate agent. He picked up a gold propelling pencil and began rolling it to and fro between his fingers.

'I'm afraid you'll soon discover that where murder is concerned privacy flies out of the window. And in this instance the conversation was highly relevant to our inquiry.'

'How?' The monosyllable was like a gunshot.

'When we last spoke to you you said – What, exactly, did Mr Ogilvy say, sergeant?' It wasn't that Thanet couldn't remember but that a notebook was occasionally a useful weapon against a hostile witness. It can be intimidating to realise that every word you say is a potential boomerang.

Lineham dutifully shuffled back through the pages. '"My wife and I discussed the matter and I decided to end my relationship with Mrs Manifest."'

'Quite,' said Thanet. 'A fairly bland description of what actually happened, wouldn't you agree?'

'I don't know what you're talking about.'

'Oh come, sir. We now know that Mrs Ogilvy had only found out about your affair with Mrs Manifest that morning, and naturally she was extremely upset about it. That evening you quarrelled and she presented you with an ultimatum: give Mrs Manifest up or your marriage was over. And the fact of the matter was that when it came to the crunch you weren't prepared to risk losing your beautiful home, your wife and your children for the sake of your mistress.'

'I don't know where you've been hearing all this stuff,' said Ogilvy. 'Oh, I see! It's that bloody girl, isn't it? Chantal. Interfering little b—' He cut himself off, realising perhaps that he had gone too far.

Thanet said nothing. It didn't worry him that Ogilvy had guessed the truth. When Chantal had told them about the quarrel she must have realised that this would get back to her employer. But Thanet didn't think it would have worried her too much. She was quite capable of standing up for herself and in any case it was Mrs Ogilvy who at the moment was calling the shots in that household. She would soon put a stop to it if Ogilvy tried to fire the girl. And if the worst did come to the worst, well, as Chantal had said, she intended moving on soon anyway.

'I don't know what the devil she's been telling you,' said Ogilvy, 'but all this stuff about ultimatums is a load of rubbish.' He placed the propelling pencil precisely in the centre of the tooled leather blotter before him as if squaring up his thoughts, then said, 'It was all very unfortunate, really.' His tone had changed, suddenly become confidential, and he leaned back in his chair, adopted a man-to-man, somewhat quizzical expression. 'Ironic. You see, it's true my wife was told about Jessica and me on Tuesday, at a coffee morning she went to. Some well-meaning so-called "friend", I suppose,' he added vindictively. 'But the point is, I'd already made up my mind before that to break it off that evening. Sickening, wasn't it?' *To think I almost got away with it*, his expression said.

'Very annoying for you,' said Thanet.

Unsure whether he was serious or not, Ogilvy gave him a suspicious look. 'So you see, there was no question of ultimatums or anything of that nature.'

'Why had you come to that decision, sir? To break it off with Mrs Manifest?'

'I don't see that's any of your business.'

Thanet simply raised his eyebrows, folded his arms and waited.

'Well, if you must know, I'd got a bit fed up with the way she was carrying on.'

'Carrying on?'

Ogilvy sighed. 'Look, it all started really because, well, to tell you the truth, I was flattered. Right from the beginning she was the one who made the running. After all, she is – was – quite well known in the area and she was a very attractive woman. And I must admit she intrigued me. She was an interesting combination, you know, of career woman and – how shall I describe it? – vulnerability. Yes, that's it. Vulnerability.'

Ogilvy looked pleased with his description, as if he had just pulled off some difficult feat of terminology.

'But?'

'But lately, well, I'd been getting more and more . . . Oh hell, this is really very difficult . . . Well, uncomfortable, about her behaviour.'

'In what way?' But Thanet could guess. How many men would enjoy going to bed with their mistress under her husband's nose, so to speak? But he wasn't going to let Ogilvy off the hook.

The estate agent shifted uncomfortably on his chair as if the seat had suddenly become too hot to sit upon. 'Put it this way. Usually, if you're sleeping with a married woman, it's all hole-and-corner stuff. Neither of you is too keen for it to get back to your partner, you know what I mean? But in this case, Jessica actually seemed to enjoy parading our . . . relationship before her husband. And to be honest, I found that downright embarrassing. Well, wouldn't you?'

'But she obviously didn't.'

'No, not in the least! That's what I mean! In fact, she actually seemed to enjoy it. Poor sod, I couldn't help feeling sorry for him.' He gave a cynical laugh. 'And that's a new one, isn't it! Feeling sorry for the husband you're cheating on! All the same,' and he leaned forward across his desk and lowered his voice, 'if you really do suspect that someone pushed her down the stairs, I'd take a long hard look at Manifest if I were you.'

'You're accusing Mr Manifest of murder?'

He backtracked immediately. 'Certainly not. I mean, not necessarily.'

'Did you see any indications of violent behaviour against his wife?'

Honesty struggled with the desire to shine the spotlight anywhere but on himself. 'Well, no, not exactly. He didn't say much. Just seemed rather . . . depressed.' Another cynical little laugh. 'Not surprising, really, is it? But he must have resented the way she was carrying on. Stands to reason, doesn't it?

'So it was her treatment of her husband that, shall we say, put you off her?'

'Well, it does make you think. I mean, if she could treat him like that . . .'

'She could treat you like that too.'

'Exactly!' Ogilvy was warming to his theme now. 'But that wasn't the only thing.'

'Oh?'

'She had a nasty temper, you know. It used to come out in all sorts of little ways, whenever she was crossed or frustrated – in a restaurant if the service was bad, for example, or if she hadn't been able to get what she wanted out of an interview. With her husband it seemed to be there all the time, ready to flare up at the slightest provocation, and I saw signs that she was beginning to lose patience with me too. She was getting very pushy, pressing me to leave Pen, go and live with her. But I never did have any intention of doing that. My wife and children are the most important things in my life.'

Not so important that you wouldn't risk losing them for the

cheap thrill of an affair with a woman you weren't even in love with, thought Thanet harshly, the image of Daisy in her red bobble hat and mini ski-suit fresh in his mind.

'I'm sure you know what I mean,' Ogilvy was saying. 'Have you got any children, Inspector?'

'Two,' said Thanet reluctantly.

'There you are, then.' Ogilvy gave a saccharine smile, as one family man to another. 'Anyway, I think it was beginning to dawn on Jessica that she wasn't going to get anywhere. So one way and the other . . .'

'You were getting a bit fed up with her.' Although the picture of Jessica that Ogilvy was painting was an unattractive one, and Thanet certainly couldn't condone the way she had treated her husband, he couldn't help a twinge of sympathy for her. It seemed that nothing had ever gone right for the woman. 'Speaking of your wife . . .'

Ogilvy frowned. 'What about her?'

'Is she in the habit of following you about?' Thanet deliberately chose to be offensive in the hope of provoking Ogilvy. He succeeded.

The estate agent's nostrils flared and he put his head down like a bull about to charge. 'Frankly, I don't see that it's any business of yours. Just leave my wife out of this, will you?'

'I'm afraid we can't do that, can we, sir?'

'Why not?'

'It's obvious, surely. She was there, only yards away from the spot where a murder was committed. '

Ogilvy jumped up and, resting his hands on the desk, leaned forward and said angrily, 'Not while I was there, it wasn't! I repeat, Inspector: Jessica Manifest was alive and kicking when I left her house that night. I can't prove it but if there is any justice in this world – which frankly I'm beginning to doubt – sooner or later you'll find out that I'm telling the truth. And as for my wife, she has no involvement in this whatsoever. And now, if you don't mind . . .'

Thanet didn't budge. 'If that is true you have no reason not to answer my questions. If you refuse, of course, we can only draw our own conclusions.'

Ogilvy took a deep breath, then slowly subsided on to his

chair. 'Very well,' he said wearily. 'But get on with it, will you? I do have a job to do.'

'When did you first notice your wife's car?'

'Just after turning out of the front gate. She told me she'd parked there deliberately, so I couldn't miss seeing her.'

'Was she in the car or out of it?'

'In.'

Was he telling the truth or not? Thanet couldn't tell.

'When you were in the house, did you go upstairs at all?'

Ogilvy looked surprised at the sudden change of direction. 'No. Why?'

'And you're absolutely certain that you shut the front door behind you?'

'Yes! I told you!'

'Did you check that it was properly shut?'

'No. I just slammed it.'

Ogilvy couldn't hide his relief as Thanet rose.

'Well, I think that's all for the moment, sir. Thank you.'

'It's very odd,' said Lineham when they were outside, 'the more we learn about her the less I like her, but the more sorry for her I feel.'

'I know. A paradox, isn't it? Who did you put on to investigating the Ogilvys' background? Bentley? It'll be interesting to see what he turns up.'

Lineham clapped a hand to his forehead. 'Oh no! I forgot to brief him! I meant to do it first thing this morning, then I was late, of course.'

'Not like you, Mike.' Was this the first of the slip-ups Thanet had been afraid might happen? He sighed inwardly. It looked as though he was going to have to tackle Lineham about his domestic situation after all. 'Anyway, no harm done, very little time has been lost. Do it when we get back.'

They were now passing Snippers.

'There's Kevin,' said Lineham.

The boy was in the window, rearranging the wigs on some model heads with improbably classic features against a swathe of black velvet. He caught sight of the two policemen outside and Thanet glimpsed a flash of fear in his eyes before he turned away without acknowledging them and busied himself with his work. Something tweaked at Thanet's memory and his stride faltered as they moved on.

Lineham had noticed. 'What?'

Thanet shook his head. 'Nothing. Well, there was something, but I don't know what it was.'

'What sort of thing?'

'I don't know.' He frowned. What could it have been?

'I thought he looked frightened when he saw us,' said Lineham.

'So did I.' Thanet was still struggling to place what it was that had disturbed him. He took a few more steps and then paused to glance back over his shoulder. From this distance the tableau in the window of Snippers looked positively surreal, the disembodied model heads with their unnaturally perfect tresses seeming to float at different heights against the dark background. Kevin bent to pick something up and briefly his hair flamed as it caught the sun. Red hair. Suddenly Thanet understood.

Lineham, who had stepped behind him to allow a woman with a shopping trolley to pass, had cannoned into him. 'Sorry, sir!'

'My fault,' said Thanet, mind in turmoil. The tumblers in his brain were turning, click click click.

'You've realised what it was,' said Lineham, recognising that look.

'Yes, I have. Look, I know it's a bit early, but let's go and have a bite, Mike, and I'll explain.'

'Where shall we go?'

'How about the Woolsack? We haven't been there for ages.'

'Fine by me.'

Thanet chose a baguette with crispy bacon and mushrooms, Lineham a ploughman's platter. English pub food, thought Thanet, seemed to get better and better. The sergeant waited until they were seated at their table before saying eagerly, 'Well?'

'You can work it out for yourself, Mike, it's really very simple. Just a matter of making the right connections. Put it this way: what colour was Jessica's hair?'

'Auburn. First thing I noticed about her. Gorgeous, wasn't it?'

'And what colour is Kevin's?'

'Carrot.' Lineham's face went blank as he saw what Thanet was getting at. 'And Kevin was adopted,' he said slowly, obviously taking in the implications.

'Exactly!'

'So the reason why Jessica left school unexpectedly that summer was because she was having a baby. And that,' said Lineham, speeding up as he warmed to his theme, 'was why she wouldn't go swimming with Juliet Barnes during the summer holidays –'

'And why she went to stay with an aunt in Bristol –'

'And stayed there when the holidays were over!' finished Lineham. 'Yes, it all fits, doesn't it!'

'A bit far out, though, don't you think, Mike?'

'I'm usually the one who says that!'

There was a pause while the food was served.

Lineham loaded a piece of french bread with cheese and pickle, popped the food into his mouth and chewed thoughtfully. 'It all depends on whether Kevin really was the prowler. If he was, then you may well be right. Adopted children often seem to want to trace their biological parents, especially their mothers, when they get to Kevin's age. And if he did, he may well have been trying to pluck up the courage to tackle her. I've often thought it must be a hell of thing, to walk up to the door of a complete stranger and say, "Hi, I'm the baby you gave up for adoption all those years ago."'

'And a tremendous shock for the mother, too. Mmm. This looks delicious.' The baguette was positively bulging with bacon and mushrooms and Thanet's mouth filled with anticipatory saliva. He took a huge mouthful.

'So,' Lineham went on, 'say he'd been hanging around, keeping an eye on her, watching for his moment. What time did we say he would have arrived on Tuesday evening? Around eight? Ogilvy claims to have left at twenty to, which fits with him arriving at the pub a few minutes later. Say he did leave the door open – Kevin would soon have noticed that it was ajar . . .'

Thanet had finished chewing and he swallowed. 'If she was still alive, wouldn't Jessica have noticed that it was open in the interim?'

'Not necessarily, if she stayed in the sitting room after Ogilvy walked out on her.'

'I suppose.'

'So if Kevin decided to investigate, pushed the door open . . . There are two possibilities, aren't there: Jessica was already dead, in which case he rings for an ambulance and gets out of there as fast as he can, or . . . Let me see . . . If she was in the sitting room as you suggest, she'd probably have heard him come in, so she calls out –'

'Comes into the hall –'

'Panics –'

'Runs upstairs –'

'Kevin follows, to try to reassure her –'

'She thinks he's chasing her, they struggle and –'

'That's it!' said Lineham. 'She falls.'

They both concentrated on their lunch for a few minutes, thinking.

'It could have happened like that,' said Lineham at last. 'If it did, he'd have panicked himself then, made that phone call and scarpered.'

'Yes, but as far as I can see our only hope of proving beyond doubt that he was behind that hedge is a saliva test on those cigarette ends. And as yet we don't even know if he smokes.'

'Easy enough to find out.'

'True. But I think the first thing to do is tackle Jessica's brother-in-law again, find out if she really did have a baby. She was living with them at the time, he'd have had to be in the know.'

Lineham groaned. 'Let's try and catch him in the open air. I don't think I could stand another session in that stinking living room.'

'We might not have any choice.'

They decided to drop in at the office before going to see Covin and had been there only a minute or two when the door opened and Mallard bounced in. Thanet never ceased to marvel at the new lease of life which the police surgeon's second marriage had given him. For years after his first wife died of lingering cancer the little doctor had been one of the loneliest, saddest men it had ever been Thanet's misfortune to meet. He had continued to work but there had been no joy in his life and he had quickly acquired the reputation of being cranky and short-tempered. Since his marriage to the cookery writer Helen Fields a few years ago, however, he was a changed man, radiating good humour and contentment. An added bonus was that from one year to the next, he never seemed to age. It was a pity, thought Thanet now, observing the police surgeon's bright eyes, clear skin and his general air of well-being, that happiness couldn't be doled out on the NHS. The geriatric wards and nursing homes would empty in no time.

'Morning both,' said Mallard, beaming. 'Thought you'd like a verbal on the PM.'

'So what's the verdict?'

'Nothing very exciting, I'm afraid, nothing unexpected. To put it in lay terms, she died of a broken neck.'

'Instantly?'

Mallard shrugged. 'Assuming that she wasn't moved after she fell, then yes. As we've said before, if anyone did move her, then it's a different story. But there's no way of telling.'

'And that's it?'

'Afraid so. Sorry I can't be of more help.' He bustled towards the door. 'Must get on.' With one hand on the door-knob he paused. 'You hoping to get this case cleared up before Saturday?'

'Ha ha,' said Thanet. 'Very funny.'

'Not going well?'

Thanet pulled a face. 'Slowly, that's all.'

'You never know. Miracles can happen. When's Bridget coming home?'

'Today.'

'Helen asked me to tell you she's finished decorating the cake, if Bridget and Joan would like to pop round to take a look.'

'Fine. Thanks, I'll tell them.'

With a wave of the hand Mallard was gone.

'Not much help there, then,' said Lineham gloomily.

'Well we didn't really expect anything else, did we? Come on, Mike. Let's go and see what Covin has to say.'

ELEVEN

'We're looking for Mr Covin.' Thanet had to raise his voice above the barking of a Labrador/Collie cross.

Covin's house was shut up and they had gone to the main house to inquire whereabouts on the farm he might be working. It was a typical Kentish farmhouse of rosy red bricks to the first floor with tilehanging above. Someone was a keen gardener: the lawns were trim, the flowerbeds immaculate and still colourful with Michaelmas daisies, late roses and dahlias. The door had been opened by one of the tallest men Thanet had ever come across. He reckoned that Covin's employer must be a good six foot five and his build matched his height. He was in his sixties with grizzled hair cropped very short and the kind of tan acquired only by those who work outdoors in all weathers. He was wearing sturdy corduroys worn thin on the thighs and knees and a padded waistcoat over a thick checked shirt. 'Quiet, Ben! Sit!' he said, and the dog subsided, reluctantly lowering its haunches on to the flagstone floor.

'Do you happen to know where Mr Covin might be, Mr . . .?' said Thanet into the blissful silence.

'Wargreave. James Wargreave,' said the farmer.

'We're investigating the death of his sister-in-law, Mr Wargreave.' Thanet produced his warrant card.

'I'm afraid you're out of luck. He's out and won't be back until around five.'

'May I ask how long he's been working for you?'

'Twenty years or so.' Wargreave frowned. 'Why? Is he in trouble?'

'Not at all. It's just that we're trying to fill in some family

126

background. I wonder, would it inconvenience you too much if we had a brief talk?'

Wargreave stood back. 'If you think it'll help.'

There was a savoury smell in the hall and a clatter of dishes from the kitchen.

'I hope we're not interrupting your lunch.'

'Oh no, we've just finished. We were washing up.'

He took them into a square sitting room which had a comfortable lived-in air. The soft furnishings were faded and threadbare in places but there were books and newspapers and some knitting bundled up on one of the armchairs as if its owner had just put it down for a moment and would soon return.

'Who is it, James?'

A little barrel of a woman appeared in the doorway drying her hands on a tea towel. She went to stand beside her husband. Jack Sprat and his wife, thought Thanet. She couldn't have been above five feet tall and with her rosy cheeks, untidy bun and voluminous apron she was almost a caricature of a farmer's wife, a model for the illustrations in children's picture books. But her eyes were bright with intelligence as she listened to her husband's explanation and Thanet guessed that she didn't miss much. Good, he thought. If anyone could sum up the Covin household, she would.

'Sit yourselves down,' she said. 'Though I can't see how we can help. We hardly knew her really, did we, James? Poor girl, what a terrible thing to happen.'

When they were all settled Thanet said, 'When, exactly, did the Covins come to work for you?'

They consulted each other with a glance.

'Nineteen seventy-eight?' said Wargreave. 'Or was it 1977?'

'It was a couple of months before Mum died, I do remember that – that was on February 27th, 1978.'

'That's right,' said her husband. 'So it must have been the beginning of January that year.'

The January after Jessica took her O levels, thought Thanet. 'And was Mrs Manifest living with them then?'

'No. She was staying with an aunt, I believe,' said Mrs Wargreave. 'Then in the spring the aunt died so she came to live with the Covins. But it was only a month or two before she moved into a bedsit, in Maidstone. You know what these teenagers are like, they all want their independence.'

'And it was more convenient for her work, of course,' said Wargreave. 'She'd found herself a job on the *Kent Messenger* and she didn't have any means of transport. She was very excited about it, I remember.'

'So you see, we hardly knew her. She never visited her sister much. I don't think she got on too well with Bernard – at least, that was my impression.'

And Thanet's impression was that Mrs Wargreave wasn't too keen on Covin either.

'How did she seem when she came here?' said Thanet.

Mrs Wargreave's forehead creased into unaccustomed folds. Smiles rather than frowns were more her line, Thanet guessed. 'In what way?'

'Was she cheerful or depressed?'

'She looked a bit peaky when she first arrived, I thought.'

Not surprising, if his theory was correct, thought Thanet. But come to think of it, why wouldn't Jessica have had an abortion? Perhaps he was barking up the wrong tree.

'But she soon picked up,' said Mrs Wargreave. 'I assumed she'd been upset by her aunt's death. She was only a young girl, after all, it must have been pretty distressing for her.'

'Where were they living before they came here?' said Lineham.

'Bernard was assistant farm manager at a farm near Headcorn,' said Wargreave. 'He went there straight from college, as I recall.'

'What was the name of his employer?'

'Pink.'

Lineham made a note.

'So he must have been working there for what, ten or twelve years?' said Thanet.

And Jessica would have been living with the Covins for six of those years, thought Thanet. Perhaps the Pinks should go on his list of people to interview. They would have seen her grow from child to teenager, might even have had some inkling of the pregnancy, if there had been one.

'Is Mr Covin a good manager?'

Wargreave shrugged. 'I've got no complaints. He's conscientious, hardworking, honest . . . I think that's as much as one can hope for these days.'

'But Mrs Wargreave wasn't too keen on Covin, I thought,' said Lineham when they were back in the car. They would return to interview Covin later. 'Perhaps she can't stand the smell of him either. They were both non-smokers, did you notice? There wasn't an ashtray in sight.'

'Mike,' said Thanet, who had been trying to work out the best way to approach the subject, 'there's something I want to talk to you about. Pull in over there, will you?'

'There' was an empty layby and after a troubled glance at Thanet Lineham did as he was asked. He switched off the engine and silence descended.

Thanet wound down his window and took a deep breath of fresh air. There was a post-and-rail fence on their left and beyond that the ground fell away to a little valley where sheep were peacefully munching away at what was left of the grass after the long hot summer. At moments like this Thanet wondered why on earth he didn't suggest moving out into the country. Now that the children were grown and easy access to public transport was not so important, it would be perfectly feasible to make a move. Perhaps he ought to suggest it? Perhaps, with Bridget's wedding, he and Joan would move into a new phase of their life together. He became aware of Lineham's expectant silence and realised that he was merely prevaricating, reluctant to broach a difficult subject. 'I was just wondering if you'd got any closer to making a decision about your mother. I don't want to intrude on a private matter, but I am concerned about you. And apart from anything else, I feel it's beginning to interfere with your work.'

Lineham sighed. 'You're right, I know you are. It's just so difficult.'

'I appreciate that. But putting off the decision isn't going to make it any easier, is it, Mike? I'm sure that by now you've looked at the options from every possible angle.'

'And some,' said Lineham with a groan. 'The trouble is, the problem just isn't going to go away. In fact, if anything it's going to get steadily worse. I mean, let's face it, her health has been gradually deteriorating over the last few years. She keeps on asking why she can't come and live with us, and it gets harder and harder to put her off.'

'And you and Louise both agree it wouldn't work?' Thanet put the question as a matter of form. He already knew the answer.

'Louise and Mum could never live happily under the same roof! They've never got on very well, as you know. They just seem to rub each other up the wrong way.'

Because they were too alike, Thanet suspected.

'But if you do as your mother suggests, sell both houses and buy a larger one with a granny annexe – like the one we saw in Ogilvy and Tate's window . . .?'

But Lineham was shaking his head. 'I still can't see it working. We're both out all day and I think what Mum really needs is company. The truth is, she's lonely and she's bored, it's as simple as that, and living in a granny annexe wouldn't help. Apart from anything else, having been alone all day she'd want to share our evening meal and spend the evenings with us, I'm sure she would. I'm very fond of Mum, you know I am, but it would drive Louise and me round the bend, never having any privacy.'

'Then you'll just have to look for some kind of alternative solution.'

'Such as? She'd never go into a home, I'm sure of that, and in any case she doesn't need to. She's perfectly capable of looking after herself.'

'What about sheltered housing, with a warden on call?'

'We've discussed that and I don't think she'd be much better off than she is now. It's true that someone would be at hand in an emergency but I honestly don't think she'd be any happier.' Lineham sighed again, a deep, despairing sigh. 'I only hope I won't end up being a burden on my children.'

'Don't we all?' said Thanet. 'Unfortunately we all end up having very little control over that particular situation. The trouble is, the perfect answer doesn't exist, it's bound to be a matter of compromise all along the line. We just have to muddle along and try to find the best solution we can, and it isn't easy. In the end it's bound to come down to choosing the least unacceptable alternative.'

'Don't I know it!'

'Wait a minute!' said Thanet suddenly. 'I've just thought of something. I remember my mother mentioning some organisation to me that she seemed to think was very good. A friend of hers had gone into one of their homes and my mother had visited her there and was very impressed.'

'I told you, Mum would never even consider a home.'

'But these aren't conventional homes at all, not the sort where the residents sit around the walls staring at a television set all day. It's coming back to me now. For a start, they only take a small number of residents – ten at the most, I think. They're really more like family homes, for people who are still fairly independent but would benefit from some degree of being looked after and from having company available to them should they want it. So far as I can recall, they have their own rooms, with their own furniture, but there's a communal dining room and sitting room and the place is run by a resident housekeeper who provides lunch and tea each day. But they're free to go shopping, go to church, visit relations, in other words live as normal a life as possible. Mum said if ever she couldn't go on living alone she'd be happy to go into one herself.'

Lineham was listening avidly but now he pulled a face. 'It all sounds too good to be true, but horribly expensive.'

'Apparently not. Mum told me that it's a charity, and that residents pay rent according to what they can afford.'

'How old is your mother now?'

'Eighty.'

'Eighty! And she still lives alone quite happily?'

'Yes. She's amazing.'

When Thanet's father had retired his parents had, like so many, decided to leave the increasingly crowded southeast and move to the West Country. They had bought a bungalow in a village near Salisbury and had settled happily into community life. Unfortunately, only four years later Thanet's father had died suddenly and unexpectedly of a heart attack and Thanet had thought his mother might return to

Sturrenden to be near him and his family. Instead she had stayed on, declaring that life in Wiltshire suited her very well and she had no intention of leaving it unless she were forced to by ill health. So far, however, she had been lucky.

'She's coming to the wedding, of course?'

'Wild horses wouldn't etc.,' said Thanet, grinning. 'We offered to go and fetch her by car but no, she said she always enjoyed the train journey. You can see so much more than from a car, she says. And as the Salisbury trains go into Waterloo she doesn't even need to cross London from one mainline station to another to transfer to the Sturrenden line. So we're meeting her at the station tomorrow afternoon.'

'Well, I just hope I'm as fit and active at eighty,' said Lineham. 'Anyway, what's this amazing outfit called?'

Thanet frowned. 'That's what I'm trying to remember. Something with a monastic flavour to it, I think, though it's not connected to any religious organisation. I can easily find out, anyway. I'll give her a ring when we get back.'

'Thanks, sir. It does sound good. Though whether Mum will listen or not is another matter.'

'You can but try. I think the thing to do is to emphasise the fact that it not a normal type of residential home at all. Best of all would be to take her to look at one, let her meet some of the residents and talk to them.'

'Always assuming there is one in this area.'

'True. Perhaps it would be sensible to find out before mentioning it to her.'

'Yes. It would be infuriating to get her all interested only to find that there just aren't any around here.'

As a matter of principle, Thanet did not usually make private telephone calls from the office, but as the matter was affecting Lineham's work, on this occasion he felt justified in doing so. His mother was surprised to hear from him during working hours but at once gave him the information he needed and said how much she was looking forward to the wedding.

'Why don't you let us come and fetch you? It would only take a couple of hours.'

'Certainly not! You've got enough on your plates, I'm sure. Besides, I've already bought my ticket and I'm really looking forward to the journey.'

'See you tomorrow evening, then.'

'The Abbeyfield Society,' he said triumphantly to Lineham as he put the phone down. 'I told you it had a monastic flavour. And its headquarters are in St Albans, so you can get the number from directory enquiries.'

'Is it OK if I ring from here, sir? By the time I get home I imagine their office will be closed.'

'Go ahead. You must try and get this sorted out.' Thanet occupied himself with some paperwork while Lineham was making his call. 'Well?' he said, when the sergeant had finished.

'Some good news and some bad. The first bit of good news is that there is an Abbeyfield House in the area, in Maidstone –'

'Excellent.'

'The bad news is that there's usually a long waiting list for places, and that they don't often come up.'

'Oh.'

'You have to wait for someone to die, I suppose.'

Thanet pulled a face. 'Quite.'

'However, the other piece of good news is that they're hoping to open a new Abbeyfield House in Sturrenden in the spring of next year. Apparently they've found suitable premises and the sale is going through at the moment.'

'That's a bit of luck. So it might be possible to get your mother's name down on a waiting list.'

'Exactly! Meanwhile, I've got the number of the Maidstone house to arrange a visit if Mum would like one. I must say, they were very pleasant and helpful.'

'Good.' Thanet couldn't help feeling pleased with himself. There was a long way to go, of course, before the matter was settled. Meanwhile one of the main obstacles, he felt, was going to be the attitude of Lineham himself. 'Look, Mike,' he said, 'before you broach the subject with your mother I think you have to settle in your own mind what you feel about this yourself. If you really do think that having to share a roof with her is out of the question, you'll just have to bring yourself to be honest and say so. For one thing it's unfair to her to keep her dangling, and for another, well, to put it bluntly, as there seems to be no way of pleasing both your mother and Louise, however painful it might be you're going to have to disappoint one of them. Otherwise you're going to end up pleasing neither.' Thanet was thankful he himself had never been in that position.

'I know. I do realise that and I'm well aware that I've been burying my head in the sand because there just didn't seem to be any way out. But this really does sound a possible solution.'

'Let's keep our fingers crossed,' said Thanet.

Back at the farm they ran Covin to earth in the packing shed, which was filled with the rich, fruity aroma of ripe apples. The packers had gone home for the day and the grading machine and conveyor belt had been switched off. The shed was a high-ceilinged structure divided to provide office and communal rest room along one side. The internal walls were glazed above waist height and a light burned in the office where Covin was busy with paperwork. Predictably, he was smoking.

'Let's try and get him outside,' whispered Lineham as they knocked at the door.

Covin raised his head, saw them through the glass and beckoned them in.

The room smelled almost as bad as the man's sitting room but Thanet had no intention of giving Covin a psychological advantage by asking him a favour right at the beginning of the interview. Lineham would have to grin and bear it. The sergeant had left the door open and remained standing nearby. Wisps of smoke curled past him into the huge empty space beyond.

'Is this important, Inspector?' Covin hadn't got up. 'I don't want to be unhelpful, but I've been out most of the day and I've got a lot of paperwork to catch up on.' He gestured at the littered desk.

'Yes, I know. We came out to see you earlier.'

Covin frowned. 'Oh?' He removed a strand of tobacco

from the tip of his tongue and wiped his finger on his trouser leg. 'What's so important?'

'We think you've been less than frank with us, Mr Covin.'

He stubbed the cigarette out in an overflowing ashtray and stood up, leaning against his desk. He folded his arms defensively. 'What are you talking about?'

An acrid smell of burning filter drifted up between them. Thanet suppressed the urge to point out that he hadn't put his cigarette out properly. The stink really was disgusting. Unobtrusively he edged away a little. 'Your sister-in-law, sir.'

There was a flicker of some emotion in Covin's eyes which, frustratingly, Thanet couldn't read. What had it been? Relief? Anger? Fear? Or perhaps it had merely been irritation?

'When we asked you why she hadn't stayed on at school to take her A levels as everyone seemed to expect, you told us she was simply fed up with school and wanted to start work, earn some money of her own.'

'So?' Covin was wary now.

'That summer, the summer she was sixteen, we understand she went to stay with an aunt in Bristol.'

'That's right. Yes.'

'Why was that?'

Covin shrugged. 'It was twenty years ago! How should I know?'

'You're saying you can't remember?'

'I imagine she felt like a change.'

'But she didn't come back afterwards, did she?'

'So? She liked it there. They got on well together.'

'I want you to think very carefully before you answer my next question, Mr Covin. I strongly advise you to tell the truth this time. Otherwise . . . Well, you do understand that when we discover someone has been lying to us we tend to look rather more carefully at that person the second time around. And if he lies again . . .'

Covin said nothing.

'So what I want to ask you is, was there another reason why Jessica did not go back to school that autumn? The reason why she didn't return to Sturrenden until the following spring?'

Covin's lips tightened.

'Make no mistake about this. We are determined to find the answer, and we can, of course, do so ourselves, with a little research. But it would save time if you were prepared to be frank with us.'

Covin still remained silent but now Thanet read uncertainty in his eyes.

'Very well. If you're not prepared to volunteer the information, perhaps you would just confirm or deny what I suggest to you. But do bear in mind what I said. The truth will emerge, sooner or later.' Thanet paused. Covin's arms were still folded and Thanet saw the tips of the man's fingers whiten as he tightened his grip in anticipation of what was coming.

Thanet's conviction that he was right was growing by the second. 'We believe that Jessica left school unexpectedly because she was pregnant, and that she went to stay with her aunt in order to have the baby out of the area.'

Covin abruptly left the desk and blundered across the room to the window. There he remained with his back to them, staring out into the fading light.

Thanet and Lineham exchanged victorious glances.

'Mr Covin?' said Thanet.

Covin apparently came to a decision. He squared his shoulders and turned. 'Yes,' he said quietly, with a sigh. 'You're right, of course.' He went back to his desk, shook a cigarette out of the pack and lit it, inhaling as greedily as if he been deprived of nicotine all day.

'And the baby was adopted.'

A long plume of smoke. 'Yes.'

'What sex was it?'

Drag, exhale. 'A boy.'

'And which adoption agency was used?'

Another drag. 'I've no idea. Madge arranged it all. With Jessica, of course.'

'Why were you so reluctant to tell us?'

A shrug. 'I promised.'

'Who? Jessica?'

'No. My wife. Well, it came down to Jessica in the end, I

136

suppose. I expect she went on at Madge to get me to promise.'

'But they're both dead now,' said Lineham. 'What does it matter?'

Covin cast him a scornful glance. 'A promise is a promise. Or it is in my book. Anyway, the kid's not dead, is he?'

Point taken, thought Thanet. 'Who was the father?'

'She wouldn't tell us.'

'As a matter of interest, why didn't she have an abortion?'

'Don't ask me. Hearts to heart with Jessica weren't exactly my line, as you might have gathered last time. I just didn't want to know.'

And that, it seemed, was as much as he could tell them. But Thanet was satisfied. It was enough to move them on one step further and that was all that mattered. He was as glad as Lineham to get back into the fresh air. They lingered beside the car, breathing deeply.

'Hope that's the last time we have to interview him,' said the sergeant, 'or I'll be claiming danger money. Anyway, it looks as though you were right.'

'Partly, anyway,' said Thanet. 'We still don't know if Kevin is the son.'

'So what next?'

'We go and see his adoptive mother again for a start. See what she can tell us.'

TWELVE

'What if Kevin's there?' Once again Lineham had to shout to make himself heard over the roar of traffic thundering past as they waited for Mrs Barcombe to answer their knock. 'He should be home from work by now.'

It was six o'clock.

'We'll have to play it by ear.'

Mingled scents of furniture polish and frying onions wafted out to compete with the reek of exhaust fumes as the door opened. One of the two men was home anyway, Thanet noted: there was only a single pair of men's slippers just inside the door.

Mrs Barcombe wasn't too pleased to see them. 'Is it important? I'm just cooking the tea.' She was still wearing the crossover apron.

'We won't keep you long.'

'Who is it, Mary?' A shaft of brighter light shone along the passageway as a door at the far end opened and the silhouette of a man appeared. The smell of frying onions intensified.

She half turned. 'It's the police again.'

'What do they want?'

'How should I know?' Then with a muffled exclamation she darted along the passage and brushed past him into the kitchen.

The man advanced. 'You'd better come in,' he said with an apologetic smile. He was in his fifties, with thinning brown hair carefully brushed to conceal incipient baldness. The subservient forward tilt of his head was probably habitual, the result of years of deference to customers. He was still dressed for work in striped shirt, discreet tie and the trousers of a suit, held up by braces. Bentall's was a good-quality shop and would expect its salesmen to uphold certain standards. They would no doubt have frowned upon the woolly carpet slippers, which looked distinctly incongruous.

Although it was still light outside the sitting room was gloomy and Barcombe put the overhead light on. In the sickly glow of a low-wattage bulb the antiseptic room looked more unwelcoming than ever. Introductions over, the three men sat down.

'Just got there in time,' said Mrs Barcombe, bustling back into the room. 'You could've kept an eye on the onions, Al. Couldn't you smell they were starting to catch?' She plumped down beside him on the settee.

'Sorry, dear.'

Thanet decided to go straight to the point. They had wasted enough time and Kevin could arrive home at any minute. He wanted to talk to the boy again, but not until he'd clarified the issue with the Barcombes.

'When we were here yesterday, Mrs Barcombe, you told us that Kevin was adopted.'

Immediately deep frown lines appeared between her brows and she exchanged an uneasy glance with her husband. 'That's right. What's it got to do with you?'

'Mary!' said her husband nervously. 'Just listen to what the Inspector's got to say.'

'How old was he when he came to you?'

'Six weeks. But I still don't see –'

'Bear with me, will you? When was this, exactly?'

She didn't hesitate. 'February 10th, 1978.' But despite her swift, almost automatic response, she was becoming agitated. Her bony fingers moved restlessly, rolling and unrolling a corner of her apron.

Thanet experienced a spurt of triumph and he caught Lineham's eye. *You see?*

'So he would have been born towards the end of December 1977.'

'Yes. Look, I think we've a right to know what all this is about.'

'I'm sorry, I'm not at liberty to tell you at the moment. Were you living in Sturrenden at the time?'

'We were living here, in this house. We've always lived here.'

'Which adoption agency did you use?'

She shot to her feet. 'That's it. That's enough. You have no right to come here poking and prying like this.'

'Mary.' Barcombe was on his feet too, a restraining hand on her arm.

She shook him off. 'Don't "Mary" me! I'll say what I like! Kevin's done nothing wrong!'

Thanet rose too. 'Look, Mrs Barcombe, I'm sorry. I can understand your getting upset –'

'Oh, you can, can you? I don't suppose you've ever had to put up with people coming into your home and asking questions about your private life, have you?'

The answer to that, of course, was that no, he hadn't. None of his family had ever been in trouble with the law, thank God, unlike those of other policemen he knew. 'We don't enjoy upsetting people, you know.'

'But you don't let that stop you, do you!'

And again, she was right. In his job you had to learn to put personal feeling aside. He had one last question to ask before giving up. 'Mrs Barcombe, has Kevin ever tried to trace his natural mother?'

Bullseye. He could tell by the agonised glance at her husband, by her sudden stillness.

'No!' she said wildly. 'I told you this morning. He's never given us a moment's worry.'

Thanet remembered the shadow behind her eyes when she had said this and now he understood it. Adoptive parents, especially those who dearly love their adopted child, as she did, must always dread the moment when the questions about the natural parents start to proliferate, must always be afraid that sooner or later the tug of blood will win over the years of unselfish devotion.

In the ensuing silence the sound of a key in the front-door lock could clearly be heard.

'There's Kev,' she said, starting towards the door.

140

'We'll need to speak to him,' said Thanet.

She ignored him and went out, shutting the door firmly behind her. There was a murmur of voices.

Thanet nodded and Lineham went to open the door. 'We'd like a word, Kevin,' he said.

The boy came in, stripping off the anorak he was wearing. His mother put out her hand and he gave it to her. 'What's up?' he said, jauntily. But his eyes belied his tone.

'We'd like to speak to Kevin alone,' said Thanet.

'No!' said his mother.

'Yes,' said Thanet.

'We have every right to stay. We're his parents. Tell them, Al.'

Barcombe, who had remained silent through most of the interview and was clearly used to letting his wife rule the roost, looked uncomfortable. 'I don't think we can do that, Mary.'

'Your husband's right, Mrs Barcombe. Kevin is no longer a minor. If you prefer, we could take him away and interview him at the Station.'

'No!' she cried. Her eyes moved in desperation from one to another, seeking a way out of the dilemma and failing to find it. Then the muscles of her face sagged and her shoulders slumped as she acknowledged defeat. She turned away, hugging Kevin's anorak to her chest for comfort. 'I'll go and get your tea ready, Kev.'

'That's right, dear,' said Barcombe, putting an arm across her shoulders. 'I don't suppose they'll be long,' he murmured as they went out.

Now all that agonised emotion had been removed the room seemed very quiet. In unspoken agreement they all sat down and Kevin at once took out a tobacco pouch, extracted a packet of cigarette papers and a few strands of tobacco and proceeded to roll a cigarette. Lineham cast a glance at Thanet in which triumph at being right was mixed with despair at the prospect of being trapped in yet another smoke-filled room.

Thanet was equally certain. In his opinion, this clinched it. So few people rolled their own cigarettes these days that he simply couldn't believe that it was a second person involved in the case who had stubbed out those butts behind the hedge opposite the Manifests' house. No, Kevin had been the watcher, he was now sure of that. But how to get him to admit it?

'Well now, Kevin,' he said. 'We've been doing a bit of checking up.'

'I'd've thought you had better things to do than waste your time on me.'

'It always pays to be thorough, doesn't it, sergeant?'

'Certainly does, sir.'

Lineham deserved full marks for not flinching as Kevin blew a long stream of smoke in his direction, Thanet thought. 'And in this case we've come up with one or two question marks. Now, you claim that you left home on Tuesday night around 8.15 and went straight to Sally's. But your mother says you left at 7.45 –'

'No she doesn't. She was mistaken. You ask her.'

So Kevin had persuaded his mother to change her story. 'And the doorman at Sally's said you arrived at 8.30.'

'So? What's a few minutes here or there?'

'A few minutes here or there, as you put it, may be very important indeed. You know the Green Man in Charthurst?'

The sudden change of subject caught Kevin unawares. He blinked and leaned forward to stub out his cigarette. 'I know where it is, yeah.'

'Been there lately?'

'How should I remember?'

'I'm not asking you to go back very far, Kevin. Only to Tuesday night.'

Kevin clamped his lips together, clearly in a dilemma. He didn't want to incriminate himself further by lying, nor did he want to admit to anything he didn't have to.

'You see, the landlord of the Green Man has been getting pretty fed up lately because people who aren't customers keep using his car park.'

Kevin ran his tongue over his upper lip.

'So he's been keeping a record of the registration numbers of offenders. Er . . . You did say you borrowed your father's car on Tuesday night, Kevin?'

Kevin's eyes were taking on the hunted expression of a rabbit hypnotised by a stoat.

'Because one of the cars parked at the Green Man in Charthurst around eight p.m. last Tuesday night was a red Nissan.' Thanet glanced at Lineham who read out the registration number. 'That is the number of your father's car, isn't it?'

The boy licked his lips again, his freckles now in stark contrast to the pallor of his skin.

'It is, isn't it? Thanet persisted.

'I . . .' Kevin croaked.

'Yes?'

'I went for a walk.'

'I see,' said Thanet, nodding. 'A walk.'

'I felt like one. A breath of air. After being cooped up all day.'

'Kevin.' Thanet was gentle, reproachful. 'Are you really expecting us to believe that you drove all the way to Charthurst to go for a walk in the dark?'

'It's quiet there,' said Kevin with the bravado born of desperation.

'There's plenty of quiet countryside much closer than that.'

A shrug. *That's my story and I'm sticking to it.*

'You knew Mrs Manifest, didn't you?'

'Not know her, exactly. She used to have her hair done at Snippers, so I've seen her in the salon.'

'You've spoken to her?'

'I've washed her hair once or twice. Look, I want to go to the toilet.'

Excellent. Kevin's bladder was playing up, a sure sign of nervousness – if Thanet needed another. Signs there already were, aplenty. Besides, Kevin's absence would give him the opportunity he had been hoping for. 'OK,' he said, with a nod at Lineham.

The two left the room and Thanet quickly took out a polythene bag and pocketed the cigarette butt.

Lineham didn't miss a trick, he noticed when they returned. The sergeant's eyes went straight to the ashtray and then met Thanet's in comprehension. Thanet was

143

amused to find that he felt as though he had received a pat on the back.

'So,' he said when they were all settled again. 'You washed Mrs Manifest's hair occasionally. Did you like her?'

An emotion which Thanet couldn't define flashed briefly in Kevin's eyes before he shrugged and said, 'She was OK.'

'Your mother tells me you're adopted, Kevin.'

A little pulse began to beat near the corner of the boy's right eye.

'Kevin?'

'So what?'

'So I wondered if you'd ever thought of trying to trace your natural mother.'

'It's none of your bloody business.'

'That may well not be true.'

Kevin gave him an intense stare. 'What are you getting at?'

'If you have tried to trace her, we'd be very interested to hear what you found out.'

'I still don't see what it's got to do with you.'

Thanet was tempted to voice his suspicions straight out, but something, some unspoken restraint seemed to be operating in his brain. 'We just want to be certain that this has nothing to do with Mrs Manifest's death, that's all.'

Kevin appeared genuinely bewildered. 'I don't know what you're talking about, I really don't. How the hell could there be any connection between my natural mum and Mrs Manifest?'

The question seemed to hover in the air between them, inviting the obvious answer.

'No!' said Kevin suddenly. 'You can't be thinking . . . No!'

'What?'

'That Mrs Manifest was . . .' He stared at Thanet and suddenly, disconcertingly, began to laugh, a few sniggers at first and then, in a release of tension, a mounting crescendo of near-hysterical laughter. Tears squeezed their way between his eyelids and began to run down his cheeks and he clutched his stomach as if in pain.

Thanet and Lineham looked blankly at each other. Did this mean the collapse of their theory?

'Kev?' The door burst open and the Barcombes came in, their faces confused. 'What's the matter? What's going on?'

Kevin shook his head, still gasping and snorting with mirth.

His mother took a handkerchief from her apron pocket and thrust it into his hand. 'Here. Wipe your face.'

He did as he was told. He was gradually calming down but little hiccups of laughter kept on escaping like gas from an underground reservoir.

His parents stood watching him, one on either side.

Anyone who had seen their concerned faces would never again doubt the love which adoptive parents can feel for their child, thought Thanet.

'Mum,' he said at last, twisting his head to look up at her. 'I think you'd better hear this. The Inspector wants to know about my natural mother.'

Their eyes all turned to Thanet, Kevin's mocking, his parents' puzzled, resentful, anxious.

'But why?' said Mrs Barcombe.

'He seems to have some fancy idea that she was Jessica Dander – Jessica Manifest!' Kevin dabbed at his eyes as he succumbed to another bout of laughter.

His parents both looked astounded.

'The *KM* reporter?' said his mother.

'The one who was found dead a couple of days ago?' said his father.

'Is that true?' said Mrs Barcombe to Thanet. 'Was she his mother?'

Thanet shrugged. *Don't ask me.* Her reaction was interesting, he thought. The fact that the police were investigating Jessica's death and that they seemed to think Kevin had some connection with it was not for her the most important issue. Later, no doubt, it would be.

She looked at Kevin. Clearly there was something she was longing to know but dared not ask.

All at once Thanet understood what was going on here. Mrs Barcombe either knew or suspected that Kevin had been trying to trace his natural mother but wasn't sure if he had succeeded. It was this uncertainty that was tormenting her.

'Oh Mum,' he said. 'Get real.'

There was fear in her eyes now and her lips moved stiffly as she said, 'How can you be sure?'

He stood up suddenly, as if propelled from his chair by an invisible force. 'Because I found out who she was, didn't I.' He turned to face them all, as if to confront his own pain. 'There, now you know. I went through the whole bloody performance, didn't I, social workers, interviews, questions, questions, questions. It took for ever, months and months and then, in the end, when I finally tracked her down, what happened? She just didn't want to know.'

Relief blossomed briefly in Mrs Barcombe's face before, for Kevin's sake, she tried to hide it. 'She didn't?'

He turned away to conceal his expression. 'Nah.'

Swiftly she crossed the room and put her arm around his shoulders. They twitched, but he didn't shake her off. 'Oh Kev,' she said. 'I am sorry.'

'Yeah, well . . .' he mumbled.

'We'll need her name and address,' said Thanet. 'We'll be very discreet,' he added.

Kevin was still clutching the handkerchief his mother had given him and now he blew his nose and shrugged. 'Why not? It's no skin off my nose.' He glanced at her. No doubt he didn't want her to hear the details. 'I'll write it down for you.'

On the way back to the car Thanet stopped suddenly and banged his fist against the wall. 'What a fool! What an idiot!' Kevin's laughter still sounded in his ears.

'What do you mean?'

'Building such an elaborate structure of theory without a shred of evidence to base it on.'

'That's not true.'

'Nothing worth speaking of, anyway.'

'I don't see it that way at all. All right, so we were wrong about Jessica being his mother, but we were right about everything else. Kevin's admitted he was in Charthurst that night and we're now virtually certain that he was watching her. What's more –'

'He'll never admit it.'

'What's more, we'll now be able to prove it. It's a bit of luck you managed to get hold of that cigarette end.'

'We *hope* we'll be able to prove it.'

'Oh come on, sir. Give over. You're just feeling negative at the moment. OK, you were partly wrong. So what?'

So my pride is dented, thought Thanet. And not for the first time. Serves me right. When am I going to learn?

It was after seven o'clock and they decided to call it a day. As he drove home through a spectacular sunset Thanet made a conscious effort to slough off his dejection and forget about the case for a while. He had been looking forward to this evening. Tomorrow the house would be bursting at the seams but tonight he and Joan and Bridget would be able to spend some time together, just the three of them.

This turned out to be a vain hope. What else should he have expected? Thanet asked himself as Bridget went to answer the phone for the umpteenth time. The talk was all of arrangements, arrangements, arrangements and like many a father before him he thought he would heave a sigh of relief when the whole thing was over. Still, it was a joy to see Bridget so happy.

He watched fondly as she returned to sit on the floor beside his chair. 'Just think,' he said, 'in two days' time you'll be an old married woman.' *And you won't be my daughter any more. First and foremost you'll be Alexander's wife.*

As if she had divined his thoughts she looked up and smiled. 'Don't worry, dad. We'll only be an hour away.'

An hour too much, as far as he was concerned. 'I'm looking forward to all those free lunches.'

'Breakfasts, lunches, dinners, the lot. You'll have to come up for weekends, let us educate you about London. You don't know what you've been missing all these years.'

'A new dimension to our lives,' said Joan, smiling.

'Just what I was thinking earlier,' said Thanet. But not in quite that way. Try as he would, he could see Bridget's marriage only as loss, not gain.

THIRTEEN

'What time's your fitting?' said Joan as she switched off the radio. They had been listening anxiously to the weather forecast for the weekend. Fortunately it sounded good.

'Ten o'clock,' said Bridget.

Joan had taken the day off and they were discussing their plans for the day over breakfast.

'It shouldn't take long, though,' Bridget added. 'It was only a very minor adjustment.'

'Good. Well, I suggest that after that we go on into the town and pick up the suits for your father and Ben from Moss Bros.'

'Wouldn't it be better to bring my dress home first, to hang it up straight away? And I'm not particularly keen on the idea of leaving it in the car while we go shopping. What if the car got stolen!'

'No doubt you'd expect me to mobilise the entire police force of the area to get it back in time!' said Thanet with a grin.

'Naturally!' said Joan. Then, to Bridget, 'But you're right. Better to hang it up as soon as possible. Back here first then, before going into town.'

'What about the service sheets?'

'Done. I collected them in the lunch hour on Wednesday.'

'That's a relief.' Bridget grinned. 'The last wedding I went to they didn't arrive until the guests were actually seated in the church.'

'Poor organisation,' said Thanet. 'No chance of that, with your mother in charge.'

'Thank goodness! What time is Gran arriving?'

'Twelve-forty-five,' said Joan. Her own mother lived only a few miles away.

'Who's meeting her?' said Thanet.

'We both are, of course!' Bridget was mildly indignant.

'Then we'll come back here for lunch and try to persuade her to have a rest before everyone else arrives.'

'Good luck,' said Thanet, finishing his coffee and rising. 'She won't want to miss a thing.'

He put his coat on and went back into the kitchen to kiss them both goodbye. 'Oh, by the way, Helen says she's finished decorating the cake, if you want to go round and take a look.'

'Oh good!' said Bridget, eyes lighting up. 'She's delivering it to the Swan tomorrow morning, but I can't wait till then. I'm dying to see it.'

'We could pop in on the way back from picking up your grandmother at the station,' said Joan. 'I'm sure she'd love to see it too. I'll give Helen a ring, check she'll be in.' She followed Thanet into the hall. 'Bye, darling. You will be able to make the dinner this evening, won't you?'

'I'll be there,' he said. 'Stop worrying!'

'And don't forget your haircut,' she called after him.

'I won't.' When on earth was he going to fit it in? he wondered. Somehow, he must. His heart sank as he remembered that Draco was due back later on this afternoon and given the opportunity would no doubt insist on being brought up to date with every last detail. Thanet resolved to avoid the office after four p.m. if at all possible.

Lineham was back on form this morning, already immersed in a report. He looked up as Thanet came in. 'I did it, sir!'

'Did what?'

'Spoke to her. My mother. Put it to her straight, like you suggested, that it just wouldn't work, her coming to live with us.'

'How did she take it?'

Lineham grimaced. 'Better than I expected, really. But she wasn't too pleased, obviously. It's not exactly an easy thing to put tactfully.'

'Did you talk to her about the Abbeyfield organisation?'

'Yes. At first she just didn't want to know, but I kept on telling her they weren't like ordinary homes and pointing out all the advantages and in the end she did at least agree to go and look at the one in Maidstone. I rang the housekeeper there and we're going over on Sunday. She sounded really nice. They have a waiting list, so it would mean the Sturrenden one in any case, and it'll be getting on for nine months, apparently, before they get that one off the ground, so there'll be plenty of time for Mum to get used to the idea. They suggest not selling her house until she's given them at least a month's trial, and I think that's reassured her – you know, that she isn't going to be shoved off into a home against her will, that it really will be ultimately her decision.'

'What did Louise think about it?'

'She's over the moon that I'm trying to get things sorted out at last. She thinks the Abbeyfield idea sound great. Let's hope it's all it's cracked up to be.'

'I hope so too!' said Thanet. 'Or I really will be in the doghouse.' But he trusted his mother's judgement and was confident that it would be. He nodded at the report Lineham was reading. 'Anything interesting?'

'Bentley's report on the Ogilvys,' said Lineham. 'Local opinion is that Mrs O. is an angel in disguise, pillar of the community, nothing too much trouble etc. etc. He's not so popular, though there was no specific complaint against him. People seem to agree that they had a bit of a sticky time during the recession – there were little signs like cutting back on help in the house and garden, changing her car to a cheaper model – but that things are picking up again now. She's gone back to a Polo from a Mini for instance.'

'Nothing of any use, then.'

''Fraid not.'

The telephone rang. Lineham answered; listened. 'Put her on. Hullo? Yes, I remember. Yes. Oh, have you?' He listened intently. 'Yes, I see. Thank you for letting us know. Yes, that's very helpful.' He put the phone down. 'You remember that neighbour who said she'd seen a young man hanging about and thought he looked familiar but couldn't place why?'

'Don't tell me! She has her hair cut at Snippers.'

'Exactly!'

'Doesn't really help, though, does it, Mike? I suppose it might be worth following up. Yes, better send someone out to get more details – exactly where and when it was that she noticed him around.'

Lineham made a quick note. 'Kevin keeps on cropping up, doesn't he?'

'Yes. But there's still no scientific evidence to connect him with Jessica yet.'

'There's the cigarette butt.'

'We hope.'

'So what do you reckon, sir? Which of them would you put your money on? Kevin, Desmond or Ogilvy?'

Thanet shook his head. 'Your guess is as good as mine. They all had the opportunity. On the face of it both her husband and Ogilvy had good reason to get involved in an argument with her but the very fact that Kevin was there at all is suspicious.'

'Downright creepy, if you ask me. Any man who makes a habit of lurking behind hedges to spy on a woman isn't normal.'

'I agree. There must be some kind of morbid fascination there. In which case . . . It's just occurred to me. If that is so, in view of the fact that Jessica was a public figure, he might well have made a habit of collecting stuff about her.'

'Kept a sort of scrapbook, you mean. Yes!' Lineham's face was alight with interest. 'Articles she wrote, photographs and so on. You're right.'

'The question is, which do we do first – interview him again, now that we have an independent witness to testify that she's seen him near Jessica's house on more than one occasion, or go and search his room, see if he has got anything like that stashed away?'

'His mother'd never let us search his room without a warrant.'

'No. And it would mean a Section 8.'

Both men were silent, thinking. The more usual Section 15 search warrant was easier to obtain than the Section 8

151

warrant, which was granted only in the case of serious crimes such as murder and if the application met certain conditions. If they applied for one, it would not be sufficient for Lineham to go before the magistrates, Thanet himself would have to do so. He must therefore be very sure of his ground.

'I think we could meet all the conditions,' he said. 'What I'm not sure about is whether we'd be justified in applying for a warrant at this juncture.'

'The trouble is, if we interview him again and he continues to deny any involvement, we'd have to let him go and he might well start feeling very nervous and decide to get rid of any incriminating material, if he has any.'

'*If* he has any. That's the trouble. We can't be sure. It's all conjecture.'

'Suspicion is all that's necessary, surely,' objected Lineham. 'After all, this is a murder case.' He began to tick the points off on his fingers. 'One: we have Jessica's belief that she was being watched, backed up by two police reports. Two: we now have an independent witness who claims to have seen Kevin lurking in the vicinity of Jessica's house. Three: we have scientific evidence to prove he had been spying on her –'

'Unconfirmed as yet. It'll be days before forensic get back to us on the saliva test.'

'Exactly! We can't afford to wait that long. Four: we have another independent witness, the pub landlord, who will swear that the Nissan has been parked at his pub on more than one occasion and that it was there on the night Jessica died. Five: Kevin actually admits that he was there, on the spot, during the period the murder was committed and so far he's only come up with the thinnest of excuses for his presence. Six: we have good reason to suspect that we might find further evidence to link him with Jessica if we search his room and that if we delay that evidence could be removed or destroyed. No, sir, there's no doubt in my mind that we'd be justified in applying for a warrant and I really don't think any magistrate is going to disagree.'

'It's true that if we interview him again before we search, he might have the opportunity to get rid of the evidence if there is any . . .' Thanet made up his mind. 'You're right,

Mike. We'll go for it.' He stood up. 'Ring the Magistrates' Clerk and tell him we'll be over at 10.30. But before we do anything else today I absolutely must go and get my hair cut.' He ran his hand over the back of his neck. 'I don't like taking time off during working hours but I really can't turn up at the wedding looking like an old English sheepdog.'

'I'll do that right away.' Lineham glanced at his overflowing in-tray. Since Tuesday night routine work had been pushed aside. 'Then I'll do a bit of catching up while you're gone.'

'Right.' Thanet hurried out and set off for the barber's at a brisk pace, hoping that there wouldn't be too much of a queue. As he turned into the High Street he ran into Mallard, almost knocking him over.

'Whoa!' said the little doctor. 'Ease up.'

'Sorry! I'm in a bit of a rush.'

'I can see that!'

'I've sneaked out to get my hair cut for tomorrow. If I don't make it I'll be in real trouble at home.'

'I've been wanting a word,' said Mallard. 'And we never seem to get a chance to talk nowadays. I'll walk with you.'

They fell into step.

Mallard gave him an assessing look. 'If you could take your mind off work for two minutes . . . I was just wondering if you felt happier now, about Alexander.'

Unconsciously, Thanet's pace slowed. Apart from Joan, the Mallards were the only people to whom he had ever confessed his reservations about Alexander. He remembered an evening not long after the two young people had first started going out together when Mallard had taken him to task about this, accusing him of being prejudiced against every boyfriend that Bridget brought home simply because he didn't want to lose her. And there had been a measure of truth in that – still was, for that matter, he thought uncomfortably, remembering his thoughts last night. Mallard had also accused him of wanting someone perfect for Bridget and had pointed out that no one ever was, that such expectations were completely unrealistic. Thanet had been left to face the uncomfortable fact that his reservations arose chiefly from his own feelings of inadequacy in the face of Alexander's superior education, earning power and upper-middle-class background.

Now he felt ill at ease as he said, 'Yes, I suppose so.'

'But you're still not sure.'

'I just feel that if he could hurt her once . . . Last time she had no warning, you know. He simply dropped her, out of the blue, just like that.' Thanet snapped his fingers. 'You know how upset she was. It took her ages even to begin to get over it. In fact, she never really did.'

'All the more reason, surely, to be thankful that he changed his mind and came back?'

Thanet shrugged. 'Perhaps. But you must see that it makes me a bit wary of him.'

'On the principle that if he did it once he can do it again.'

'Precisely.'

'But as I recall, Luke, the reason he gave for breaking it off on that occasion was that he felt he wasn't ready for the commitment. Leaving Bridget's feelings aside for the moment, wouldn't you regard that as a pretty responsible decision to take? Surely you'd prefer him to be sure of his feelings before marrying her, rather than rush into marriage without proper thought, like so many youngsters nowadays – as the soaring divorce rate demonstrates only too clearly?'

How can I leave Bridget's feelings aside? 'That's what Joan says.'

'Sensible woman, your wife!'

Some oranges had fallen off the display in front of a greengrocer's shop and were rolling across the pavement. They stooped to pick them up.

'Thanks,' said the shop assistant as they handed them back. 'Cheers.'

Thanet had been thinking over what Mallard had said. 'It wasn't so much the fact that he broke it off,' he said as they moved on, 'as the way he did it. It was so abrupt, such a shock for her. There'd been no warning at all.'

'According to her.'

Thanet stopped. 'What are you saying?'

'Just that there may well have been signs, but that she may

not have wanted to read them. You know perfectly well that we often see only what we want to see and that love, as they say, is blind. A cliché, maybe, but none the less true.'

'I never thought of it like that,' said Thanet. They resumed their walk, which had slowed down to a snail's pace as they neared their destination. 'It's true that she was head over heels. Still is, for that matter, as I said.'

'Which is just as it should be. And in my opinion, so is he. If you ask me, Bridget is a very lucky girl.'

'You think so?'

'Oh come on, Luke! It's not very often one comes across a young man who has all of Alexander's qualities. He's hardworking, honest, sincere, likeable, very able, he's earning a good living and, to cap it all, has a sense of humour. Truthfully, now, what more could you ask?'

Thanet gave a sheepish grin. 'Not much, I suppose.'

They came to a halt beneath the barber's striped pole. Peering in, Thanet was relieved to see that there were only two people waiting.

'I tell you this,' said the little doctor. 'I've never had any children, as you know, more's the pity, but if I had had a daughter I would have been very happy to see her married to Alexander.'

'You would?'

'I swear it! And it's not often I go out on a limb like this, as you know.'

That was true. Thanet was touched by the fact that Mallard had gone out of his way to try and reassure him – and had succeeded in doing so. Somehow he felt easier in his mind. He trusted Mallard's judgement; he always had. 'Thanks, Doc, I appreciate this.'

Expressions of gratitude had always embarrassed Mallard. 'See you at the church,' he said gruffly, and with a wave of his hand, was gone.

By the time Thanet got back to the office it was twenty past ten. They hurried across to the Magistrates' Court and had a brief discussion with Graham Ticeman, the Magistrates' Clerk, who satisfied himself that all the conditions pertaining to a Section 8 warrant applied. The magistrates had been alerted to the fact that an application was to be made and had agreed to hear it at the end of the current case. Meanwhile, Thanet and Lineham slipped into the courtroom and sat at the back as usual. Thanet was pleased to see that the chairman today was Felicity Merridew, a magistrate of long standing with a reputation for sound judgement and impartiality. She was a tiny woman in her sixties with neatly cropped silver hair and a remarkable air of authority for one so small of stature. They didn't have long to wait as the case was just finishing and in a matter of minutes they were taken into the retiring room to present their application.

The other two magistrates were male and towered over their chairman as they came in. She greeted Thanet and Lineham with a smile and said, 'Right, Inspector Thanet. Let's proceed.'

Thanet took the oath and then laid forth his arguments for the application. All three magistrates listened carefully. When he had finished Mrs Merridew glanced at the Clerk. 'Are you happy about this, Mr Ticeman? You've satisfied yourself that the conditions have all been met?'

'Yes, ma'am.'

'Is there any advice you wish to give?'

He shook his head.

She consulted her fellow magistrates with raised eyebrows. They too shook their heads. 'Very well, Inspector. Your application is granted.'

'Great!' said Lineham, outside.

'All right, Mike. No need to say "I told you so."' But Thanet, too, was pleased that it had gone so smoothly.

A quarter of an hour later they were knocking yet again at the Barcombes' now familiar front door. No reply. They knocked again; waited. Still no answer.

He and Lineham exchanged glances of dismay. They were all geared up to search, eager to find out if their guess was going to pay off. Thanet had no intention of forcing an entry. Perhaps she had gone shopping.

He took a step backwards to peer up at the façade of the house and felt the slipstream tug at him as a lorry passed close behind.

Lineham grabbed his arm. 'Careful, sir.'

'There's something different about the house. It's the curtains. The net curtains have been taken down. Knowing her, she probably washes them once a week.' Thanet stepped close to the window and shielded his eyes with his hand as he peered inside, but there was nothing of interest to see. The front room looked as sterile and uninviting as ever. 'Try again, Mike. Knock harder.'

Lineham did as he was asked and they both strained their ears to catch any sound of movement from within. Nothing. They were about to turn away when Lineham put his hand on Thanet's arm. 'Just a sec.'

Sure enough, a moment later the door opened. Mrs Barcombe, surprisingly, didn't look as unwelcoming as Thanet had expected. Perhaps she felt grateful to them for precipitating Kevin's outburst last night. It must be a great relief to her to know at last that there was no danger of losing him to the woman who had given him away at birth. Her attitude would change, no doubt, when she heard why they had come.

'Have you been waiting long? I was in the garden, hanging out my nets.' As usual she was wearing a crossover apron, a different one this time. With her standards of hygiene Thanet wouldn't be surprised if she had a different one for each day of the week. Her hands, he noticed, looked red and raw. Not surprising, considering the punishing routine to which she no doubt subjected them.

'We've only been here a few minutes,' he said. 'May we come in?'

'I suppose.'

Into the barren sitting room again, looking curiously denuded without its curtains.

'Actually, it's Kevin's room we've come to take a look at,' he said.

Her expression became hostile in a flash. Her only chick had been threatened. She shook her head vehemently. 'You've got no right to do that. You'd better go.' She turned to open the door, gestured them out.

'We have a search warrant, Mrs Barcombe,' said Thanet.

He sympathised with her need to protect the child she loved, but there was nothing he could do about that. In a murder case it was inevitable that innocent people got hurt along the way and sadly it was often he who had to inflict the pain. Over the years he had had to resign himself to the fact that this was unavoidable but unlike some policemen he had never been able to anaesthetise himself against it.

She stared at him. It was clear that she had been completely unprepared for this and had no idea what to do. 'But why?' she said at last.

'Because we need to look at Kevin's room and we knew that you probably wouldn't allow us to do so without one.'

She shook her head. 'I didn't mean that. Last night, I was more interested in what Kev was telling me than why you were here. I tried to get him to explain, after, but he wouldn't. Just said it was all a mistake. But here you are again and now you want to search his room. I just don't understand what Kev has to do with that Jessica Dander.'

'I'm sorry,' said Thanet. And he meant it. If they were right, she had more shocks coming to her. 'You'll have to ask Kevin to explain.'

'But he won't! I told you! Please, Inspector!'

'I'm sorry,' Thanet repeated. 'I'm afraid I can't do that. And now we'd like to see Kevin's room, please.'

Defeated, she turned to lead the way upstairs.

'Just tell us where it is, Mrs Barcombe. We'd prefer you to remain downstairs.' With her obsessive tidiness he didn't want her breathing down their necks, clicking her tongue over every move they made.

'I'm afraid it's rather untidy,' she said. 'Kevin only lets me clean up once in a blue moon.'

And it was true that he needn't have worried. Her indulgence towards Kevin evidently extended even to allowing him to make as much of a mess of his room as he liked.

'I'm amazed she lets him get away with this,' said Lineham, wrinkling his nose in distaste at the stale, unwashed odour as they picked their way through the dirty discarded pants, socks, shirts and jeans dropped, presumably where he took them off, all over the floor. The bedside table was cluttered with empty cans and dirty mugs with mould growing over the bottom. Motoring and fashion magazines were scattered across the unmade bed and the wastepaper basket nearby was overflowing with empty crisp packets and the wrappers of chocolate bars and biscuits.

'The power of love,' said Thanet, looking around. 'Just think what it must cost her, with her obsession for cleanliness, to leave things in this state. I have heard that adoptive parents find it harder to discipline an adopted child than one of their own, on the grounds that criticism may be taken as rejection.'

'Well I wouldn't put up with this mess from one of ours, I can tell you! Where do we start?'

'Let's kick all this stuff into a corner, to begin with.' Thanet had no intention of picking up Kevin's dirty clothes with his bare hands, but all this clutter was distracting.

That done, they set to, beginning conventionally with chest of drawers, wardrobe and bed. They examined the posters on the walls, dismantled the few framed photographs of family holidays and then moved on to a close examination of the fitted carpet, which proved to be professionally fixed with gripper rods.

'Nothing,' said Lineham gloomily, sitting back on his heels. 'Looks as though we were wrong. There's not one single thing here to connect him to Jessica.'

Thanet glanced at the hatch in the ceiling. He could think of more than one case where a loft had yielded up interesting secrets. 'If there is anything incriminating, he wouldn't have put it where his mother was likely to come across it on one of her occasional cleans.'

Lineham followed his gaze and they scrambled to their feet.

'Wonder if there's a loft ladder,' said Lineham. The hatch was just too high for him to reach but there was a wooden chair in the corner piled with dirty jeans and T-shirts and Lineham tipped them off and positioned it below the hatch. This was hinged on one side and as he lowered it a ladder swung sweetly down. 'Great!' he said.

'If there is anything hidden up there it won't be too far in,' said Thanet. 'He wouldn't have wanted to go clumping about in the loft and making his parents ask questions about what he was up to.'

By now Lineham was three-quarters of the way up the ladder, standing with head and shoulders in the opening. 'There's a light,' he said, and switched it on.

'Well?' said Thanet impatiently. He longed to be up there himself, but the sergeant had been too quick off the mark.

'The floor is boarded for a few yards around the hatch,' said Lineham. 'And there's the usual sort of junk, boxes and bits of leftover carpet and so on.'

There was a series of scraping sounds as he moved things about. 'Hang on,' he said suddenly.

'What?'

'There's a loose section of board here.'

A rattling sound, and then, 'Aaah.'

'"Ah" what?' said Thanet, by now in a frenzy of suspense and impatience.

'Eureka, I think!' said Lineham.

He switched off the light and began to descend.

FOURTEEN

As Lineham came down the last few rungs he handed his find to Thanet. It consisted of two items, a blue hard-covered scrapbook with thick pages, of the type readily bought in any large newsagent's, and an orange folder. When he had stowed away the ladder and closed the hatch they both sat down on the edge of the bed to take a closer look.

'Bingo!' breathed Lineham.

And here it was, the proof they needed of Kevin's obsession with Jessica Manifest, which had begun, it seemed, some six months ago. The scrapbook opened with an article written about her last Easter on the occasion of her winning an award. Then came many more, this time written by her and obviously clipped from the *Kent Messenger*. All were dated. Interspersed with these were photograph after photograph, taken in various public places. Many of them had been cut so that only Jessica remained.

'She was right, wasn't she?' said Thanet. 'He had been following her, and for some time. He obviously took these photographs himself, mostly on Sundays, I imagine. Her husband was probably with her, that's why they've been cut.'

'Yes,' said Lineham. 'That one was taken at the County Show, don't you think?'

Thanet agreed. 'And this is in the white garden at Sissinghurst. Last June, by the look of it. The rose pergola is in full bloom.'

'And I recognise that pub too. Yes, it's the Three Chimneys at Biddenden.'

Thanet opened the folder. Here were two more articles

161

clipped from the *KM*, both of recent date and obviously waiting to be pasted in.

'I wonder if there's any undeveloped film in his camera?'
said Lineham. This was hanging over one of the knobs on the
headboard of the bed. He unhooked it, opened the case and
examined it. 'It's on number 16 of a 24-exposure film,' he
said with satisfaction. 'With any luck there'll be more of her
in here.'

'Good thinking, Mike. Write out a receipt for the camera,
to give to his mother.' Thanet stood up. 'I think we've got
enough to pull him in, don't you?'

Mrs Barcombe was standing at the bottom of the stairs
looking anxiously up as they emerged from Kevin's room.
She looked even more worried when she saw what they were
carrying. 'That's Kevin's camera!' she cried. 'You can't have
that!'

'Don't worry, he'll get it back,' said Thanet. 'Here's a
receipt.'

She snatched it from him. 'And what have you got there?'
She made a grab for the scrapbook but Lineham held it out
of her reach. 'That's not Kevin's! I've never seen it before!'
And then, illogically, 'You've no right to take his things
away!'

'We're very sorry to have disturbed you, Mrs Barcombe.'
Thanet edged past her in the narrow hall. 'We're leaving
now.'

It was a guilty relief to escape from her anxiety and frustration.

Outside he cast an anxious glance at the sky, which had
clouded over. 'I hope the weather forecasters haven't got it
wrong again. They promised us a fine weekend.' As soon as
they got back to the car he radioed in to give the order for
Kevin to be picked up.

Earlier Lineham had dispatched two women detectives,
new but very capable additions to the team, to interview
Kevin's natural mother, with strict instructions to be tactful
and not to proceed if she were married and her husband or
family were around. Back at the office, while they were waiting for Kevin to arrive, WDC Tanya Phillips gave them a

verbal report. She was in her mid twenties, a stocky girl with an engaging smile and a mop of unruly dark curls.

'She wasn't too pleased, needless to say, when she found out we'd come about Kevin. Tried to show us the door. Fortunately we were inside by then and as there didn't seem to be anyone else around we decided it was worth persisting. When she discovered that all we wanted was verification (a) that Kevin is her son and (b) that he had contacted her recently, and that that really would be the end of the matter as far as we were concerned, she gave in.'

'And he was and he did?'

'Yes. About a month before Easter. She went on and on about what a shock it had been and how he had ruined her subsequent holiday in Majorca, turning up out of the blue like that.'

'She's married?'

'Yes, with two children, a boy and a girl.'

'What's she like?' Though Thanet could guess, from the little Tanya had already said.

WDC Phillips pulled a face. 'I must say I didn't take to her, sir. A bit of a hard-faced bitch, if you want my honest opinion.'

Poor Kevin. What a disillusionment. No doubt he had woven all sorts of elaborate fantasies about what his mother would be like. 'What does her husband do?'

'I didn't ask. Should I have?'

'No, don't worry. It really doesn't matter.'

'They're quite well off, I should think. Detached house, car of her own, nice clothes, spends a lot on her hair and make-up . . .'

'I get the picture.' She hadn't wanted her nice cosy set-up disturbed. And, in a way, who could blame her?

Except that he did. He did. 'Anyway, I gather she sent Kevin packing.'

'In no uncertain terms, I should think. She just didn't want to know.'

'Right. Thanks, Tanya. About a month before Easter,' he said to Lineham when she had gone. 'That's interesting, isn't it?'

'It is, isn't it? Are you thinking what I'm thinking?'

'That he substituted one obsession for another? It does seem likely, doesn't it? It must have been a pretty shattering disappointment. He must have expended so much emotional energy in tracing her, spent so much time thinking about her . . . When all that was suddenly taken away from him he might well have needed something else to take its place.'

'Are you suggesting that Jessica Manifest was a sort of mother substitute, sir?'

'No, not at all. Well, not necessarily. Just that nature abhors a vacuum and an interest in another woman would fill his mind, prevent him from brooding on his disappointment.'

'Interesting that he should choose someone so much older than him, though.'

'Yes. The question is . . .'

'What?'

'Well, if Ogilvy did leave the door open that night and Kevin did go in . . .'

'She'd be frightened, seeing a strange man in the house.'

'Yes. But how would he see her reaction?'

'You mean, would he take it as another rejection?'

'Exactly.'

'In which case, it might have made him flip.'

'It's a possibility, isn't it?'

The phone rang and Lineham answered it. 'Kevin's here.'

'Good.' Thanet sprang to his feet. He felt eager, buoyed up with optimism, certain that at last they were about to learn what had actually happened in that quiet country backwater on Tuesday night. He tucked the scrapbook under his arm. 'Let's see what he has to say for himself.'

Kevin was slumped at the table in one of the interview rooms, arms folded protectively across his chest, his expression a mixture of sulkiness, fear and defiance.

Thanet had decided that the time for pussyfooting around was over. The hard edges of the scrapbook pressing against his side were a comforting reassurance that this time he had some powerful ammunition. He marched into the room and slammed the book down on the table.

Kevin jumped and as he recognised the scrapbook his face

164

became the colour of tallow, the freckles standing out against his sudden pallor.

'Right!' Thanet snapped as he and Lineham sat down. 'A quiet country walk, you said, didn't you, Kevin? That's why you were in Charthurst on Tuesday night?'

Silence. The boy's eyes were riveted to the scrapbook.

'We don't like it when people lie to us, Kevin, not one little bit. It makes us suspicious, very suspicious indeed. And when they lie to us more than once, as you have . . .'

Kevin opened his mouth, then shut it again.

'Because you have, haven't you? First of all you lied to us about not going to Charthurst at all on Tuesday night, and now we find you've been lying to us again. You assured us that as far as you were concerned Jessica Dander was only another customer, and not one that you'd had much to do with at that. But now, what do we find carefully hidden away in the loft above your bedroom where you thought no one would ever find it?' Thanet opened the scrapbook. 'An article about Jessica Dander. Articles by Jessica Dander. Photographs of Jessica Dander, lots of them – private photographs, taken by you.' Thanet nodded at Lineham and the sergeant held up the camera.

'Yours, I believe,' he said.

Kevin leaned forward for a closer look, opened his mouth then closed it again, clearly torn between denying that the camera was his and losing an expensive object if he did so.

Cupidity won. 'What if it is?' he muttered. Then, 'You've got no right to take my things away! Stealing, that's what it is. I want to make a complaint.'

'Your mother has a receipt for the camera,' said Thanet. 'But in fact you can have it back right now, once Sergeant Lineham has removed the film.'

Lineham did so, then put the camera on the table.

Kevin snatched it up and examined it, as if looking for damage.

'We're looking forward to getting that film developed, aren't we, sergeant? So.' Thanet sat back and folded his arms. 'What have you got to say for yourself now?'

Silence. Then Kevin laid the camera carefully down and

fished in the pocket of his anorak for his tin of tobacco.

'No!' snapped Thanet. 'Put that away. This isn't a cocktail party!' He leaned forward. 'I don't think you quite realise the seriousness of your position, Kevin. We're talking about murder here, the worst crime in the book. Believe me, we won't be so easily fobbed off this time. You are not going to walk out of here unless and until we know the truth – and who knows? Maybe not even then. So you'd better get on with it.'

Kevin lifted his chin and shrugged. 'OK.'

Thanet found it difficult to hide his astonishment and he sensed Lineham stir beside him. He certainly hadn't expected Kevin to cave in so quickly.

'Get me off the hook, won't it? Anyway, there's no point in keeping mum any longer, is there, not now you know about, well . . .' He nodded at the scrapbook. 'I ain't done nothing wrong,' he added defiantly.

'Really.' Thanet tapped the scrapbook. 'You don't call following a woman, spying on her, frightening her, something wrong?'

'Not really. It ain't a crime, anyway, is it?'

'It soon will be.' At last there was going to be legislation to make stalking a statutory offence. Not before time, in most people's opinions. 'So tell me exactly what happened on Tuesday night.'

And out it all poured. It was as if Kevin had been longing to tell somebody his story and until now had been denied an audience. It is not very often, after all, that the average person has so dramatic a tale to tell.

Kevin had, as his mother originally stated, left the house on Tuesday evening at around 7.45. By the time he had walked to where his father's car was garaged and driven to Charthurst it was just after eight o'clock. He parked at the Green Man and, having checked that there was no one about to notice him, took up his usual position behind the hedge. As he hurried past the end of Willow Way he noticed that Jessica's front door was open.

Thanet interrupted him for the first time. 'You're sure about that?'

'Certain.'

'Go on.'

'Well, I'd only been behind the hedge a coupla minutes when this geezer comes out. He hesitates, like, on the doorstep, as if he was trying to make up his mind about something, then he hurries off down the road towards the pub and a minute or two later an engine starts up and I hear a car go off.'

'It was definitely a man?'

'Yep.'

'Did you recognise him?' If Kevin had been watching Jessica for months he must by now know most of the people in her life by sight if not by name.

But if he had, he was not yet ready to say so. 'I think he was trying to make up his mind whether or not to close the door behind him.' He leaned forward eagerly. 'I been thinking about it, see. And I reckon he thought, if I leave it open, perhaps someone else'll get in and that'll muddy the waters.'

'Hmm.' Thanet was non-committal. 'Go on.'

'Well, I waited a few minutes and then I thought I'd better go take a look. Well, I mean to say, it was a bit funny, wasn't it, the front door being open like that, specially at night, in the dark. Anybody could've just walked in. And I got to thinking perhaps there was something wrong, perhaps something had happened to her . . .' His voice tailed off. 'Can I have a fag now?' he said abruptly.

'Go ahead.' Thanet was interested to note the tremor in Kevin's hands as he rolled his cigarette. He made a bad job of it too and the loose paper flared up as he struck a match to it. He guessed that despite the apparent ease with which the boy had told his story until now, Kevin was dreading the next part. 'Go on,' he said gently.

Kevin spat out a loose shred of tobacco then gave him an assessing glance. 'So I went across, didn't I? It was all quiet in the house, no radio or telly on. It was like in them films, when you've got this terrific build-up to what's going to be on the other side of the door.' He stubbed out his cigarette viciously.

It was a gesture of anger and of something more.

Repudiation? But of what? Thanet wondered. Of reality, perhaps. Until the moment when Kevin had pushed open that door he had been keyed up, excited, playing a part in a drama which had no real emotional impact because it was unrelated to his feelings. But if the boy, for whatever reason, had for months been focusing his thoughts, his hopes, his aspirations perhaps, on Jessica, what a shock the sight of her lifeless body must have been.

He was right. Kevin had put his elbows on the table and buried his face in his hands. 'And there she was,' he said in a muffled voice. 'It was horrible. She was all – crumpled. Broken. I never seen a dead person before. And she was always so alive.' His head came up suddenly and Thanet experienced a powerful pang of compassion at the pain in the boy's face. 'Did you know her?' he said.

Thanet shook his head. 'Only by sight.'

'She was great,' said Kevin. 'Really great. I always used to wash her hair, you know – beautiful hair, she had, long and thick and that amazing colour . . . And we'd talk. You know the great thing about her?'

Thanet shook his head.

'She made you feel you had . . . what's the word? Potential. Yeah, that's it. Potential. As though you could do whatever you wanted to do, if you only wanted it enough and were prepared to work hard enough. She had a pretty bad time of it herself when she was little, you know.'

'Yes, I know.'

'And look how she ended up! It's not fair! It's bloody well not fair!'

'You really liked her, didn't you, Kevin?'

'Yes I bloody did! She was . . . She was . . .' He shook his head, as if Jessica's qualities defied description. '. . . great,' he finished.

'It must have been a terrible shock for you.'

'You can say that again.' Now that the worst was over Kevin's bravado was creeping back.

'Did you touch her at all, move her?'

'No!' He was horrified. 'What would have been the point? Anyone could see she was dead, with her eyes all staring like

168

that.' He shuddered. 'All I could think of was to get out of there, quick.'

'Was it you who rang for an ambulance?'

'Yeah, it was.'

'Why?'

'What d'you mean?'

'Well, as you said, she was obviously dead, nothing could be done for her.'

'But I couldn't just walk out and do nothing, leave her there like that, could I?'

'No, I don't suppose you could.'

'And I remembered to pick up the receiver in my hand-kerchief,' said Kevin proudly.

Police procedurals on TV had much to answer for, thought Thanet.

Lineham shifted restlessly beside him. Thanet knew why. There was one burning question which as yet remained unanswered.

'Kevin,' he said, 'I asked you just now if you recognised the man you saw come out of Jessica's house, but you didn't reply. Did you know who he was?'

Kevin nodded and now his face was grim. 'He's some sort of relation of hers. Farm manager at Hunter's Green Farm, over at Nettleton.'

Thanet and Lineham looked at each other. 'Bernard Covin!' said Lineham.

FIFTEEN

'That's a turn up for the book!' said Lineham, when Kevin had gone. The boy could not be shaken. The man he saw come out of Jessica's house that night was Bernard Covin, and his description of him certainly matched. His interest in Covin had first been aroused when he saw him talking to Jessica in Sturrenden High Street one day. It was obvious that they knew each other well and a couple of weeks later, after seeing Covin in a pub, he had decided to follow him home. He had eventually discovered that Covin had in fact been married to Jessica's sister, now dead.

Thanet guessed that Kevin had originally suspected that Jessica might be involved with Covin and had followed him out of jealous interest. He wondered what the boy had thought of her affair with Ogilvy. 'We'd better take another look at Covin's statement,' he said. Though he could remember perfectly well what the man had told them: Covin and his daughter had had supper together before she left to drive to Reading. She had asked him to give her aunt a ring to apologise for not having managed to visit her to say goodbye before leaving for the new term and he had done so, about 7.30. When he got Jessica's answering machine he had rung off and had then spent the rest of the evening watching television.

They both read Covin's statement through again, but found nothing new or ambiguous in it.

'Presumably, having failed to get through on the phone, he then went round instead,' said Lineham.

'But why? It was scarcely an urgent message, was it? And how did he get to Charthurst anyway?' said Thanet. 'Karen had taken his car. He must have borrowed a farm vehicle.'

They looked at each other in sudden comprehension.

'That white pick-up parked at the Green Man!' said Lineham.

'A bit slow on the uptake, weren't we?' said Thanet. 'We really ought to have followed that up before. We knew about Kevin's father's Nissan and Ogilvy's Mercedes but we just didn't follow up on the Ford.'

'I suppose that was because Covin told us his daughter had borrowed his car, so we just assumed he'd be without transport.'

Will I never learn, thought Thanet? 'Just shows how dangerous assumptions can be. And of course we're making another, in assuming it was Covin who was driving that Ford.'

'It does seem likely, though, doesn't it? He must have got there somehow.'

'We really should have made an effort to trace that pick-up before, then we might have made the connection with Covin, if there is one. Anyway, assuming it was Covin that Kevin saw come out of the house, why on earth do you suppose he left the door open?'

'Maybe Kevin's right, sir. Maybe Covin did just want to muddy the waters.'

'Which waters? Nobody even knew he was there.'

'Maybe he didn't want to ring for an ambulance himself because he didn't want to get involved, but thought that if he left the door open someone else might notice and go to investigate – which is, in fact, what happened.'

'But why bother? Presumably he knew that sooner or later her husband would come home and find her. And in fact, if she did die as the result of a quarrel or whatever, I'd have thought he'd prefer to delay the discovery of the body rather than hasten it. No, it doesn't make sense.'

'Perhaps he hoped that when the police heard the door had been left open they might think it was a burglary that went wrong.'

'The last thing a burglar would have done is leave it open,

surely, and draw attention to the fact that something was amiss? And it was the fact that the door was open that alerted us to the possibility that it hadn't been a straightforward accident.'

'Perhaps he just acted unwisely on the spur of the moment. He'd have been anxious to get away. I don't suppose he'd have had time to work out all the pros and cons.'

'You're probably right, Mike. Ah well, no doubt we'll find out eventually. Anyway, as far as the case is concerned we don't seem to have got much further, do we? All we've achieved is to add one more to our list of suspects.'

'You don't think we can cross Kevin off, then?'

'I think we still ought to keep an open mind as far as he's concerned. Though I'm inclined to believe his story, aren't you?'

'Yes, I am. I imagine he didn't tell us about Covin before because he didn't want to admit to having been there in the first place.'

'Quite.'

'And at least we're gradually getting a clearer picture of what happened that night.'

'True.' But Thanet was determined to feel pessimistic. The truth was, he was still feeling put out that his beautiful theory had been proved wrong and Kevin had turned out to be someone else's son, not Jessica's. It had been such a neat, satisfying explanation. He sighed. He ought to know by now that life wasn't like that, it was muddled and messy and explanations were rarely neat and even more rarely satisfying.

'What's the matter, sir?'

'There was I, thinking we were going to have this case all nicely sewn up before the wedding, and we're practically back to square one. Come on, Mike. Let's see what culinary delights the canteen has to offer today. I don't know about you but I feel distinctly in need of nourishment.'

Over dried-up shepherd's pie and watery cabbage they chewed over Covin's involvement in the case.

'I still can't see why he went over to see her,' said Thanet for the third time. He kept on coming back to this. He dug down into his pie, seeking for any sign of mince beneath the

172

thick topping of potato. 'It really wouldn't have mattered if he hadn't passed on Karen's message until the next day. Honestly, these caterers really ought to be prosecuted under the Trade Descriptions Act. There's barely a couple of tea-spoonfuls of meat under this potato!' It was a general grumble that since the canteen had switched to outside cater-ers standards had plummeted.

Lineham grinned. 'A dicy one, that, sir. Precisely how much mince should there be in a shepherd's pie?'

Thanet grunted, then there was silence while they both considered possible reasons for Covin's visit.

'Unless . . .' said Lineham suddenly.

'What?'

'I was thinking . . .'

'Come on, spit it out, Mike.'

'Well, I was just thinking. What if that phone call wasn't to have been a message from Karen at all. What if it had been about something else entirely?'

Thanet stared at him. 'Something sufficiently urgent for him to go over there when she failed to answer the phone, you mean? But what?'

Lineham lifted his shoulders. 'Search me. Just an idea.'

'Yes,' said Thanet slowly. All at once he was aware of the beginnings of a familiar sensation in his head, almost of pres-sure building. His pulse speeded up. 'Let me think, let me think,' he muttered.

'Perhaps he intended putting a note through her door?'

Intent upon trying to formulate the idea that was just beyond his grasp, Thanet scarcely heard him. He froze with his fork half way to his mouth, as illumination came.

Of course!

He automatically popped the cabbage into his mouth and chewed without tasting.

Could it be true?

'Sir?' said Lineham, alerted. He was used to Thanet's brain-waves and had seen that look more times than he could remember.

Thanet's eyes came into focus again. 'Yes?'

'What were you thinking?'

Thanet shook his head. 'I'm not sure I want to risk telling you, after the last fiasco.'

'Oh come on, sir! You can't leave me in suspense!'

Thanet still hesitated. He didn't relish the prospect of being wrong again. But Lineham had never been one to gloat over someone else's mistakes and it really wouldn't be fair to keep him in the dark. 'All right. What if . . .?'

Lineham's eyes opened wide as Thanet explained. 'But, sir, we haven't a single shred of evidence to suggest that might be true.'

'That doesn't mean to say it isn't. We got our wires crossed in exactly the same way in the Parnell case, don't you remember?'

'Yes, I do. But Covin said –'

Thanet knew exactly what Lineham was going to say. 'I know what Covin said! But he might well have been lying about that too.'

'I suppose,' said Lineham. But it was obvious that he still wasn't convinced. 'Anyway,' he said, 'even if it is true, it might have no bearing on the case.'

'*Might* is the operative word, Mike.'

'I don't see how it could.'

'That's because we haven't got to the bottom of it all yet.' Thanet was becoming exasperated. 'You know perfectly well that something we don't understand is often explicable in the light of later evidence.'

'True.' But Lineham was still grudging.

'I think it's worth following up, anyway. We'll put Tanya on to Southport.'

Lineham knew when there was no point in arguing. 'Right, sir.'

'And then we'll go and see the Pinks.'

'The Pinks?'

'Covin's former employers, Mike. Wake up!'

'But why, sir?'

'Because they'll be able to fill us in on the background, obviously!'

'But isn't it more important to go and tackle Covin?'

'All in good time, Mike. The more weapons we have tucked

under our belt the better equipped we'll be.' He stood up. 'Where did the Wargreaves say they lived?'

'Near Headcorn,' Lineham muttered, obviously convinced that Thanet was going off on a wild goose chase.

'Shouldn't be too difficult to find out exactly where.'

No more difficult than consulting the telephone directory, in fact, and half an hour later they were turning in to the entrance to Barn End Farm. Thanet was relieved to see that the clouds which had blown up earlier had cleared away. Perhaps it would be a fine day tomorrow after all.

'Must have been a step up for Covin to get the job at Hunter's Green Farm,' said Lineham as they pulled up in front of the farmhouse and got out of the car. His moods never lasted long and he was already back to his usual ebullient self.

Thanet agreed. This farmhouse was smaller and the outbuildings less extensive. There were children's toys lying about and a black-and-white puppy came bouncing around the corner of the house barking shrilly, closely pursued by a little boy of about four. He stopped when he saw the strangers and, like little Daisy Ogilvy, put his thumb in his mouth.

'Hello,' said Lineham, trying to stop the puppy climbing up his trouser leg. 'Where's your mummy?'

The boy turned and ran off the way he had come. Thanet and Lineham followed. The puppy was still barking and jumping up and down at Lineham as they walked.

'He's taken a fancy to you, Mike,' said Thanet with a grin, raising his voice to make himself heard.

'Why on earth can't people keep their dogs under control?' said Lineham, trying to fend the animal off.

'I've got a nasty feeling we might be disappointed here,' said Thanet. 'If the boy's parents are the owners they'd be much too young to be the Pinks we want to see.'

'Could be the son,' said Lineham. 'The old man might have retired. Down, boy! Down!'

They had to pass the kitchen window to get to the back door. There was a young woman inside, watching them. Thanet raised a hand in greeting and she nodded but made no move to open the door. They waited a few moments and then went back to the window. She was leaning forward across the sink, waiting for them.

'Identification,' she mouthed.

Thanet nodded and they both pressed their warrant cards against the window.

A moment later she unlocked the door and opened it. She was holding the little boy by the hand. 'Sorry,' she said, raising her voice above the noise the dog was still making. 'But you can't be too careful these days, especially in a place like this. Quiet, Tess!'

The dog ignored her.

'I couldn't agree more,' said Thanet.

To Lineham's relief she bent down and seized the puppy by the collar. 'I apologise for Tess,' she said. 'She's only six months old and not very civilised yet. Just a moment.' She dragged the dog off and they heard a door open and close.

'Mrs Pink?' said Thanet when she returned, relieved to be speaking at a normal pitch again.

'Yes?' Her expression changed and she glanced from one to the other. 'There's nothing wrong, is there? My husband hasn't had an accident?'

'Oh no, not at all.'

As Lineham had suggested she was the daughter-in-law of the Pinks who had been Covin's employers. Her father-in-law had retired four years previously, and he and his wife had moved into a development of retirement homes on the edge of the village. Ten minutes later Thanet and Lineham were turning in between the imposing wrought-iron gates at the entrance to The Beeches, a retirement complex set in what had obviously once been the spacious grounds of a large Victorian house which was visible over to the left behind a screen of young trees. Such developments had sprung up everywhere over the last ten to fifteen years as it had dawned on builders that the one sector of the housing market which was going to expand rather than shrink in the immediate future was custom-built accommodation for the elderly. The complexes varied enormously in price and quality, as might be expected, but this was obviously an upmarket version, built in the local vernacular of brick and tilehanging in a setting of carefully preserved mature trees and well-kept lawns and flowerbeds. Thanet and Lineham followed a curving drive to the rear of the block of buildings then made for the warden's flat. Their knock was answered by a pleasant middle-aged woman.

'It's not bad news, I hope?' she said, when Thanet had introduced himself and asked for the Pinks.

'No, not at all, I assure you.'

'Good. Only Mrs Pink isn't too well. She's not long out of hospital.'

'We'll try not to tire her.'

This seemed to satisfy her. 'I'll take you along.'

'That isn't necessary, really.'

But she insisted. 'I'd like to make sure they're not alarmed.' She smiled. 'It's not often we get a visit from the police.'

The Pinks' home was a surprise. From the outside the cottages looked small but inside they were unexpectedly spacious. The warden asked them to wait while she went in, then reappeared with an elderly man whose leathery complexion criss-crossed by a myriad of fine lines at once proclaimed that he had spent his working life in the open air, rain or shine. He greeted them apprehensively then led them through a large square sitting room into a heated conservatory where his wife was sitting with one bandaged foot propped up on a footstool. 'Here they are, dear,' he said.

'Please don't worry,' said Thanet, anxious to allay their obvious anxiety. 'The only reason we've come to see you is that we think you might be able to help us with some information about a former employee.'

As if by magic their faces cleared and Mrs Pink invited Thanet and Lineham to sit down.

'Who d'you mean?' said her husband, when they were all settled.

Thanet had arranged that Lineham would begin this interview. 'Someone who worked for you over twenty years ago, sir,' said the sergeant. 'A man called Bernard Covin.'

'Oh, I see,' said Pink. And to his wife, 'It must be about Jessica.'

'Oh,' she said. 'We heard about it on the radio.' She looked tired and drawn and from time to time would ease the bandaged foot into a new position, lifting her leg with both hands. A pair of aluminium crutches stood against the wall nearby. 'And there's an article in the *KM* today.'

Of course, it was Friday, thought Thanet. He should have remembered to check the newspaper, though he doubted that they would learn anything new from it.

'Terrible, wasn't it?' she said. 'Poor little scrap.'

Thanet realised she was remembering Jessica as the child she had known.

'You remember her, then,' said Lineham.

'Of course!' she said. 'She came to live with her sister and Bernard when her mother died. You couldn't help feeling sorry for her. She always looked as if a puff of wind would blow her away, so thin and pale she was.'

'How did she get on with her brother-in-law?'

She shrugged. 'Didn't have much to do with him, as far as I could see. Very fond of her sister she was, though. She was a lovely girl, Madge. I was sorry to see her go, when they moved away. Too good for him, I always thought.'

'I never could see why you didn't like him, myself,' said her husband. 'He was a good worker, was Bernard.'

Another shrug. 'I just never took to him. How is Madge?' she said to Lineham.

'She died, I'm afraid,' he said. 'Of breast cancer, I believe. A couple of years ago.'

Her face had clouded. 'Oh, I am sorry. What about her little girl? What was her name?'

'Karen. But not so little now,' said Lineham with a smile. 'She's nearly twenty and studying at Reading University.'

'Twenty!' said Mrs Pink. 'You can't credit it, the way time speeds up as you get older!'

'Did you know Karen as a baby?' said Lineham. 'We thought the Covins left here just before she was born.'

'Not before. Just after, actually. Not that Madge was here when the baby arrived, so I didn't see her until she was about three months old, when Madge brought her to see me. She was so proud of her! She'd been so excited when she found she was pregnant! They'd been married six or seven years by then, you see, and had more or less given up hope. Mind, she didn't have a very easy time. First she had terrible morning sickness and then she got high blood pressure and had to rest a lot. In fact, I hardly saw her for the last three or four months. She never went out, except when Bernard took her to the ante-natal clinic. Those were the only times I caught a glimpse of her, when she was passing in the car.'

'You didn't go and see her?'

'I tried, a few times, but she would never answer the door. In the end I gave up. I assumed she just didn't feel like socialising, that she'd no doubt get back to normal after the baby was born. As she did. She certainly seemed all right when she brought the baby to see me, as I say.'

'What did you mean, "Not that Madge was here"? Where was she?'

Thanet was glad that Lineham had picked this up.

'She was in Bristol – it was Bristol, wasn't it, Bob?'

They were well away now, engrossed in their story. Like many elderly people who don't get out much they obviously enjoyed having an audience.

Her husband nodded. 'Yes. It's all a bit complicated. Madge and Jessica had this aunt, you see, who lived in Bristol. The previous summer holidays Jessica went to stay with her and they got on so well she decided to stay on. But in the middle of December Jessica apparently rang to say the aunt had been taken ill and would Madge come and help. Well, Jessica was only sixteen so presumably Madge felt she had to go.'

'She wouldn't have been very happy about it, I imagine,' said Mrs Pink. 'She had this problem with high blood pressure, the baby was due at the beginning of January and apart from anything else she'd been very busy trying to get everything packed up ready for the move.'

'The move to Hunter's Green Farm, you mean?' said Lineham.

179

'Yes,' said Pink. 'Bernard had put in for the job in November and just before that phone call from Jessica he heard he'd got it. He was over the moon, of course, it was a step up for him.'

'But I shouldn't think Madge was too pleased,' Mrs Pink put in. 'It meant she'd be moving house just around the time the baby was born and I'm sure she wouldn't have felt well enough to cope.'

'The job started in the new year,' said her husband. 'So they were supposed to move on January 1st.'

'Anyway, as Bob says, Madge presumably didn't feel she had any choice and off she went to Bristol,' said Mrs Pink. 'And lo and behold, the baby chose to arrive early – probably because of all the upheaval. So just before Christmas Bernard gets a phone call to say Madge had gone into labour. Well, naturally he left right away, and the next day we heard the baby had arrived and it was a little girl.'

'Bernard stayed on for another week and then had to come home by himself to do the move.'

'The aunt was still ill, you see, so Madge felt she couldn't leave Jessica to cope alone. That was why I didn't see Karen until she was three months old.'

'So when Mrs Covin did come back she went straight to Hunter's Green Farm?' said Lineham.

'Yes.'

'And when was that?'

Mrs Pink frowned. 'I'm not sure. Early in February, I believe.'

'So the baby would have been about six weeks old.'

'Something like that, I imagine.'

So there it was. Thanet felt a thrill of triumph. He was right this time, he just knew it.

Outside Lineham said, 'All right, all right, don't say it. I was wrong!'

'We're not a hundred per cent certain yet, Mike.'

'We soon will be.'

And they were. Back at the office WDC Phillips was waiting for them, fax in hand. 'This just came through, sir.'

'Well?' He almost snatched it from her in his eagerness.

And there it was, the proof he needed. The information on the birth certificate was unequivocal:

Name of child: Karen Mary.
Date of birth: 21.12.77.
Name of mother: Jessica Mary Dander.

SIXTEEN

'Well done, Tanya,' said Thanet, handing the fax to Lineham. 'I didn't think you'd get a response so quickly.'

'Well, I did lay it on a bit thick, sir, the urgency, I mean. A murder case and so on. But the girl was very helpful. Apparently she deals exclusively with police inquiries. And the fact that it was an unusual surname helped.'

'Good.'

'I was a bit puzzled when you told me to ring Southport. I've never had occasion to make this sort of inquiry before and I always thought the records were held at St Catherine's House. That's where I'd have rung if you hadn't told me otherwise.'

'They only have the Index to the Register there,' said Lineham. 'And they don't deal with telephone inquiries anyway. You have to go along in person and it's always packed out. This is a much better system.'

'She said the father's name does not appear on the certificate if the child is born out of wedlock unless he agrees.'

'Presumably he didn't,' said Lineham. 'Anyway,' he said to Thanet, waving the fax, 'we got what we wanted. You were right, weren't you, sir?'

'So far, anyway.' Thanet dismissed WDC Phillips with a smile and a nod.

'Though I still can't see that it gets us any further.'

Thanet grinned. 'To be honest, Mike, neither can I, at the moment.' It had done much to restore his confidence, however, and he felt optimistic as they now set off to interview

Covin. He hoped Covin would be there this time. Not wishing to put him on his guard they had deliberately refrained from ringing to check.

'Hope we won't have a wasted journey,' said Lineham, tuning in to his thoughts.

'So do I.'

But they were out of luck, it seemed. Hunter's Green Farm appeared deserted.

'I suppose they're all out in the orchards,' said Lineham.

'Let's try the packing shed.'

Inside the shed the scene was very different from yesterday evening, when they had run Covin to earth in the glass-walled office. The grading machine and conveyor belts were working and as soon as they stepped inside the hum of machinery met their ears. The rich, fruity aroma of ripe apples was even stronger and there was an atmosphere of bustle and activity. Most of the workers were women, all wearing dark green overalls and a cap-cum-headscarf which covered their hair.

'No idea,' said one of them in response to their inquiry as to Covin's whereabouts. 'Mick Landy might know.' She pointed. 'Over there.'

Landy was operating a small fork-lift truck, moving boxes of apples to stack them on pallets. 'He's gone to take his dad to the dentist's. His parents haven't got a car.' He was a very tall, lanky young man, all knees and elbows as he hunched over the controls in the confined space. He was wearing a baseball cap the wrong way around.

Landy hadn't switched off the engine and once again Thanet found himself shouting. 'Is he coming back this afternoon?'

'Yes. He said he'd be back before I knocked off.'

'Could we step into the office for a few minutes, sir?' At this rate he wouldn't have any voice left for his speech tomorrow!

'Sure.' Landy twisted the ignition key, removed his cap and wiped his forehead on the back of his sleeve. Then he led the way to the office, which still stank of Covin's cigarettes. He shut the door behind them and the noise faded to a muted roar.

'What sort of car is Mr Covin driving at the moment?' said Lineham. 'We understand his daughter has borrowed his.'

'That's right. He's using the pick-up. He often does.' Landy grinned. 'Doesn't have to pay for the petrol.'

The pick-up was white, apparently, and a Ford. Thanet and Lineham exchanged glances of satisfaction.

'Where do you live, sir? On the farm?' Lineham asked.

He was obviously thinking that if, like Covin, Landy also had a tied cottage, it was possible that he might have seen or heard Covin go out on Tuesday night.

No such luck.

'In the village. Why?'

'So you wouldn't by any chance know if Mr Covin used the pick-up on Tuesday night, after Karen left to drive to Reading?'

'What's this all about?' Landy was wary now.

Thanet felt a spurt of excitement. Landy did know, obviously, but was reluctant to say so in case it caused Covin trouble.

'Just answer the question, please, sir.'

'You'll have to ask him, won't you?'

It was a struggle for Lineham to persuade Landy to talk but he managed it in the end.

Apparently Landy had been using the pick-up on Tuesday afternoon and Covin had told him not to bother to return it until next day, but at just after 7.30 that evening he had rung to ask him to bring it back right away. He said he had arranged to go out that evening and had forgotten that Karen would be borrowing his car to drive her stuff back to Reading. It wasn't until he was ready to go that he remembered Landy had the Ford. He was already late, he said, so could Landy hurry up. He would drop him back at his own house before going on to his appointment. Landy had done as he asked.

'So how did he seem?' said Lineham.

'A bit on edge, I suppose,' said Landy reluctantly.

'Did he say where he was going?'

'Didn't say much at all. Just thanks and sorry for disturbing my evening.'

'Didn't you wonder what it was all about?'

184

'No point, was there? It was none of my business. If he wasn't going to tell me, I wasn't going to ask.'

'Did you see which direction he drove off in, after dropping you?'

'The Ashford direction.'

The way he would have to go to get to Charthurst.

On the point of leaving Thanet turned. 'D'you happen to know if Karen usually drove herself back to Reading at the beginning of term?'

'Funny you should ask that. No, Bernard usually takes her.'

'So, what now?' said Lineham when they were outside. 'Do we wait?'

Thanet was thinking about something else. 'I don't know,' he said. Then, putting his mind to the question, 'Yes. He's due back soon and if we went to his parents' house, we might miss him. We don't want him arriving back here in the interim and hearing from Landy that we've found out he was lying about not going out on Tuesday night. I want to catch him unprepared.' He took out his pipe and tobacco. It was too good an opportunity to miss. 'I think I'll take a little stroll down the track.'

Lineham fell into step beside him. 'Anyway,' he said, 'we now not only have an eye-witness who saw him come out of Jessica's house around the time she died, but a second witness to connect him with the pick-up and a third to swear the pick-up was parked at the pub.'

'Not *the* pick-up,' said Thanet, his thoughts still focused elsewhere. '*A* pick-up.'

'Oh, come on, sir. A *white Ford* pick-up. Isn't that enough?'

'A registration number would have been even better.'

'But it's enough to bring him in.'

'To bring him in, yes. But not to charge him, obviously.'

'D'you think this appointment he mentioned to Landy was with Jessica?'

'I shouldn't think so. She had a date with Ogilvy, so she wouldn't have arranged to see Covin as well. I doubt that he had an appointment at all, it was just an excuse he gave to Landy for wanting the pick-up in a hurry.'

'So what was suddenly so urgent?'

'Ah, now I've just been thinking about that.'

'Oh?' said Lineham.

'Yes. What if –'

'Here he comes, sir.' The pick-up had just turned into the track.

Thanet sighed. He'd just got his pipe going nicely and he'd been looking forward to trying out this new idea of his on Lineham.

'Can we talk to him outside, sir?' said Lineham as they turned to walk back. 'I don't think I can face that sitting room again.'

Thanet shook his head. 'Sorry, Mike. It would be inappropriate. Too informal.'

Covin raised a hand in salute as he drove past.

'Besides,' said Thanet, 'I should think that any minute now the farm workers will be knocking off. It would be impossible to talk with people streaming past.'

Now it was Lineham's turn to sigh.

Covin parked in front of the packing shed and came back to meet them, the inevitable cigarette dangling from his lips.

'We'd like another word, sir, if we may,' said Thanet, reluctantly knocking out his pipe on the heel of his shoe.

'No need to put your pipe out, Inspector. You're welcome to smoke inside.' But despite the apparent geniality his eyes were wary.

Thanet smiled inwardly as he imagined Lineham's reaction if he had accepted the invitation.

Having been shut up all day the sitting room smelled worse than ever. Lineham made a little gagging sound of disgust as they went in and Thanet gave him a warning glance. He sympathised, but the sergeant really would have to learn to keep quiet about this.

Covin lit another cigarette from the stub of the one he had been smoking. 'I hope this won't take too long, Inspector. I've got things to attend to before people knock off.'

Thanet ignored this. 'Do you often drive that pick-up, sir?'

'Sometimes. Why?'

'And on Tuesday evening?'

Covin's eyes narrowed above the coils of smoke. 'What are you getting at?'

'Remind me what you said you did on Tuesday evening.'

'I told you. I had supper with my daughter and after she left I watched television.'

'All evening?'

'All evening.'

'So you claim that you definitely weren't driving that pick-up on Tuesday evening?'

'Look, what is all this about?'

'And you definitely did not visit your sister-in-law's house that night?'

'No! I said, what's this all about?'

Thanet leaned forward. 'I'll tell you what it's all about, Mr Covin. We don't like it when witnesses lie to us, that's what. Especially when it involves something as serious as murder.'

'What do you mean?' But the bravado had gone out of Covin's voice.

'One,' said Thanet, ticking the points off on his fingers, 'we have a witness to say that far from sitting innocently at home watching television that night, you actually rang him around 7.30 on Tuesday evening to ask him to bring the pick-up over because you needed it urgently to go out. Two, the landlord at the Green Man in Charthurst swears that that same pick-up was illegally parked on his forecourt around eight o'clock that evening.' This was stretching the truth a little, but still . . . 'And three,' said Thanet with emphasis, 'we also have a witness who swears that he saw you – you, Mr Covin – coming out of your sister-in-law's house at about five past eight that evening.' He stopped.

Silence.

'Well, Mr Covin?'

'They're lying,' said Covin. His fingers were trembling as he lit up again.

'What, all of them?'

Silence again.

'I don't think a jury would be likely to accept your word against theirs, do you?'

Covin still said nothing, just puffed furiously, sucking the smoke into his lungs as if his life depended on it.

Thanet wondered what would happen if they took his cigarettes away. They couldn't do that here, of course, and anyway Thanet didn't believe in gratuitous cruelty. But back at the station, perhaps, as a last resort . . .? 'Especially when we could actually prove to them that you had already lied to us about something else.'

Covin jumped up. 'I don't have to listen to this! I'm not under arrest, am I? Right, then, that's it. Enough. I'd like you to leave now.'

'By all means,' said Thanet pleasantly, getting up with a glance at Lineham, who followed suit. 'We'll continue the interview at the Station, shall we?'

'What d'you mean?'

'Simply that you have a choice: we can continue here or there, whichever you wish. But make no mistake, Mr Covin, I have no intention of terminating this interview until I am satisfied.'

Covin stared at him, chewing the inside of his lip. Then he tossed his head in disgust, sat down and shook out yet another cigarette.

The two policemen sat down again.

'I'm glad you've decided to be cooperative,' said Thanet. 'Now, where was I?'

'You were telling Mr Covin that he wouldn't stand much chance of being believed in Court, in view of the fact that we could prove he'd lied to us about something else,' said Lineham.

'Ah yes,' said Thanet. 'That's right.' He waited. 'Aren't you going to ask what that something else was, sir?'

Covin compressed his lips as if to prevent words escaping. Clearly he was longing to ask but terrified of knowing the answer.

'Very well,' said Thanet. 'When you confirmed that your sister-in-law had given birth to an illegitimate child when she was sixteen, you told us that the baby was a boy.'

Covin stared at him, the colour seeping from his naturally ruddy complexion.

188

'When in fact,' said Thanet, 'it was a girl.' He nodded at Lineham, who took the fax from the pages of his notebook, unfolded it and laid it on Covin's lap.

Covin looked at it and then at Thanet. It was as if he had been struck dumb, the muscles of his face and organs of speech paralysed.

No. He was waiting, Thanet realised, to see how much more they knew. Very well. 'That was quite a smokescreen you put up, wasn't it, pretending that it was your wife who was pregnant, arranging for Jessica to go away before her pregnancy began to show and then making sure your wife was away when the baby was due so that you could go through the charade of rushing to her bedside. Just as a matter of interest, did the aunt with the convenient illness ever exist, or was she just a figment of someone's fertile imagination?'

Covin didn't answer.

'But anyway, it's all ancient history now. Twenty years is a long time. Why bother to go on lying about it now?'

Covin still didn't respond.

'Mr Covin,' said Thanet softly. 'Is Karen aware that she is adopted?'

Covin jumped. In his absorption the cigarette had burned down to his fingers. He stubbed it out and found his voice at last. He ignored Thanet's question. 'How did you find out?'

'We went to talk to your former employers, the Pinks. It wasn't too difficult to work out what had happened. Of course, at the time, the deception worked well – has continued to work, for that matter, all these years. But my guess is that on Tuesday something happened to change the situation, and that was why you went rushing over to see your sister-in-law.'

Bernard stared at him.

'Karen found out, didn't she?' said Thanet softly.

'No!' said Covin desperately. Then he buried his face in his hands. He mumbled through his fingers.

'Sorry?' said Thanet. He thought he had caught the word 'accident'. Was this a confession? He glanced at Lineham who raised his eyebrows and mouthed *Caution*?

Thanet shook his head and ignoring Lineham's puzzled frown said to Covin, 'What did you say?'

Covin sat up and reached for his cigarettes. 'I said, it was an accident,' he said wearily.

It *was* a confession.

'Sir!' said Lineham but again Thanet shook his head. 'Go on.'

'Jessica had been threatening to tell Karen,' said Covin. 'We'd all agreed from the beginning that we never would. I was afraid that if Karen found out she'd turn against me, for keeping it from her. She's . . .' He faltered and briefly his face crumpled as if he were about to dissolve into tears. 'She's all I have left now my wife is gone. I was desperate to stop her finding out, so as soon as she'd left I got Landy to bring the pick-up over and drove to Charthurst.'

Already questions were buzzing in Thanet's brain but he said nothing. There'd be plenty of time later. If Covin was willing to talk he had no intention of stopping him.

'I got there around eightish. I parked at the pub because the road was up in front of Jessica's house. When she let me in –' He stopped.

'Yes?' prompted Thanet.

'I tried to persuade her to change her mind, but she wouldn't listen.' Covin was speaking more slowly now. 'In the end she told me to go –'

'Where was this conversation taking place?' Thanet interrupted for the first time.

'In the sitting room.'

'I see. Go on.'

'We were both pretty worked up by then and she ended up by saying she'd made up her mind and nothing was going to stop her. She stalked out of the room into the hall and started to go up the stairs. I followed her. I . . I caught her by the arm and she must have lost her balance. She fell. It was horrible. I couldn't believe it. I never intended to hurt her, honestly!'

'And where was she, exactly, when she fell?'

'About halfway up, I suppose.'

'I see.' Thanet's eyes met Lineham's. The sergeant no doubt had an equally clear picture in his mind of Jessica's shoe lying against the staircase wall, three steps down from the top.

They were both startled by a slow handclap from the door of the sitting room.

'Well done, Dad. Good try.'

A girl was standing with her hands on her hips, a slight figure in jeans and sweatshirt. Karen. Knowing her parentage Thanet briefly wondered how she could have failed to notice her resemblance to her mother over all these years. There was Jessica's slightly pointed nose, and lips that were too thin for beauty. But her eyes were hazel instead of green, her hair brown not chestnut. Perhaps she had resembled her aunt, her adoptive mother, too. Genes often skipped about in the generations.

He could guess what she meant by 'good try'.

SEVENTEEN

Thanet glimpsed relief then horror on Covin's face before Covin cried 'Karen!' and erupting from his seat went rushing across to seize her by the elbow and attempt to steer her out of the room.

The horror Thanet could understand, but relief? No, that was beyond him.

Karen tried to shake him off. 'Dad! Let go!'

'I really don't think this is a good place for you to be right now, love,' said Covin. He was trying to sound calm but merely succeeded in sounding desperate.

'We have no objection to Miss Covin being present, if she wishes,' said Thanet.

Karen finally managed to free herself from Covin's grasp. 'There you are, Dad. That's all right, then.'

'Inspector,' said Covin, turning to face Thanet. 'I've changed my mind. I think it would be better to continue this interview at the Police Station.'

'I'll come with you,' said Karen. 'I think the Inspector would be interested in what I have to say.'

They all looked at Covin who seemed to shrink before their eyes. It was as if all the air had suddenly been sucked out of him.

'You won't stop me, Dad,' she said softly, and put her hand on his arm.

He looked directly into her face for the first time, a long searching look, and she stared back. The air between them was dense with emotion, charged with words unspoken, explanations long delayed. 'No,' he said finally. 'I can see I won't.'

She tucked her arm through his and led him to the sofa where they sank down on to it, side by side.

Thanet introduced himself and Lineham, before saying, 'As you've no doubt gathered, we're investigating the death of your . . . of Mrs Jessica Manifest, or Jessica Dander as she was professionally known. I don't know how much you heard just now . . .'

'Most of it,' Karen said. 'I parked around the back and came in through the back door. Dad's a shocker, he never locks it.'

'Karen –' said Covin.

'Shh,' she said, and squeezed his arm. 'You're not stupid, Inspector,' she went on. 'You wouldn't have reached your present rank if you were. So you must realise Dad's story is as full of holes as a colander.' She laid a warning hand on Covin's arm as he made a movement of protest. 'It's no good, Dad. I told you, I've made up my mind.'

'I had noticed certain discrepancies,' said Thanet.

'And I suspect you can guess why.'

'He was trying to protect you,' said Thanet, catching a reproachful glance from Lineham. *Why didn't you tell me?* He'd have to explain, later. 'I assume you've come back to sort things out.'

'Yes. And to return the car, of course. I couldn't hang on to it indefinitely.'

'We're all ears,' said Thanet. He couldn't believe it. The case was going to be cleared up in time for the wedding after all! There was going to be no coercion, no persuasion, no manipulation, just a straightforward confession, and all he had to do was sit back and listen! The only problem was, he wasn't sure if he wanted to hear it. He suspected that this was going to be one of those cases where he understood only too well why the crime had been committed, even had a sneaking sympathy for the perpetrator.

'It all began,' said Karen, 'because my roommate and I are planning to go Interrailing around Europe next summer and I needed a passport of my own.'

And there it was, the key to the whole puzzle, something so simple and so obvious. Why on earth didn't I catch on before? thought Thanet, castigating himself. I knew about the Interrailing plans, Lineham told me, early on.

'And for that, of course, I needed my birth certificate.'

Thanet glanced at the photographs, his gaze lingering on the one of Karen in ski outfit. 'Hadn't you been abroad before?'

'Oh yes, a number of times. But first on my parents' passports, then on a group passport, for school trips. This is the first time I'd needed one of my own.'

Once again Thanet was kicking himself. He'd known about passport arrangements for children too, from personal experience, but again it hadn't clicked.

'I'd been nagging Dad to let me have my birth certificate for ages but first he kept on coming up with the excuse that he hadn't had time to look, then he kept on promising to look but never seemed to get around to it. When it got to the point where I was due to leave for the new term and he still hadn't produced it I said I was fed up with waiting and I was going to send off for a copy.'

'This was on Tuesday evening?'

'Yes, at supper. So, of course, he finally had to tell me the truth.'

So far she had appeared calm, composed. Now for the first time there was a tremor in her voice.

Thanet glanced at Covin. The man hadn't said a single word, he realised, ever since his bid to continue the interview back at Headquarters had failed. Covin was hunched into a corner of the sofa staring down at his hands, the picture of defeat and grim resignation. He wasn't smoking either, Thanet noticed. Perhaps he was beyond consolation.

Someone hammered on the front door. 'Bernie?'

Thanet recognised Landy's voice.

Covin glanced at Thanet for permission before going to deal with the inquiry and there was a murmured conversation in the hall.

In the interval no one spoke. There was a tacit agreement, it seemed, to wait for Covin to return before continuing.

194

When he had done so Thanet said, 'The truth being . . .?'
It had to be spelled out. There was no room for misunderstandings and further false assumptions at this juncture.

Karen took a deep breath and began to talk.

Thanet could imagine it all so clearly:

'Oh Dad, you promised you'd find it before I went back, you really did. I've been asking you for months.'

'I know. But there's no hurry, is there? There's plenty of time before next summer.'

'It seems as though there's plenty of time, but you know as well as I do that if I'm not here to keep on at you, you'll never get around to it. I really can't see the difficulty. There are only a limited number of places you'd have put a birth certificate, surely. I'm sorry, I really don't want to wait any longer. I think the easiest thing would be for me to send off for a copy.'

'No! There's no need for that!'

'Isn't there? When did I first ask you to look it out for me? In July? That's three months ago! No, forget it. I'll see to it myself.'

'Karen –'

'Yes?'

'I . . . To be honest . . . To tell you the truth . . . I suppose I've just been putting off the evil hour.'

'What d'you mean, "evil hour"?'

'I . . . The reason I haven't produced it . . .'

'You mean, you do know where it is? You do? So what are you trying to say?'

'I didn't want to give it to you because I knew that when you saw it . . . Oh, it was stupid of me, I know that. Like I said, I was just putting it off, that's all. Pointless!'

'Putting what off? Dad, you're frightening me! Tell me!'

'Telling you . . . telling you that you were adopted . . . Karen, love, don't look at me like that!'

'But why didn't you tell me before? I mean, my God, Dad, everybody, but everybody knows you should always tell adopted children the truth, right from the beginning, practically as soon as they're old enough to talk! You know, all that stuff about really really wanting a baby and picking her out because she was so special . . . What? Why are you shaking your head?'

195

'That's the point, love, it wasn't like that.'

'What do you mean, it wasn't like that? You mean, you didn't pick me out? What did you do? Find me under a blackberry bush or something?'

'No, of course not!'

'Well, what did you mean?'

'That's one of the reasons why we never told you. It was all so complicated. When I said "adopted" I didn't actually mean legally adopted.'

'Dad, for crying out loud! I just can't believe this is happening!'

'Calm down, love.'

'Calm down! How can you expect me to be calm? Suddenly my parents are not my parents any more and I'm not even legally adopted? So who am I? And what about my mother? Who was she? Her name must be on that certificate. I want to see it.'

'All in good time, love. I might as well tell you now, myself. She was – is – your aunt Jessica.'

'My aunt Jessica? Auntie Jessica is my mother?'

And then had come the explanations, how Madge had longed for children but after years of trying had still failed to conceive, how she had seen Jessica's baby as the perfect answer, a child of her own blood, how they had managed to deceive everyone into thinking the child was theirs.

Throughout Karen's account of this conversation Covin hadn't moved. It was as if he were in a state of suspended animation, waiting for something. But for what? Thanet wondered. Simply for Karen to finish, for this painful narration to be over? But no, she had stopped talking now and that air of frozen anticipation still seemed to encase the man like a shroud.

'It must all have been a terrible shock for you,' said Thanet.

'You can say that again! To find out that my mother was really my aunt and my aunt my mother, that everyone I loved and trusted had been deceiving me since the day I was born! It was as if . . . as if . . . Oh, I don't know. As if the foundations of my world had suddenly been knocked away. How could you do that to me?' she cried, addressing her father directly for the first time since she had begun her story. 'Can you even begin to imagine how I felt – how I feel?'

Now, at last, he moved. 'I'm sorry, love,' he whispered. The look he gave her was full of contrition, true, but there was more to it than that, a hunger to *know*.

And that must be it, of course, thought Thanet. Covin was longing to find out exactly what had happened at Jessica's house that night. Thanet's guess was that after all these revelations Karen's hurt and anger had been so intense that her overwhelming need had been to go and confront her mother. No doubt she had just grabbed the keys to her father's car and taken off – and afterwards had driven straight on to Reading. No wonder her father had been 'on edge', as Landy put it, when he delivered the pick-up to him.

'Anyway,' said Karen, confirming what Thanet had been thinking, 'naturally I couldn't possibly just swan off to college leaving everything in the air like that. I had to see Jessica first; there were things I really needed to know. So I just took Dad's car keys and went. I was in such a state, I can't tell you . . . I don't remember anything about the journey.'

Thanet was aware that Lineham had stirred and he could guess what the sergeant was thinking. *Not a good idea to drive when you're in that condition.* Lineham was very hot on road safety. He glanced at him, willing him to keep quiet. He didn't want to interrupt the flow of Karen's story.

Lineham must have got the message because he settled down again.

'Anyway,' she went on, 'it wasn't until I got there that it occurred to me she might not be in. It simply never entered my head. It was as if I needed to see her so much she just couldn't *not* be there, if you see what I mean. I was so relieved when I saw the lights were on and then, when she answered the door . . . It was odd. She's always been a part of my life, but it was as if I was seeing her for the first time.

197

Not my aunt, but my *mother.*' Karen shook her head. 'I just couldn't seem to make the transition. Mum – my real mother – was dead. I couldn't speak, I just stood there.'

'*Karen? What is it? What's the matter? Come in.*'

EIGHTEEN

'She took me by the arm,' said Karen, 'and tugged me in. I shook her off. I couldn't bear her to touch me.'

'*Karen, what is the matter. Look, come into the sitting room and sit down.*'

'*No! I'm not here for a cosy little chat!*'

'*What, then?*'

'*Dad's just told me the truth.*'

'*What do you mean, the truth?*'

'*That you . . . That you're my . . . my mother.*'

'*Oh God, no! The bastard! He swore he'd never tell!*'

'*I think you'll have to be careful how you use that word around me in future. And is that all you can say, anyway? Not, "Oh, I'm so sorry, Karen, I really didn't want to hand you over to someone else like an unwanted Christmas present." Or, "It really broke my heart to give you away, but I had no choice"?*'

'*Well, I'm sorry you're upset, of course I am.*'

'*And that's it? You're sorry I'm upset, full stop?*'

'*It'll only make things worse if I'm hypocritical about it.*'

'*What do you mean, hypocritical? Oh, I see. You're saying you never wanted me in the first place, right?*'

'*No, I'm not saying that . . .*'

'*Well what are you saying?*'

'*I suppose if I'm honest . . . Let me put it another way. How many teenagers who discover they're pregnant actually want the baby? At least I had you, didn't I? I didn't have an abortion.*'

'*And I'm supposed to be grateful?*'

'*It's better to be alive than dead, isn't it? Look, I don't think*'

199

there's any point in continuing this conversation. We'll talk again when you've calmed down.'

'Don't you dare turn away from me like that! What makes you think you have the right to dictate terms anyway? Don't you think it's about time I had my say?'

'I'm not saying you shouldn't! I'm just saying that it might be better to wait to talk about this until you've calmed down.'

'Better for whom? For you, you mean! No, you're just trying to wriggle out of an uncomfortable situation, aren't you? It must be so inconvenient to have your illegitimate child turn up after all these years, asking awkward questions! Well, you needn't think you're going to get rid of me as easily as that! I came here for an explanation and I'm not leaving until I've had it!'

'All right, all right! If you insist. But please, can't we at least sit down and talk sensibly about this? I really can't see why you're being so aggressive. You had a good home, didn't you? Parents who loved you?'

'Yes, of course. But . . .'

'There you are, then. I really did try to do my best for you, in the circumstances.'

'But why the charade of Mum pretending to be pregnant, all those elaborate arrangements?'

'It just seemed better that way, that's all.'

'That's no answer!'

'Well, it's all the answer you're going to get, so you might as well make up your mind to be satisfied with it!'

'How dare you say that! Don't you think I'm entitled to an explanation?'

'I'm sorry, I refuse to be interrogated like this.'

'And why have I never been told the truth until now?'

'That was the agreement. In fact, the agreement was that you never would be and Bernard never should have broken it.'

'But you must have realised I'd need to see my birth certificate at some time in my life?'

'Your birth certificate? Is that what happened? You saw your birth certificate? Oh God, how stupid can you get? Would you believe, that simply never occurred to us?'

●　　　●　　　●

200

It might seem difficult to credit, thought Thanet, but he could see how it might have come about. Preoccupation with the here and now could well have blinded them to an eventuality in the distant future. Otherwise they could easily have overcome the problem by Jessica giving Madge's name as her own when she had the baby in Bristol. A hospital has to notify the local registrar of a baby's birth, but if the medical staff had been given the wrong information this would presumably simply have been passed on and entered on the birth certificate. And why hadn't it occurred to them later? Well, it all happened twenty years ago. They must long since have been lulled into a sense of false security, have decided that any risk of discovery was past. For the first time he wondered how Jessica must have felt, seeing her child grow up under her sister's roof, unaware of her true parentage. According to Karen's account of their conversation it hadn't bothered her in the least. It sounded as though Jessica had been entirely devoid of maternal feelings. She certainly hadn't produced any more offspring. Though it was possible that on Tuesday evening she had been so unprepared for the situation that the only way she had been able to deal with Karen's attack was by keeping a tight rein on that unpredictable temper of hers, aware that this might make her seem hard and unfeeling but prepared to take the risk. She might in any case have thought it pointless to do otherwise. It was, after all, a little late in the day for a touching mother-and-daughter reconciliation.

'Anyway, what did you mean, that was the agreement, that I would never be told the truth. What agreement?'

'The condition on which I agreed to hand you over.'

'You mean . . . Oh, I see. I understand now. You mean, you'd really intended to have an abortion, but because Mum put pressure on you, begged you to let her have me, you agreed on condition that no one should ever know I was yours!'

'I think that just about sums it up, yes.'

'But why was it so important to you that no one should know? Why would it have been so dreadful simply to have me *and let it be known that your sister was bringing me up?'*

'We thought it would be confusing for you, if you knew you had two mothers, so to speak.'

'Oh come on, don't give me that! Children are brought up by their grandmothers, by stepmothers, by foster mothers . . . I'm sorry, I simply can't accept that. And it couldn't have been because of the stigma. I know it was twenty years ago, but it wasn't exactly the dark ages, was it?'

'Oh, for God's sake, Karen, do stop going on! Isn't it enough that I had you, that I made sure you had a good home, people who really cared about you? It wasn't much fun, you know, being pregnant at sixteen and having to leave school when I'd hoped to go to university.'

'Oh, tough! You could have gone later. Lots of people take a year out.'

'Some year out! Believe me, having a baby is a bit different from backpacking to India. It changes you, eats away at your motivation as far as academic work is concerned. And it's all very well burbling on about it not being the dark ages and so on, but just think how many girls still feel as I did, even now, these days, when you trip over single mothers at every turn. It all depends on the individual and on her circumstances. How often do you read of some poor infant being abandoned in a telephone box or in a carrier bag on a rubbish heap? At least I made sure you were well cared for. So don't give me that stuff, don't try to minimise the problems I had and the difficulties I went through. You can't begin to imagine how it feels until it happens to you.'

'And you can't begin to imagine how it feels to be that child, can you? To know that your own mother was so ashamed of having you that she would go to any lengths to keep her pregnancy quiet.'

'I did what I thought was best.'

'"I, I, I." Yes, best for you. The truth is, Jessica, you've never really considered anyone but yourself. You are completely and utterly selfish and self-centred.'

'How dare you speak to me like that! I'm not listening to this one moment longer!'

●

'We'd been standing in the hall until then,' said Karen, 'but suddenly she just shot off up the stairs. I was furious and I went after her. "Oh yes, you will," I said. "There's something else I need to know." She was nearly at the top by then and suddenly she twisted around and almost spat at me. "And I can guess what that is!" she said.'

So could Thanet.

And so, too, could Covin. The man's hands suddenly clenched into fists so tightly that the knuckles gleamed white. Clearly he was bracing himself.

And then at last Thanet understood what it was that Covin had been waiting to find out. He understood, too, why the moment Karen had flung out of the house that evening Covin had gone straight to the telephone to ring Jessica. He had not only wanted to warn her that Karen now knew the truth, he had wanted to make a desperate plea that Jessica should not tell her the rest of it. His relief at Karen's unexpected return was also now explained: he had been afraid that their estrangement might be permanent.

'I suppose you want to know who your father was. Well, you won't have far to look. Just turn around and go home again.'
'You mean –'

Covin let out a sound between a sob and a gasp and buried his head in his hands. Karen looked down at the bent head, then laid a tentative hand on his shoulder and said, 'I'm sorry, Dad. But I have to tell them how it was, so they can understand what happened.' Covin half raised his head but didn't look up at her.

'Yes. Bloody Bernard, that's who. Couldn't keep his hands off his little sister-in-law, could he.'
'No!'
'No point in screaming at me. Like it or not, it's true.'
'It's not!'

'And then, well, that was when it happened. So fast that it's still all really a blur. She swung around to climb the last couple of stairs and I grabbed for her, to try and stop her. She tried to jerk aside, to avoid my hand and that . . . that was when she lost her balance and . . . and –'

Up until now Karen's composure had been remarkable. During the intervening days she must have relived the events of Tuesday night so often that she had been able to relate them almost as if they had happened to someone else. Now, at last, her control cracked. Her face contorted and Thanet glimpsed the tears which suddenly gushed from her eyes before she too buried her face in her hands. 'It was horrible,' she sobbed. 'Horrible.'

As if Karen's collapse had been a signal Covin straightened up and put his arms around her, began to rock her as if she were a child. 'Hush, love,' he said. 'Hush.'

They seemed oblivious of the presence of the two policemen.

Thanet and Lineham exchanged uncomfortable glances and Lineham raised his eyebrows, jerking his head towards the door.

Thanet hesitated. Father and daughter needed some time alone together, to begin to come to terms with what had happened. On the other hand he couldn't afford to miss the rest of Karen's story. Well, he could at least give them the illusion of privacy. He rose quietly; Lineham followed suit and silently they left the room. Thanet adjusted the door so that it was slightly ajar and they waited in the hall. He didn't like eavesdropping but in this instance felt that it was the best compromise he could make.

Karen was still crying, great gasping gulps of pent-up emotion. Covin continued to soothe her, to murmur in her ear, to stroke her back.

In view of what Thanet had just learned it did cross his mind to wonder if there was a sexual element in their embrace, but he quickly dismissed the suspicion. The solace which Karen was seeking and the tenderness displayed by Covin were, he was certain, untainted by any unnatural element.

At last her sobs abated. 'Oh Dad,' she said, 'it was horrible. I can't tell you.'

'I've been so worried about you.'

'I know. I'm sorry. I'm so sorry.'

'Shh. I'm the one who should be apologising.'

'Her face . . . Her eyes . . . I can't get them out of my mind.'

'It wasn't your fault. She must have seen how upset you were. She shouldn't have lost her temper.'

'But I said such horrible things! And I can't help thinking, over and over again, that that was the only conversation I shall ever have with my real mother, and look how it ended! I'll never forgive myself, never.'

'Karen.' Covin raised her up so that she was facing him, tilted her chin gently with one finger so that she was looking directly into his face. 'Karen. Get this straight. Madge was your mother, your true mother. Oh, not biologically perhaps, but in every other way. She certainly couldn't have loved you more if she had borne you herself.'

'I know that. I do, really. But, Dad . . .'

'What?' There was a shadow in his face now. He could tell what she was going to ask him.

'What she said . . . about you. Was it true?' She knew, really; Covin's reaction just now had been all the confirmation she required. But she still needed to hear it from him.

'Yes. But Karen – you must understand, and I swear this is the truth, it only happened the once. I was bitterly ashamed of myself at the time, but later, when it brought me you, I found I couldn't really regret it.'

'Did Mum know?'

Covin shook his head. 'Jessica always refused to tell her who your father was.'

'I've thought about it such a lot this week.' Karen put a hand up to her temple and massaged it. 'There's been so much to think about . . . Finding out I was adopted and then, well, there's no point in pretending I wasn't shocked, horrified even, at first, when Jessica told me about you. I didn't want to believe it. But later, well, that was what I wanted to tell you. Later, when it had all had time to sink in, I found I was actually glad.'

'Glad!'

'Yes. Glad that you really are my father. It meant that although at first I felt the whole of my past had been just one big lie, in fact a great big chunk of it, my relationship with you, had survived more or less intact. It's the one thing I can salvage out of all this.'

'Oh Karen, you can't imagine how relieved I am to hear you say that.'

'That was why I had to come back, to put things right with you.'

'I'm so glad you did. I was afraid I might have lost you for good.'

'You won't get rid of me as easily as that!'

The tone of the conversation had lightened so much that Thanet decided it was time to go back in. So engrossed were they with each other that they barely glanced up as he and Lineham returned to their seats and he wondered if they had even registered that they had been left alone for a while.

It was time to lower the emotional temperature. 'So, Karen,' he said briskly, 'you're saying Mrs Manifest's fall was an accident.'

She nodded.

'Then why on earth didn't you say so right away?' said Covin, reaching for his cigarettes and lighting up.

Back to normal, thought Thanet.

'I just panicked, I suppose,' said Karen. 'I was in such a state I was incapable of thinking straight. And I was frightened. Although I knew it had been an accident it still felt as though it was my fault, that it was I who'd killed her.'

'Because you'd been so angry with her earlier, you mean?' said Thanet. 'Perhaps you felt as though you'd almost willed it to happen.'

'Yes, that's it exactly! I hadn't thought of it like that, but you're right.'

'But why didn't you at least call an ambulance before you left?' said her father.

'I told you. I just panicked. I was terrified. It was obvious she was dead. No one alive ever has that terrible blank, fixed stare . . . I just ran, jumped into the car and drove off.'

'I saw you,' said Covin.

'Really? Did you? I didn't realise that. I didn't see you. I think I was more or less incapable of noticing anything.'

'You went rushing across the road and into the car as I was coming around the bend in the lane behind you. I didn't know whether to follow you or not.'

Thanet could understand Covin's dilemma. He must have been torn between his desire to know whether or not Jessica had told Karen he really was her father, and the need to set matters right between them.

'I thought you might be going home again,' said Covin. 'So I thought I'd better have a quick word with Jessica first.'

'Did either of you touch the body?' said Lineham.

They shook their heads in unison.

'So why didn't you ring for an ambulance, sir?' said Thanet.

'Obviously I didn't want to get involved!' said Covin. 'Just in case Karen might somehow be dragged into it. So far as I knew, no one had seen either of us there and I wanted it to stay that way. That was why I left the door open, as I found it.'

'Did I leave it open?' said Karen. 'I didn't realise.'

Such a trivial matter, thought Thanet, with such far-reaching consequences. If she hadn't, there would have been no reason for Kevin to go into the house to investigate, no phone call to arouse suspicion. It would also have saved the police a great deal of time and fruitless effort. Still, he wasn't complaining. He would be able to put the case entirely out of his mind for the wedding.

The wedding!

He glanced at his watch. Six-thirty! He would barely have time to get home and change before the dinner at the Black Swan.

Quickly he arranged for both father and daughter to come in to make their statements next morning, then wound up the interview and left.

'Why the sudden rush?' said Lineham as they hurried to the car.

Thanet explained. Then he grinned.

'What's so funny?'

'I was thinking that at least I've got a good excuse for not going back to the office, if the Super complains I haven't brought him up to date! By the way, I'm sorry I didn't put you in the picture about Karen. I was just going to tell you when Covin arrived back, remember?'

'I really couldn't understand why you wouldn't let me caution him.'

'Yes, well, I'd guessed what was coming by then.' A moment or two later, Thanet groaned. 'Oh, no!'

'What's the matter?'

'I've just remembered. I'll never be ready in time. The house will be crawling with people. The bathroom'll be permanently occupied and I'll have to keep on stopping to be sociable.'

Lineham grinned. 'I'd rather you than me.'

NINETEEN

Even from the outside, Thanet's house proclaimed that something unusual was afoot. Although it was not yet fully dark, lights blazed from uncurtained windows in every room and figures could be seen moving about inside. Thanet's parking space in the drive had been left empty but cars lined the kerb in front of the house and Thanet wondered who they could all belong to.

Inside the atmosphere was charged with that special electricity generated by a high pitch of expectation. There was noise, laughter, movement all over the house. For a moment Thanet felt himself a stranger in his own home and then Joan appeared at the top of the stairs. She was all ready to go out, in a dress he hadn't seen before. It was in one of her favourite colours, a deep, rich blue, with fluid, feminine lines which enhanced the figure she had only ever lost briefly, during her pregnancies.

'Luke!' she cried. 'There you are. I was getting worried.'

'Yes, sorry darling. I'll –'

'Dad! Hi!' said Ben, emerging from the kitchen with a tray of coffee mugs. He looked unfamiliar.

'You've had your hair cut!' Thanet said.

'So've you.'

They grinned at each other.

'Couldn't let the side down, could we?' said Ben.

'Who're all those for?' Thanet nodded at the mugs.

'Just some friends who've dropped in. And the two grandmas of course. I went and fetched Granny Bolton earlier. They're having the time of their lives.'

209

The grandparents on both sides were to join them at dinner.

'I'll just say hullo.' The buzz of laughter and conversation swelled as Thanet opened the living-room door.

Ben was right, he saw at once. Joan's mother and his, both also dressed ready to go out, were sitting on either side of the fire like twin icons, their faces animated as they listened to the chatter all around them. 'Some' friends was an understatement, he thought. Bridget and Ben had both attended local schools and their friends seemed to have 'dropped in' in force tonight. There were half a dozen youngsters crammed on to the settee and every inch of carpet seemed to be covered by bodies seated or supine. Thanet knew most of them and there was a chorus of greeting. His mother raised a hand to wave at him. 'I'll talk to you later, dear. You go and change now.'

Thankfully, he escaped.

'Oh, there you are, Dad!' said Bridget, emerging from her room as he went by. 'We were getting worried in case you'd been held up.' She was wearing a brief velvet dress with long tight sleeves in a green so dark it was almost black.

'You look gorgeous,' he said.

Ignoring eve-of-the-wedding convention, she and Alexander had opted to join their parents and grandparents for this initial meeting between the two sets of in-laws. Thanet had dreaded the prospect of handing Bridget over to a bride-groom with a hangover but things had changed, it seemed, since he got married. Alexander's stag 'night' had been a day's go-karting with some friends, and Bridget's had been lunch in Calais on a day trip to France. In any case, he and Joan had been relieved that the young people had opted to join them tonight. It should smooth the way.

'I see Lucy's arrived,' he said. She had been one of the familiar faces downstairs.

'Yes. I'm so glad she could get away to be bridesmaid, we've known each other such a long time. Did you meet Thomas, her fiancé?'

'No. I only put my head around the door.'

'He seems really nice. I hadn't met him before.'

'Good.'

'Luke!' called Joan impatiently.

'Coming.'

She was waiting for him in their bedroom. 'It's five past seven already,' she said. 'We really ought to leave by twenty past.'

They were supposed to be meeting the Highmans at 7.30.

'Don't fuss!' Thanet said. 'It won't matter if we're a few minutes late. It's not considered polite to be dead on time.' He spotted his hired dress suit for the wedding hanging on the back of the door. 'Good grief. Do I really have to wear that tomorrow?'

'Luke! Let's concentrate on the here and now, shall we? Just tell me what you're going to wear tonight and I'll get it out while you have a shower. I've made sure the bathroom's free.'

'I always did think it would be nice to have a valet,' he said with a grin.

'Get a move on!' she said.

By the time he came back his clothes were all laid out on the bed. He dressed quickly and was hurrying towards the stairs when he stopped dead. Passing Bridget's room he had glimpsed a ghostly white shape in the darkness. Her wedding dress. Slowly he retraced his steps and went in.

There it was, hooked over the door of her wardrobe, shrouded in protective polythene, a symbol of the great change that was to take place in his daughter's life, in all their lives, tomorrow.

Contemplating it he was overcome by a complicated blend of emotions – a sense of loss, of yearning for the days of her childhood now gone for ever, all mixed up with a heartfelt desire for her happiness with this stranger who had stepped into their lives to steal her from them.

He sighed, shook his head, squared his shoulders. It was time to face the first stage of his ordeal.

They were all four waiting for him in the hall. Ben appeared at the living-room door. He wasn't coming with them tonight and neither were Alexander's brother and sister. The party, it was felt, would have been too unwieldy. 'Have a good time,' he said.

And, astonishingly, they did. Right from the start the evening went with a swing. Everyone was in a good mood, determined to make these new relationships work, and despite his fears Thanet found the Highmans unpretentious and very easy to get along with. They were full of praise for Bridget and he found that his fears for her future began to ease. At least she was marrying a man from a stable family background and he felt that these people would do their best to welcome her and make her feel at home in their very different social circumstances.

'There you are!' said Joan, when they had taken her mother home and they were at last back in the privacy of their own room. Downstairs the party was still going strong and Bridget had slipped in to join her friends. 'Now be honest. It wasn't as bad as you expected, was it?'

'You're just saying ,"I told you so!"'

'I certainly am. Unzip me, will you? But seriously, I really liked Alexander's parents, didn't you?'

'Yes, I did,' said Thanet, complying. 'You look wonderful in this dress.'

'I hoped you'd like it . . . So, do I take it that you're not as worried about tomorrow now?'

'Marginally less, I suppose.'

'Pessimist!' she said, slipping on her dressing gown to avoid embarrassing encounters on the way to the bathroom. When she came back she said, 'How's the case going, by the way? I didn't have time to ask you earlier. I assume there's going to be no problem tomorrow?'

'It's all over bar the shouting.'

'Already! Luke! Well done! You must be delighted.' She gave him a long look. 'No? Not delighted?'

'Well, I'm pleased it's over, yes, of course. But it was all a bit of a letdown really, a lot of work to no good purpose. It turned out to be an accident after all.'

'Really?'

Now it was Thanet's turn to go to the bathroom and as soon as he returned she said, 'So what happened? This week's been so hectic we've hardly had a chance to talk about it.'

'What stage was I at last time we discussed it?'

Joan got into bed, plumped up the pillows behind her and leaned back against them, obviously settling down for a long talk. 'You were asking me about Kevin and Snippers. You thought he might be involved.'

'That seems ages ago!' Thanet eyed his morning coat uneasily as he undressed. He was going to feel so self-conscious wearing it that he'd never be able to act naturally.

'It was the night before Bridget came home. Wednesday, then.'

'Only the day before yesterday! Such a lot has happened since then.'

'Tell me,' said Joan.

'You don't want to hear this now, surely. You must be exhausted.'

'I'm wide awake, as a matter of fact.'

And Thanet had to admit, she looked it.

'I'm over stimulated, probably. And there's no point in trying to go to sleep until everyone has settled down. I just hope they won't be too late getting to bed. Bridget needs her beauty sleep. No, a bed-time story is just what I need to stop me worrying about all the things that might go wrong tomorrow.'

'Nothing's going to go wrong,' said Thanet. 'And if it does, well, it'll just go down in the annals of the Thanet family as something amusing that happened at Bridget's wedding.'

'So,' she said. 'Go on. Begin, as they say, at the beginning. What made you suspect it might not be an accident in the first place?'

Thanet got into bed beside her and put his arm around her. She settled her head into the hollow of his shoulder.

'Two things really.' And he told her about the phone call and the open door, went on to explain how to begin with he had naturally suspected first Jessica's husband then her lover. 'But then we found that neither of them could have made that phone call. Believe it or not, they actually alibied each other!'

She laughed. 'Really?'

'Yes.' Thanet explained about the Ogilvys' visit to the Harrow, the landlord's testimony that he had seen Desmond Manifest open the door as if to come in, then change his mind when he saw them. 'And that was only three or four minutes after the phone call – which was made from Jessica's number, incidentally. There was no way Manifest could have got to the pub in that space of time, it's a good ten minutes' walk. And he did walk, we checked.'

'I see.'

'That didn't let either of them off the hook as far as Jessica's death was concerned, of course. Ogilvy could have killed her before going to the pub and her husband could easily have slipped back to the house after Ogilvy had left. But meanwhile I got sidetracked by Kevin. He'd borrowed his father's car that night and it had been seen parked near Jessica's house. He had admitted driving to Charthurst that evening – to go for a country walk, he said!'

'Excuses don't come much thinner than that!'

'Quite. Anyway, we already knew that he was adopted – his mother told us so the first time we interviewed her. And I'd been puzzled why Jessica, who'd been such a promising student and had been expected to stay on at school and even go to university, had left for no apparent reason at sixteen and had instead gone off to live with an aunt in Bristol. Then I realised that both Jessica and Kevin had red hair –'

'So you jumped to the conclusion that he was her illegitimate child, that he had traced her, and that this was why he had been watching her – to pluck up the courage to approach her. And, presumably, that he had done so on the night she died and it had all gone disastrously wrong.'

'Exactly.'

'All seems quite logical to me.'

'That's what I thought. And at first it seemed I was right. I went to see Bernard Covin, her brother-in-law, and he confirmed that yes, she had had a baby, a boy, and it had been put up for adoption. But as it turned out, I was wrong. When we checked we found that Kevin had already traced his natural mother, who had refused to have anything to do with him. Kevin's interest in Jessica had been precisely what we originally thought it was, a rather unhealthy obsession with her.' And Thanet told Joan about the scrapbook they had found in the loft above the boy's bedroom.

Joan made a little moue of distaste and said, 'So it had all been a waste of time.'

'Well, yes and no. I was mortified at the time, that I'd been so convinced I was on the right track.' He grinned. 'Actually, it served me right, for thinking I'd been so clever.'

'Nonsense, darling. You're always too ready to put yourself down, if you ask me.'

'You're biased,' said Thanet, dropping a kiss on the top of her head. 'Anyway, as it turned out, although I was wrong about Kevin being Jessica's son, I was in fact still heading in the right direction. When we confronted Kevin with the scrapbook, in order to get himself off the hook he told us he'd seen a man coming out of Jessica's house around about the time she died.'

'And you believed him? He wasn't just trying to save his own skin?'

'Mike and I both thought he was telling the truth.'

'Did he know who the man was?'

'Bernard Covin.'

'Aha! The brother-in-law. The plot thickens!'

'Precisely. Now there were already several things that puzzled me about Covin. We knew he had rung Jessica that evening. According to him, he had supper with his daughter Karen, Jessica's niece, who was going back to Reading that evening for the start of the new term –'

'At the university, you mean?'

'Yes.'

'Like Ben. I wonder if they know each other? Oh, sorry. Go on. Yes, she was going back to Reading that evening . . .'

'And she'd asked him to give her aunt a ring to apologise for not having managed to get over to say goodbye to her before she left.'

Joan frowned. 'Strange.'

'That's what I thought. But even more strange was the fact that when he got Jessica's answerphone he actually went over straight away to see her. We didn't discover this at first. He told us he'd stayed in watching television all evening. We believed him because we knew Karen had borrowed his car. Stupid of me.'

'So how did he get there?'

'Took one of the farm vehicles, of course. Anyway, when Kevin told us he'd seen Covin come out of Jessica's house I just couldn't stop puzzling away at why? Why ring Jessica immediately after Karen left, as if the matter was urgent, and then why go rushing over when he couldn't get a reply? Unless something had happened between him and Karen at supper that evening.'

'Some kind of argument, you mean?'

'I didn't know. Just some kind of upset. But if there had been, I thought that might explain something else which had puzzled me – why Karen had driven herself back to Reading, in her father's car.'

'You mean you'd have expected him to drive her?'

'Yes. Wouldn't you? Unless she had a car of her own, that is. But she hasn't.'

'That was odd, I agree.'

'But if they'd had a row . . .'

'Yes, I see. She might have gone rushing off on impulse.'

'Exactly. In which case, I had to ask myself what the row could have been about?'

'And as he immediately rang Jessica and then went dashing off to see her, you couldn't help thinking there must have been some connection.'

'You should have joined the police force, darling.'

'I doubt it. I still can't see what the connection might be.'

'That's because you don't know all the facts. But I did, and that was the point at which I began to put two and two together. I already knew Jessica's sister had tried to conceive for years before succeeding. I also knew that Jessica had had a baby while staying with an aunt in Bristol. Then I learned that while she was away her sister had gone to stay with the same aunt – who was supposedly ill – and that in fact the timing of the two births had coincided.'

'I see now! You're saying that Jessica's sister didn't really have a baby at all, that Karen Covin is Jessica's daughter and that Covin lied to you about the baby's sex. To put you off the scent, presumably. But why?'

'The adoption was an informal arrangement. And – this

216

was the point – Karen had never been told any of this. In fact, I discovered this afternoon that Jessica only agreed not to have an abortion, but to have the baby and let her sister bring it up, if the Covins swore to secrecy. That was why they had to mount such an elaborate charade – they not only had to get Jessica out of the area so no one would suspect she was pregnant, but Madge too when her supposed baby was due. There was no way they could have got away with it otherwise.'

'Because of hospital records, health visitors and midwife's visits after the birth, you mean.'

'That's right. In fact, Madge had to stay away until some weeks after the baby was born while Covin changed his job and moved to a different area.'

'Because if they'd stayed in the same place their doctor and local midwife would have wondered why they'd never had an inkling of Madge's pregnancy.'

'Quite. I imagine they claimed their health records had been lost in the move, so that they could make a fresh start with no questions asked.'

'Very ingenious.'

'And it worked. For twenty years.'

The front door closed quietly downstairs and a moment or two later cars started up and were driven away. Shortly afterwards there were whispers on the stairs, stealthy movements on the landing.

Joan glanced at the clock. Ten to twelve. 'Not too bad, I suppose. And they are trying to be quiet, bless them. So,' she said, 'what went wrong? Are you suggesting that the upset over supper was because Covin finally told Karen she was adopted? But why on earth should he choose that particular evening? I mean, just before she was due to go back to university for the start of a new term was hardly the best timing, was it?'

'That's what I simply couldn't understand. Until Karen herself told me. And this was really the key to the whole puzzle. Apparently she wanted to apply for a passport, and needed her birth certificate.'

'Aaah.'

'She'd been trying to get her father to hand it over for

months, but he kept making excuses. So finally she told him not to bother. She said she was fed up with waiting and she would send away for a copy.'

'So then he had to tell her. He wouldn't have wanted her to find out when he wasn't around to explain. Not surprising she was upset. Is he fond of her?'

'Very.'

'I may be dim, but I still don't understand why it was so important for him to go and see Jessica that evening. What did he say, when you told him you had a witness who'd seen him coming out of her house that night?' Joan yawned. Her eyelids were beginning to droop.

'He confessed.'

'What? Just like that?'

'Just like that.'

'He actually admitted he'd pushed her down the stairs?'

'Something like that.'

'Well. I'm amazed. And confused. I thought you said it was an accident.' She eased herself away from him and slid down in the bed, yawning again.

'It was.'

'Darling, you're being infuriating. Would you please spell out in words of one syllable exactly what did happen?'

Thanet was enjoying teasing her, keeping her in suspense. 'I'm sure you can work it out for yourself.'

'Luke!'

'Just think. Imagine the scene at supper that night. Covin has just told Karen the truth. She's upset, naturally, confused, angry, hurt. She feels betrayed. So she rushes out to the car. But just think: would she have driven straight to Reading?'

Joan sat up with a jerk 'She went to see Jessica!' she said triumphantly. 'And she either told Covin where she was going or he guessed that that was what she was going to do. That was why he rang Jessica, to warn her! And that was why he went racing over to Charthurst when he couldn't get through on the phone!'

Thanet grinned up at her. 'Told you you could work it out for yourself.'

'But when he got there he found that Jessica was dead. Did he actually see Karen there?'

'Not in the house. He just got there in time to see her drive away.'

'So he confessed because he was afraid she was responsible for Jessica's death. But how do you know all this? He wouldn't have told you, surely. It would have defeated the whole object of the exercise, as far as he was concerned.' She slid back down in the bed. 'In fact, I still don't understand why you say you now *know* it was an accident.'

'Because while we were interviewing Covin this afternoon, Karen arrived back.'

'And told you exactly what did happen?'

'Yes.' Thanet related Karen's story.

Joan listened in silence until Thanet got the part where Jessica told Karen who her father was. 'Oh no!' she said. 'What a way to find out. Poor kid.'

Thanet then described how the accident had happened.

'You can see it all, can't you?' said Joan sleepily. 'Poor kid,' she repeated. 'What a dreadful few days she must have had.'

'And poor Jessica,' said Thanet. 'I've learned quite a lot about her over the last few days and I can't say I much like what I've heard. But I can't help feeling sorry for her. First she lost her father, then her mother and then when she goes to live with her sister, her brother-in-law gets her pregnant. Then, when she did at last get married, her husband loses his job and she loses her home. It must have seemed to her that sooner or later everything would be taken away from her. Perhaps that was why she hung on to her husband.'

'Mmm.'

'And it's only just occurred to me. Maybe that was why she had affairs. Maybe she was so convinced that sooner or later Desmond would desert her too that in some strange way she was almost compelled to try and make it happen.' Perhaps that was also why she had turned on her husband physically, if what the Bartons had said was true. 'I don't suppose she ever knew just how much he loved her, how well he understood her, and the degree to which he was therefore able to forgive her. People said, you know, that she had a very short fuse and I suppose that's understandable, after what she'd been through. Desmond told us himself that he felt she was just plain angry with the way life had treated her and that beneath the surface the anger was always simmering away, waiting to erupt.'

He glanced at Joan, expecting her to comment, but she was fast asleep.

He sighed. 'Well, I suppose you could say that on Tuesday evening it erupted once too often.'

TWENTY

'Luke? Wake up! Tea.' Joan's voice.

Thanet opened one eye and murmured his thanks. He squinted at the clock. Seven-fifteen.

She was already dressed and bustling about, drawing curtains. She peered anxiously at the sky. 'It looks as though it's going to be fine, thank goodness,' she said.

Thanet remembered. Bridget's wedding day. The prospect of his speech loomed ahead and he groaned inwardly. 'You're up early.' Usually, on Saturdays, they had a lie-in until 7.30.

'I want to give Bridget breakfast in bed today, as a special treat.'

'You'll spoil her.' But his tone was indulgent.

'Not for much longer.' She came to sit on the edge of the bed. 'Oh Luke, I do so want today to be perfect for her.'

'It will be, I'm sure. And as I said last night, if anything does go wrong, it'll be something to look back on later and laugh about.'

'But I don't want anything to go wrong! It's every mother's nightmare on her daughter's wedding day.'

'You've done everything possible to make sure it won't. You can't do more. Now why don't you just keep telling yourself that, and try to enjoy it? The one sure way of spoiling it for her is to go around looking anxiety-ridden all day!'

'You're right!' she said. She put her arms around him and gave him a hug and a lingering kiss.

'Mmm,' he said. 'You don't suppose there's time . . .'

'Not this morning. Tonight.'

'Something to look forward to!' he said with a grin. He and Joan had always enjoyed a healthy sex life.

She jumped up. 'Meanwhile, drink your tea. I'm going to prepare that breakfast tray.'

When she had gone he eyed his morning coat again. He was slowly getting used to the idea of wearing it. All the other principal actors in the drama were going to be similarly attired after all. Perhaps it wouldn't be as bad as he had feared.

He hopped out of bed, fetched the cards on which he had prepared his speech and ran through it quickly. Yes, it would do, he thought. And now it might be an idea to get into the bathroom first. Bridget had claimed it for nine o'clock so at some point there was going to be a queue.

Gradually the house began to come alive. Bridget's breakfast tray complete with ceremonial single rose in vase was taken up to her and before long the kitchen was crowded with people eating cereal, making toast and drinking cups of tea and coffee. The post arrived, with yet more cards from wellwishers, then came the bouquets, the tray of buttonholes for Thanet and the ushers. Inexorably, it seemed to Thanet, the momentum gathered pace. The ceremony was to be at midday and before long it was time for everyone to change. Joan and the bridesmaids were due to leave at 11.30 and by 11.15 he and Joan were ready in their unfamiliar finery. She was wearing a Jean Muir dress and jacket in fine aquamarine wool crepe. She had agonised over buying it. 'How can I possibly justify spending so much money on one outfit?'

'If you can't splash out on your only daughter's wedding, when can you?'

'Never?' she'd said, and laughed.

But she had given in and now, as she took a final look in the mirror, Thanet said softly, 'It was worth every penny, wasn't it?'

She smiled. 'It certainly makes me feel special enough to be the mother of the bride.'

'Mrs Thanet?' Lucy's voice. 'The taxi's here.'

'Coming.' She turned and gave Thanet a quick kiss. 'See you in the church.'

He went down with her and waved them off, then stood waiting for Bridget in the hall. The sight of her as she came downstairs, a vision in cream silk, floating veil secured by a tiara of miniature roses, brought tears to his eyes. 'You look absolutely beautiful, Sprig,' he said, reverting to her childhood nickname.

For once she didn't object to it. 'Well done, Dad,' she said with a teasing grin. 'That's what every bride wants to hear.'

En route to the church she sat serenely, clearly determined to enjoy every moment of the day. He kept on glancing at her, trying to reconcile the bride-woman beside him with the baby, the toddler, the schoolgirl she had been.

At the church they posed for photographs before moving to the entrance porch. The organ launched into the opening chords of Mendelssohn's famous wedding march and as he led her proudly down the aisle familiar, smiling faces floated past as if in a dream. He saw Alexander turn to greet her with a loving look and then the ceremony began with the solemn, time-honoured words of the traditional 1662 marriage service.

'Dearly beloved, we are gathered together here in the sight of God, and in the face of this congregation, to join together this Man and this Woman in holy matrimony . . .'

Please, let them be happy, he prayed. *Don't let them become a divorce statistic. Give them the strength to overcome the difficulties which lie ahead, the perseverence to work at their relationship when it would be so much easier to give up.*

And here was his cue, the words which for him and him alone had a very special significance: 'Who giveth this Woman to be married to this Man?'

Thanet stepped forward, took Bridget's hand and gave it to the priest, who laid it gently in Alexander's.

Look after her, Alexander, Thanet urged silently.

There, it was done. For him it was a truly significant act.

It was time, finally, to let go.

ABOUT THE AUTHOR

Dorothy Simpson is a former French teacher who lives in Kent, England, with her husband. Their three children are all married. This is her fourteenth Luke Thanet novel. Her fifth, *Last Seen Alive*, won Britain's prestigious Silver Dagger Award. Her most recent Thanet novels are *A Day for Dying*, *No Laughing Matter*, and *Wake the Dead*.

Printed in the United States
By Bookmasters